POOLSIDE

A
MELCHER
MEDIA
DURABOOK™

POOLSIDE

Published in the UK by
Dorling Kindersley Limited
80 Strand, London WC2R ORL
www.dk.com
in association with
MELCHER MEDIA
124 West 13th Street
New York, NY 10011
www.melcher.com

PUBLISHER: Charles Melcher
ASSOCIATE PUBLISHER: Bonnie Eldon
EDITOR IN CHIEF: Duncan Bock
PROJECT EDITOR: Holly Rothman
ASSISTANT EDITOR: Lindsey Stanberry
PRODUCTION DIRECTOR: Andrea Hirsh
DESIGNED BY: P*h*.D, www.phdla.com

09 08 07 10 9 8 7 6 5 4 3 2 1
Printed in China

A CIP catalogue record for this book is available from the British Library
ISBN-13: 978-1-59591-010-3
ISBN-10: 1-59591-010-7
First Edition

CONTENTS

RAFT IN WATER, FLOATING *by* A. M. HOMES

A. M. HOMES (b. 1961) made her name with The Safety of Objects, *a brazenly subversive story collection in which unruly and perverse desires surprised middleclass parents and their children. In "Raft in Water, Floating," published in* The New Yorker *in 1999, Homes revisits the backyards of suburbia. Here, a teenage girl literally drifts away from her self-absorbed family via a mysterious swimming pool.*

SHE IS LYING ON A RAFT IN WATER. Floating. Every day when she comes home from school, she puts on her bikini and lies in the pool—it stops her from snacking.

"Appearances are everything," she tells him when he comes crashing through the foliage, arriving at the edge of the yard in his combat pants, thorns stuck to his shirt.

"Next time they change the code to the service gate, remember to tell me," he says. "I had to come in through the Eisenstadts' and under the wire."

He blots his face with the sleeve of his shirt. "There's some sort of warning—I can't remember if it's heat or air."

"I might evaporate," she says, then pauses. "I might spontaneously combust. Do you ever worry about things like that?"

"You can't explode in water," he says.

Her raft drifts to the edge.

He sits by the side of the pool, leaning over, his nose pressed into her belly, sniffing. "You smell like swimming. You smell clean, you smell white, like bleach. When I smell you, my nostrils dilate, my eyes open."

"Take off your shirt," she says.

"I'm not wearing any sunblock." he says.

"Take off your shirt."

He does, pulling it over his head, flashing twin woolly birds' nests under his arms.

He rocks her raft. His combat pants tent. He puts one hand inside her bathing suit and the other down his pants.

She stares at him.

He closes his eyes, his lashes flicker. When he's done, he dips his hand in the pool, splashing it back and forth as though checking the water, taking the temperature. He wipes it on his pants.

"Do you like me for who I am?" she asks.

"Do you want something to eat?" he replies.

"Help yourself."

He gets cookies for himself and a bowl of baby carrots from the fridge for her. The bowl is cold, clear glass, filled with orange stumps. "Butt plugs," he calls them.

The raft is a silver tray, a reflective surface—it holds the heat.

"Do you have any idea what's eating me?"

"You're eating yourself," he says.

A chunk of a Chips Ahoy! falls into the water. It sinks.

She pulls on her snorkel and mask and stares at the sky. The sound of her breath through the tube is amplified, a raspy, watery gurgle. "Mallory, my malady, you are my Mallomar, my favorite cookie," he intones. "Chocolate-dipped, squishy...You were made for me."

She flips off the raft and into the water. She swims.

"I'm going," she hears him say. "Going, going, gone."

At twilight an odd electrical surge causes the doorbells all up and down the block to ring. An intercom chorus of faceless voices sings a round of "Hi, hello. Can I help you? Is anybody out there?"

She climbs out of the pool, wet feet padding across the flagstone. Behind her is a Japanese rock garden, a retaining wall holding the earth in place like a restraining order. She sits on the warm stones. Dripping. Watering the rocks. In school, when she was little, she was given a can of water and a paintbrush—she remembers painting the playground fence, watching it turn dark and then light again as the water evaporated.

She watches her footprints disappear.

The dog comes out of the house. He puts his nose in her crotch. "Exactly who do you think you are?" she asks, pushing him away.

There is the outline of hills in the distance; they are perched on a cliff, always in danger of falling, breaking away, sliding.

Inside, there is a noise, a flash of light.

"Shit!" her mother yells.

She gets up. She opens the sliding glass door. "What happened?"

"I flicked the switch and the bulb blew."

She steps inside—cool white, goose bumps.

"I dropped the plant," her mother says. She has dropped an

African violet on its head. "I couldn't see where I was going." She has a blue gel pack strapped to her face. "Headache."

There is dark soil on the carpet. She goes to get the Dustbuster. The television in the kitchen is on, even though no one is watching: "People often have the feeling there is something wrong, that they are not where they should be...."

The dirt is in a small heap, a tiny hill on the powder-blue carpet. In her white crocheted bathing suit, she gets down on her hands and knees and sucks it up. Her mother watches. And then her mother gets down and brushes the carpet back and forth. "Did you get it?" she asks. "Did you get it all?"

"All gone," she says.

"I dropped it on its head," her mother says. "I can't bear it. I need to be reminded of beauty," she says. "Beauty is a comfort, a reminder that good things are possible. And I killed it."

"It's not dead," she says. "It's just upside down." Her mother is tall, like a long thin line, like a root going down.

In the front yard they hear men speaking Spanish, the sound of hedge trimmers and weed whackers, frantic scratching, a thousand long fingernails clawing to get in.

There is the feeling of a great divide: us and them. They rely on the cleaning lady and her son to bring them things—her mother claims to have forgotten how to grocery-shop. All they can do is open the refrigerator door and hope there is something inside. They live on the surface in some strange state of siege.

They are standing in the hallway outside her sister's bedroom door. "You don't own me," her sister says.

"Believe me, I wouldn't want to," a male voice says.

"And why not, aren't I good enough?" her sister says.

"Is she fighting with him again?"

"On speakerphone," her mother says. "I can't tell which one is which, they all sound the same." She knocks on the door. "Did you take your medication, Julie?"

"You are in my way," her sister says, talking louder now.

"What do you want to do about dinner?" her mother asks. "Your father is late—can you wait?"

"I had carrots."

She goes into her parents' room and checks herself in the bathroom mirror—still there. Her eyes are green, her lips are chapped pink. Her skin is dry from the chlorine, a little irritated. She turns around and looks over her shoulder—she is pruny in the back, from lying on the wet raft.

She opens the cabinet—jars, tubes, throat cream and thigh cream, lotion, potion, bronze stick, cover-up, pancake, base. She piles it on.

"Make sure you get enough water—it's hot today," her mother says. Her parents have one of those beds where each half does a different thing; right now her father's side is up, bent in two places. They both want what they want, they need what they need. Her mother is lying flat on her face.

She goes back out to the pool. She dives in with a splash. Her mother's potions run off, forming an oil slick around her.

Her father comes home. Through the glass she sees the front door open. She sees him moving from room to room. "Is the air filter on?" His voice is muffled. "Is the air on?" he repeats. "I'm having it having it again—the not breathing."

He turns on the bedroom light. It throws her parents into relief; the sliding glass doors are lit like a movie screen. IMAX Mom and Dad. She watches him unbutton his shirt. "I'm sweating," she hears him say. Even from where she is, she can see that he is wet. Her father calls his sweat "proof of his suffering." Under his shirt, a silk T-shirt is plastered to his body, the dark mat of the hair on his back showing through. There is something obscene about it—like an ape trying to look human. There is something embarrassing about it as well—it looks like lingerie, it makes him look more than naked. She feels as if she were seeing something she shouldn't, something too personal.

Her mother rolls over and sits up.

"Something is not right," he says.

"It's the season," she says.

"Unseasonable," he says. "Ben got a call in the middle of the afternoon. They said his house was going downhill fast. He had to leave early."

"It's an unpredictable place," her mother says.

"It's not the same as it was, that's the thing," her father says, putting on a dry shirt. "Now it's a place where everybody thinks he's somebody and nobody wants to be left out."

She gets out of the pool and goes to the door, pressing her face against the glass. They don't notice her. Finally, she knocks. Her father opens the sliding glass door. "I didn't see you out there," he says.

"I'm invisible," she says. "Welcome home."

She is back in the pool. Floating. The night is moist. Vaporous. It's hard to know if it's been raining or if the sprinkler system is acting up. The sky is charcoal, powdery black. Everything is a little fuzzy around the edges but sharp and clear in the center.

There is a coyote at the edge of the grass. She feels it staring at her. "What?" she says.

It lowers its head and pushes its neck forward, red eyes like red lights.

"What do you want?"

The coyote's legs grow long, its fur turns into an overcoat, it stands, its muzzle melts into a face—an old woman, smiling.

"Who are you?" the girl asks. "Are you friends with my sister?"

"Watch me," the old woman says. She throws off the coyote coat—she is taller, she is younger, she is naked, and then she is a man.

She hears her mother and father in the house. Shouting.

"What am I to you?" her mother says.

"It's the same thing, always the same thing, blah, blah, blah," her father says.

"Have you got anything to eat?" the coyote asks.

"Would you like a carrot?"

"I was thinking of something more like a sandwich or a slice of cheese pizza."

"There are probably some waffles in the freezer. No one ever eats waffles. Would you like me to make you one?"

"With butter and syrup?" he asks.

The girl nods.

He licks his lips, he turns his head and licks his shoulder and then his coyote paws. He begins grooming himself.

"Be right back," she says. She goes into the kitchen, opens the freezer, and pulls out the box of waffles.

"I thought you were on a diet," her mother says.

"I am," the girl says, putting the waffles in the toaster, getting the butter, slicing a few strawberries.

"What's this called, breakfast for dinner?"

"Never mind," the girl says, pouring syrup.

"That's all you ever say."

She goes back outside. A naked young woman sits by the edge of the pool.

"Is it still you?" the girl asks.

"Yes," the coyote says.

She hands the coyote the plate. "Usually we have better choices, but the housekeeper is on vacation."

"Yum, Eggos. Want a bite?"

The girl shakes her head. "I'm on a diet," she says, getting back onto her raft.

The coyote eats. When she's finished she licks the plate. Her tongue is incredibly long, it stretches out and out and out, lizardly licking.

"Delish," she says.

The girl watches, eyes bulging at the sight of the tongue—hot pink. The coyote starts to change again, to shift. Her skin goes dark, it goes tan, deep like honey and then crisper brown, as if it is burning, and then darker still, toward black. Downy feathers start to appear, and then longer feathers, like quills. Her feet turn orange, fold in, and web. A duck, a big black duck, like a dog, but a duck. The duck jumps into the pool and paddles toward the girl, splashing noisily.

"These feet," she says. "They're the opposite of high heels and still they're so hard to control."

They float in silence.

She sees her sister come out of her room. She watches the three of them, her mother, father, and sister, through the glass.

She floats on the raft.

Relaxed, the duck extends her neck, her feathers bleach white, and she turns into a swan, circling gracefully.

Suddenly, she lifts her head, as if alerted. She pumps her wings. Her body is changing again, she is trading her feathers for fur, a black mask appears around her eyes, her bill becomes a snout. She is out of the water, standing on the flagstone, a raccoon with orange webbed feet. She waddles off into the night.

Below ground there is a shift, a fissure, a crack that ricochets. A tremor. The house lights flicker. The alarm goes off. In the pool the water rolls, a small domestic tidal wave sweeps from one end to the other, splashing onto the stones.

The sliding glass door opens, her father steps out, flashlight circling the water. He finds her holding on to the ladder.

"You all right?" he asks.

"Fine," she says.

"Come on out now," he says. "It's enough for one day. You're a growing girl—you need your beauty sleep."

She climbs out of the pool.

Her father hands her a towel. "It's a wonder you don't just shrivel up and disappear."

PARADISE *by* EDNA O'BRIEN

EDNA O'BRIEN's (b. 1932) literary breakthrough, The Country Girls Trilogy, *was banned in her native Ireland for its frank mix of sex and Catholicism. Now, more than four decades and twenty books later, O'Brien is one of the most celebrated Irish authors since James Joyce. From her collection* A Fanatic Heart, *"Paradise" transports us to a luxurious Mediterranean villa where a young woman, intent on pleasing her older lover but threatened by his snarky entourage, must decide whether to sink or swim.*

IN THE HARBOR WERE THE FOUR BOATS. Boats named after a country, a railroad, an emotion, and a girl. She first saw them at sundown. Very beautiful they were, and tranquil, white boats at a distance from each other, cosseting the harbor. On the far side a mountain. Lilac at that moment. It seemed to be made of collapsible substance so insubstantial was it. Between the boats and the mountain a lighthouse, on an island.

Somebody said the light was not nearly so pretty as in the old days when the coast guard lived there and worked it by gas. It was automatic now and much brighter. Between them and the sea were four fields cultivated with fig trees. Dry yellow fields that seemed to be exhaling dust. No grass. She looked again at the four boats, the fields, the fig trees, the suave ocean; she looked at the house behind her and she thought, It can be mine, mine, and her heart gave a little somersault. He recognized her agitation and smiled. The house acted like a spell on all who came. He took her by the hand and led her up the main stairs. Stone stairs with a wobbly banister. The undersides of each step bright blue. "Stop," he said, where it got dark near the top, and before he switched on the light.

A servant had unpacked for her. There were flowers in the room. They smelled of confectionery. In the bathroom a great glass urn filled with talcum powder. She leaned over the rim and inhaled. It caused her to sneeze three times. Ovaries of dark-purple soap had been taken out of their wrapping paper, and for several minutes she held one in either hand. Yes. She had done the right thing in coming. She need not have feared; he needed her, his expression and their clasped hands already confirmed that.

They sat on the terrace drinking a cocktail he had made. It was of rum and lemon and proved to be extremely potent. One of the guests said the angle of light on the mountain was at its most magnificent. He put his fingers to his lips and blew a kiss to the mountain. She counted the peaks, thirteen in all, with a plateau between the first four and the last nine.

The peaks were close to the sky. Farther down on the face of the mountain various juts stuck out, and these made shadows on their neighboring juts. She was told its name. At the same moment she overheard a question being put to a young woman, "Are you interested in Mary Queen of Scots?" The woman, whose skin had a beguiling radiance, answered yes overreadily. It was possible that such radiance was the result of constant supplies of male sperm. The man had a high pale forehead and a look of death.

They drank. They smoked. All twelve smokers tossing the butts onto the tiled roof that sloped toward the farm buildings. Summer lightning started up. It was random and quiet and faintly theatrical. It seemed to be something devised for their amusement. It lit one part of the sky, then another. There were bats flying about also, and their dark shapes and the random fugitive shots of summer lightning were a distraction and gave them something to point to. "If I had a horse I'd call it Summer Lightning," one of the women said, and the man next to her said, How charming. She knew she ought to speak. She wanted to. Both for his sake and for her own. Her mind would give a little leap and be still and would leap again; words were struggling to be set free, to say something, a little amusing something to establish her among them. But her tongue was tied. They would have known her predecessors. They would compare her minutely, her appearance, her accent, the way he behaved with her. They would know better than she how important she was to him, if it were serious or just a passing notion. They had all read in the gossip columns how she came to meet him; how he had gone to have an X-ray and met her there, the radiographer in white, committed to a dark room and films showing lungs and pulmonary tracts.

"Am I right in thinking you are to take swimming lessons?" a man asked, choosing the moment when she had leaned back and was staring up at a big pine tree.

"Yes," she said, wishing that he had not been told.

"There's nothing to it, you just get in and swim," he said.

How surprised they all were, surprised and amused. Asked where she had lived and if it was really true.

"Can't imagine anyone not swimming as a child."

"Can't imagine anyone not swimming, period."

"Nothing to it, you just fight, fight."

The sun filtered by the green needles fell and made play on the dense clusters of brown nuts. They never ridicule nature, she thought, they never dare. He came and stood behind her, his hand patting her bare pale shoulder. A man who was not holding a camera pretended to take a photograph of them. How long would she last? It would be uppermost in all their minds.

"We'll take you on the boat tomorrow," he said. They cooed. They all went to such pains, such excesses, to describe the cruiser. They competed with each other to tell her. They were really telling him. She thought, I should be honest, say I do not like the sea, say I am an inland person, that I like rain and roses in a field, thin rain, and through it the roses and the vegetation, and that for me the sea is as dark as the shells of mussels, and signifies catastrophe. But she couldn't.

"It must be wonderful" was what she said.

"It's quite, quite something," he said shyly.

At dinner she sat at one end of the egg-shaped table and he at the other. Six white candles in glass sconces separated them. The secretary had arranged the places. A fat woman on his right wore a lot of silver bracelets and was veiled in crepe. They had cold soup to start with. The garnishings were so finely chopped that it was impossible to identify each one except by its flavor. She slipped out of her shoes. A man describing his trip to India dwelt for an unnaturally long time on the disgustingness of the food. He had gone to see the temples.

Another man, who was repeatedly trying to buoy them up, threw the question to the table at large: "Which of the Mediterranean ports is best to dock at?" Everyone had a favorite. Some picked ports where exciting things had happened, some chose ports where the approach was most beguiling, harbor fees were compared as a matter of interest; the man who had asked the question amused them all with an account of a cruise he had made once with his young daughter and of how he was unable to land when they got to Venice because of inebriation. She had to admit that she did not know any ports. They were untouched by that confession.

"We're going to try them all," he said from the opposite end of the table, "and keep a logbook." People looked from him to her and smiled knowingly.

That night behind closed shutters they enacted their rite. They were both impatient to get there. Long before the coffee had been brought they had moved away from the table and contrived to be alone, choosing the stone seat that girdled the big pine tree. The seat was smeared all over with the tree's transparent gum. The nuts bobbing together made a dull clatter like castanets. They sat for as long as courtesy required, then they retired. In bed she felt safe again, united to him not only by passion and by pleasure but by some more radical entanglement.

She had no name for it, that puzzling emotion that was more than love, or perhaps less, that was not simply sexual, although sex was vital to it and held it together like wires supporting a broken bowl. They both had had many breakages and therefore loved with a wary superstition.

"What you do to me," he said. "How you know me, all my vibrations."

"I think we are connected underneath," she said quietly. She often thought he hated her for implicating him in something too tender. But he was not hating her then.

At length it was necessary to go back to her bedroom, because he had promised to get up early to go spearfishing with the men.

As she kissed him goodbye she caught sight of herself in the chrome surface of the coffee flask which was on his bedside table—eyes emitting satisfaction and chagrin and panic were what stared back at her. Each time as she left him she expected not to see him again; each parting promised to be final.

The men left soon after six; she heard car doors because she had been unable to sleep.

In the morning she had her first swimming lesson. It was arranged that she would take it when the others sat down to breakfast. Her instructor had been brought from England. She asked if he'd slept well. She did not ask where. The servants disappeared from the house late at night and departed toward the settlement of low-roofed buildings. The dog went with them. The instructor told her to go backward down the metal stepladder. There were wasps hovering about and she thought that if she were to get stung she could bypass the lesson. No wasp obliged.

Some children, who had been swimming earlier, had left their plastic toys—a yellow ring that craned into the neck and head of a duck. It was a duck with a thoroughly disgusted expression. There was as well a blue dolphin with a name painted on it, and all kinds of battleships. They were the children of guests. The older ones, who were boys, took no notice of any of the adults and moved about, raucous and meddlesome, taking full advantage of every aspect of the place—at night they watched the lizards patiently and for hours, in the heat of the day they remained in the water, in the early morning they gathered almonds, for which they received from him a harvesting fee. One black flipper lurked on the bottom of the pool. She looked down at it and touched it with her toe. Those were her last unclaimed moments, those moments before the lesson began.

The instructor told her to sit, to sit in it, as if it were a bath. He crouched and slowly she crouched, too. "Now hold your nose and put your head under water," he said. She pulled the bathing cap well over her ears and forehead to protect her hairstyle, and with her nose gripped too tightly she went underneath. "Feel it?" he said excitedly. "Feel the water holding you up?" She felt no such thing. She felt the water engulfing her. He told her to press the water from her eyes. He was gentleness itself. Then he dived in, swam a few strokes, and stood up, shaking the water from his gray hair. He took her hands and walked backward until they were at arm's length. He asked her to lie on her stomach and give herself to it. He promised not to let go of her hands. Each time, on the verge of doing so, she stopped: first her body, then her mind refused. She felt that if she was to take her feet off the ground the unmentionable would happen. "What do I fear?" she asked herself. "Death," she said, and yet, it was not that. It was as if some horrible experience would happen before her actual death. She thought perhaps it might be the fight she would put up.

When she succeeded in stretching out for one desperate minute, he proclaimed with joy. But that first lesson was a failure as far as she was concerned. Walking back to the house, she realized it was a mistake to have allowed an instructor to be brought. It put too much emphasis on it. It would be incumbent upon her to conquer it. They would concern themselves with her progress, not because they cared, but like the summer lightning or the yachts going by, it would be something to talk about. But she could not send the instructor home. He was an old man and he had never been abroad before. Already he was marveling at the scenery. She had to go on with it. Going back to the terrace, she was not sure of her feet on land, she was not sure of land itself; it seemed to sway, and her knees shook uncontrollably.

When she sat down to breakfast she found that a saucer of almonds had been peeled for her. They were sweet and fresh, reinvoking the sweetness and freshness of a country morning. They tasted like hazelnuts. She said so. Nobody agreed. Nobody disagreed. Some were reading papers. Now and then someone read a piece aloud, some amusing piece about some acquaintance of theirs who had done a dizzy, newsworthy thing. The children read the thermometer and argued about the penciled shadow on the sundial. The temperature was already in the eighties. The women were forming a plan to go on the speedboat to get their midriffs brown. She declined. He called her into the conservatory and said she might give some time to supervising the meals because the secretary had rather a lot to do.

Passion-flower leaves were stretched along the roof on lifelines of green cord. Each leaf like the five fingers of a hand. Green and yellow leaves on the same hand. No flowers. Flowers later. Flowers that would live a day. Or so the gardener had said. She said, "I hope we will be here to see one." "If you want, we will," he said, but of course he might take a notion and go. He never knew what he might do; no one knew.

When she entered the vast kitchen, the first thing the servants did was to smile. Women in black, with soft-soled shoes, all smiling, no complicity in any of those smiles. She had brought with her a phrase book, a notebook, and an English cookery book. The kitchen was like a laboratory—various white machines stationed against the walls, refrigerators churtling at different speeds, a fan over each of the electric cookers, the red and green lights on the dials faintly menacing, as if they were about to issue an alarm. There was a huge fish on the table. It had been speared that morning by the men. Its mouth was open; its eyes so close together that they barely missed being one eye; its lower lip gaping pathetically. The fins were black and matted with oil. They all stood and looked at it, she and the seven or eight willing women to whom she must make herself understood. When she sat to copy the recipe from the English book and translate it into their language, they turned on another fan. Already they were chopping for the evening meal. Three young girls chopped onions, tomatoes, and peppers. They seemed to take pleasure in their tasks; they seemed to smile into the mounds of vegetable that they so diligently chopped.

There were eight picnic baskets to be taken on the boat. And armfuls of towels. The children begged to be allowed to carry the towels. He had the zip bag with the wine bottles. He shook the bag so that the bottles rattled in their surrounds of ice. The guests smiled. He had a way of drawing people into his mood without having to say or do much. Conversely he had a way of locking people out. Both things were mesmerizing. They crossed the four fields that led to the sea. The figs were hard and green. The sun played like a blow lamp upon her back and neck. He said that she would have to lather herself in suntan oil. It seemed oddly hostile, his saying it out loud like that, in front of the others. As they got nearer the water she felt her heart race. The water was all shimmer. Some swam out, some got in the rowboat. Trailing her hand in the crinkled surface of the water she thought, It is not cramp, jellyfish, or broken glass that I fear, it is something else. A ladder was dropped down at the side of the boat for the swimmers to climb in from the sea. Sandals had to be kicked off as they stepped inside. The floor was of blond wood and burning hot. Swimmers had to have their feet inspected for tar marks. The boatman stood with a pad of cotton soaked in turpentine ready to rub the marks. The men busied themselves—one helped to get the engine going, a couple put awnings up, others carried out large striped cushions and scattered them under the awnings. Two boys refused to come on board.

"It is pleasant to bash my little brother up under water," a young boy said, his voice at once menacing and melodious.

She smiled and went down steps to where there was a kitchen and sleeping quarters with beds for four. He followed her. He looked, inhaled deeply, and murmured.

"Take it out," she said, "I want it now, now." Timorous and whim mad. How he loved it. How he loved that imperative. He pushed the door and she watched as he struggled to take down his shorts but could not get the cord undone. He was the awkward one now. How he stumbled. She waited for one excruciating moment and made him wait. Then she knelt, and as she began he muttered between clenched teeth. He who could tame animals was defenseless in this. She applied herself to it, sucking, sucking, sucking, with all the hunger that she felt and all the simulated hunger that she liked him to think she felt. Threatening to maim him, she always just grazed with the edges of her fine square teeth. Nobody intruded. It took no more than minutes. She stayed behind for a decent interval. She felt thirsty. On the window ledge there were paperback books and bottles of sun oil. Also a spare pair of shorts that had names of all the likely things in the world printed on them—names of drinks and capital cities and the flags of each nation. The sea through the porthole was a small, harmless globule of blue.

They passed out of the harbor, away from the three other

boats and the settlement of pines. Soon there was only sea and rock, no reedy inlets, no towns. Mile after mile of hallucinating sea. The madness of mariners conveyed itself to her, the illusion that it was land and that she could traverse it. A land that led to nowhere. The rocks had been reduced to every shape the eye and the mind could comprehend. Near the water there were openings that had been forced through by the sea—some rapacious, some large enough for a small boat to slink in under, some as small and unsettling as the socket of eyes. The trees on the sheer faces of these rocks were no more than the struggle to be trees. Birds could not perch there, let alone nest. She tried not to remember the swimming lesson, to postpone remembering until the afternoon, until the next lesson.

She came out and joined them. A young girl sat at the stern, among the cushions, playing a guitar. She wore long silver spatula-shaped earrings. A self-appointed gypsy. The children were playing I Spy but finding it hard to locate new objects. They were confined to the things they could see around them. By standing she found that the wind and the spray from the water kept her cool. The mountains that were far away appeared insubstantial, but those that were near glinted when the sharp stones were pierced by the sun.

"I find it a little unreal," she said to one of the men. "Beautiful but unreal." She had to shout because of the noise of the engine.

"I don't know what you mean by unreal," he said.

Their repertoire was small but effective. In the intonation the sting lay. Dreadfully subtle. Impossible to bridle over. In fact, the unnerving thing about it was the terrible bewilderment it induced. Was it intended or not? She distinctly remembered a sensation of once thinking that her face was laced by a cobweb, but being unable to feel it with the hand and being unable to put a finger on their purulence felt exactly the same. To each other, too, they transmitted small malices and then moved on to the next topic. They mostly talked of places they had been to and the people who were there, and though they talked endlessly, they told nothing about themselves.

They picnicked on a small pink strand. He ate very little, and afterward he walked off. She thought to follow him, then didn't. The children waded out to sea on a long whitened log, and one of the women read everybody's hand. She was promised an illness. When he returned he gave his large yellowish hand reluctantly. He was promised a son. She looked at him for a gratifying sign but got none. At that moment he was telling one of the men about a black sloop that he had loved as a child. She thought, What is it that he sees in me, he who loves sea, sloops, jokes, masquerades, and deferment. What is it that he sees in me who loves none of those things?

Her instructor brought flat white boards. He held one end, she the other. She watched his hands carefully. They were very white from being in water. She lay on her stomach and held the boards and watched his hands in case they should let go of the board. The boards kept bobbing about and adding to her uncertainty. He said a rope would be better.

The big fish had had its bones removed and was then pieced together. A perfect decoy. Its head and its too near eyes were gone. On her advice the housekeeper had taken the lemons out of the refrigerator, so that they were like lemons now rather than bits of frozen sponge. Someone remarked on this and she felt childishly pleased. Because of a south wind a strange night exhilaration arose. They drank a lot. They discussed beautiful evenings. Evenings resurrected in them by the wine and the wind and a transient goodwill. One talked of watching golden cock pheasants strutting in a back yard; one talked of bantams perched on a gate at dusk, their forms like notes of music on a blank bar; no one mentioned love or family, it was scenery or nature or a whippet that left them with the best and most serene memories. She relived a stormy night with an ass braying in a field and a blown bough fallen across a road. After dinner various couples went for walks, or swims, or to listen for children. The three men who were single went to the village to reconnoiter. Women confided the diets they were on, or the face creams that they found most beneficial. A divorcée said to her host, "You've got to come to bed with me, you've simply got to," and he smiled. It was no more than a pleasantry, another remark in a strange night's proceedings where there were also crickets, tree frogs, and the sounds of clandestine kissing. The single men came back presently and reported that the only bar was full of Germans and that the whiskey was inferior. The one who had been most scornful about her swimming sat at her feet and said how awfully pretty she was. Asked her details about her life, her work, her schooling. Yet this friendliness only reinforced her view of her own solitude, her apartness. She answered each question carefully and seriously. By answering she was subscribing to her longing to fit in. He seemed a little jealous, so she got up and went to him. He was not really one of them, either. He simply stage-managed them for his own amusement. Away from them she almost reached him. It was as if he were bound by a knot that maybe, maybe, she could unravel, for a long stretch, living their own life, cultivating a true emotion, independent of other people. But would they ever be away? She dared not ask. For that kind of discussion she had to substitute with a silence.

She stole into their rooms to find clues to their private selves—to see if they had brought sticking plaster, indigestion pills, face flannels, the ordinary necessities. On a dressing table there was a wig block with blond hair very artfully curled. On the face of the block colored sequins were arranged to represent the features of an ancient Egyptian queen. The divorcée had a baby's pillow in a yellow muslin case. Some had carried up bottles of wine and these though not drunk were not removed. The servants only touched what was thrown on the floor or put in the wastepaper baskets. Clothes for washing were thrown on the floor. It was one of the house rules, like having cocktails on the terrace at evening time. Some had written cards which she read eagerly. These cards told nothing except that it was all super.

His secretary, who was mousy, avoided her. Perhaps she

knew too much. Plans he had made for the future.

She wrote to her doctor:

I am taking the tranquillizers but I don't feel any more relaxed. Could you send me some others?

She tore it up.

Her hair got tangled by the salt in the sea air. She bought some curling tongs.

One woman, who was pregnant, kept sprinkling baby powder and smoothing it over her stomach throughout the day. They always took tea together. They were friends. She thought, If this woman were not pregnant would she be so amiable? Their kind of thinking was beginning to take root in her.

The instructor put a rope over her head. She brought it down around her middle. They heard a quack-quack. She was certain that the plastic duck had intoned. She laughed as she adjusted the noose. The instructor laughed, too. He held a firm grip of the rope. She threshed through the water and tried not to think of where she was. Sometimes she did it well; sometimes she had to be brought in like an old piece of lumber. She could never tell the outcome of each plunge; she never knew how it was going to be or what thoughts would suddenly obstruct her. But each time he said, "Lovely, lovely," and in his exuberance she found consolation.

A woman called Iris swam out to their yacht. She dangled in the water and with one hand gripped the sides of the boat. Her nail varnish was exquisitely applied and the nails had the glow of a rich imbued pearl. By contrast with the pearl coating, the half-moons were chastely white. Her personality was like that, too—full of glow. For each separate face she had a smile, and a word or two for those she already knew. One of the men asked if she was in love. Love! she riled him. She said her good spirits were due to her breathing. She said life was a question of correct breathing. She had come to invite them for drinks but he declined because they were due back at the house. His lawyer had been invited to lunch. She chided him for being so busy, then swam off toward the shore, where her poodle was yapping and waiting for her. At lunch they all talked of her. There was mention of her past escapades, the rows with her husband, his death, which was thought to be a suicide, and the unpleasant business of his burial, which proved impossible on religious grounds. Finally, his body had to be laid in a small paddock adjoining the public cemetery. Altogether an unsavory story, yet preening in the water had been this radiant woman with no traces of past harm.

"Yes, Iris has incredible willpower, incredible," he said.

"For what?" she asked, from the opposite end of the table.

"For living," he said tartly.

It was not lost on the others. Her jaw muscle twitched.

Again she spoke to herself, remonstrated with her hurt: "I try, I try, I want to fit, I want to join, be the someone who slips into a crowd of marchers when the march has already begun, but there is something in me that I call sense and it balks at your ways. It would seem as if I am here simply to smart under your strictures." Retreating into dreams and monologue.

She posed for a picture. She posed beside the sculptured lady. She repeated the pose of the lady. Hands placed over each other and laid on the left shoulder, head inclining toward those hands. He took it. Click, click. The marble lady had been the sculptor's wife and had died tragically. The hands with their unnaturally long nails were the best feature of it. Click, click. When she was not looking he took another.

She found the account books in a desk drawer and was surprised at the entries. Things like milk and matches had to be accounted for. She thought, Is he generous at the roots? The housekeeper had left some needlework in the book. She had old-fashioned habits and resisted much of the modern kitchen equipment. She kept the milk in little pots, with muslin spread over the top. She skimmed the cream with her fat fingers, tipped the cream into small jugs for their morning coffee. What would they say to that! In the evenings, when every task was done, the housekeeper sat in the back veranda with her husband, doing the mending. They had laid pine branches on the roof, and these had withered and were tough as wire. Her husband made shapes from soft pieces of new white wood, and then in the dark put his penknife aside and tickled his wife. She heard them when she stole in to get some figs from the refrigerator. It was both poignant and untoward.

The instructor let go of the rope. She panicked and stopped using her arms and legs. The water was rising up over her. The water was in complete control of her. She knew that she was screaming convulsively. He had to jump in, clothes and all. Afterward they sat in the linen room with a blanket each and drank brandy. They vouched to tell no one. The brandy went straight to his head. He said in England it would be raining and people would be queueing for buses, and his eyes twinkled because of his own good fate.

More than one guest was called Teddy. One of the Teddys told her that in the mornings before his wife wakened he read Proust in the dressing room. It enabled him to masturbate. It was no more than if he had told her he missed bacon for breakfast. For breakfast there was fruit and scrambled egg. Bacon was a rarity on the island. She said to the older children that the plastic duck was psychic and had squeaked. They laughed. Their laughing was real, but they kept it up long after the joke had expired. A girl said, "Shall I tell you a rude story?" The boys appeared to want to restrain her. The girl said, "Once upon a time there was a lady, and a blind man came to her door every evening for sixpence, and one day she was in the bath and the doorbell rang and she put on a gown and came down and it was the milkman, and she got back in the bath and the doorbell rang and it was the bread man, and at six o'clock the doorbell rang and she thought, I don't have to put on my gown it is the blind man, and when she opened the door the blind man said, 'Madam, I've come to tell you I got my sight back.' " And the laughter that had never really died down started up again, and the whole mountain was boisterous with it. No insect, no singing bird was heard on that walk. She had to watch the time. The children's evening meal was earlier. They ate on the back veranda and she often went there and stole an anchovy or a piece of bread so as to avoid getting too drunk before dinner. There was no telling how late dinner would be. It depended on him, on whether he was bored or not. Extra guests from neighboring houses came each evening for drinks. They added variety. The talk was about sailing and speeding, or about gardens, or about pools. They all seemed to be intrigued by these topics, even the women. One man who followed the snow knew where the best snow surfaces were for each week of every year. That subject did not bore her as much. At least the snow was nice to think about, crisp and blue like he said, and rasping under the skis. The children could often be heard shrieking, but after cocktail hour they never appeared. She believed that it would be better once they were married and had children. She would be accepted by courtesy of them. It was a swindle really, the fact that small creatures, ridiculously easy to beget, should solidify a relationship, but they would. Everyone hinted how he wanted a son. He was nearing sixty. She had stopped using contraceptives and he had stopped asking. Perhaps that was his way of deciding, of finally accepting her.

Gulls' eggs, already shelled, were brought to table. The yolks a very delicate yellow. "Where are the shells?" the fat lady, veiled in crepe, asked. The shells had to be brought. They were crumbled almost to a powder but were brought anyhow. "Where are the nests?" she asked. It missed. It was something they might have laughed at, had they heard, but a wind had risen and they were all getting up and carrying things indoors. The wind was working up to something. It whipped the geranium flowers from their leaves and crazed the candle flames so that they blew this way and that and cracked the glass sconces. That night their lovemaking had all the sweetness and all the release that earth must feel with the long-awaited rain. He was another man now, with another voice—loving and private and incantatory. His coldness, his dismissal of her hard to believe in. Perhaps if they quarreled, their quarrels, like their lovemaking, would bring them closer. But they never did. He said he'd never had a quarrel with any of his women. She gathered that he left his wives once it got to that point. He did not say so, but she felt that must have been so, because he had once said that all his marriages were happy. He said there had been fights with men but that these were decent. He had more rapport with men; with women he was charming but it was a charm devised to keep them at bay. He had no brothers, and no son. He had had a father who bullied him and held his inheritance back for longer than he should. This she got from one of the men who had known him for forty years. His father had caused him to suffer, badly. She did not know in what way and she was unable to ask him, because it was information she should never have been given a hint of.

After their trip to the Roman caves the children came home ravenous. One child objected because the meal was cold. The servant, sensing a certain levity, told her master, and the story sent shrieks of laughter around the lunch table. It was repeated many times. He called to ask if she had heard. He sometimes singled her out in that way. It was one of the few times the guests could glimpse the bond between them. Yes, she had heard. "Sweet, sweet," she said. The word occurred in her repertoire all the time now. She was learning their language. And fawning. Far from home, from where the cattle grazed. The cattle had fields to roam, and a water tank near the house. The earth around the water tank always churned up, always mucky from the trampling there. They were farming people, had their main meal in the middle of the day, had rows. Her father vanished one night after supper, said he was going to count the cattle, brought a flashlamp, never came back. Others sympathized, but she and her mother were secretly relieved. Maybe he drowned himself in one of the many bog lakes, or changed his name and went to a city. At any rate, he did not hang himself from a tree or do anything ridiculous like that.

She lay on her back as the instructor brought her across the pool, his hand under her spine. The sky above an innocent blightless blue, with streamers where the jets had passed over. She let her head go right back. She thought, If I were to give myself to it totally, it would be a pleasure and an achievement, but she couldn't.

Argoroba hung from the trees like blackened banana skins. The men picked them in the early morning and packed them in sacks for winter fodder. In the barn where these sacks were stored there was a smell of decay. And an old olive press. In the linen room next door a pleasant smell of linen. The servants used too much bleach. Clothes lost their sharpness of color after one wash. She used to sit in one or another of these rooms and read. She went to the library for a book. He was in one of the Regency chairs that was covered with ticking. As on a throne. One chair was real and one a copy, but she could never tell them apart. "I saw you yesterday, and you nearly went under," he said. "I still have several lessons to go," she said, and went as she intended, but without the book that she had come to fetch.

His daughter by his third marriage had an eighteen-inch waist. On her first evening she wore a white trouser suit. She held the legs out, and the small pleats when opened were like a concertina. At table she sat next to her father and gazed at him with appropriate awe. He told a story of a dangerous leopard hunt. They had lobster as a special treat. The lobster tails, curving from one place setting to the next, reached far more cordially than the conversation. She tried to remember something she had read that day. She found that by memorizing things she could amuse them at table.

"The gorilla resorts to eating, drinking, or scratching to bypass anxiety," she said later. They all laughed.

"You don't say," he said, with a sneer. It occurred to her that if she were to become too confident he would not want that, either. Or else he had said it to reassure his daughter.

There were moments when she felt confident. She knew in her mind the movements she was required to make in order to pass through the water. She could not do them, but she knew what she was supposed to do. She worked her hands under the table, trying to make deeper and deeper forays into the atmosphere. No one caught her at it. The word "plankton" would not let go of her. She saw dense masses of it, green and serpentine, enfeebling her fingers. She could almost taste it.

His last wife had stitched a backgammon board in green and red. Very beautiful it was. The fat woman played with him after dinner. They carried on the game from one evening to the next. They played very contentedly. The woman wore a different arrangement of rings at each sitting and he never failed to admire and compliment her on them. To those not endowed with beauty he was particularly charming.

Her curling tongs fused the entire electricity system. People rushed out of their bedrooms to know what had happened. He did not show his anger, but she felt it. Next morning they had to send a telegram to summon an electrician. In the telegram office two men sat, one folding the blue pieces of paper, one applying gum with a narrow brush and laying thin borders of white over the blue and pressing down with his hands. On the white strips the name and address had already been printed. A motorcycle was indoors, to protect the tires from the sun, or in case it might be stolen. The men took turns when a telegram had to be delivered. She saved one or the other of them a journey because a telegram from a departed guest arrived while she was waiting. It simply said "Adored it, Harry." Guests invariably forgot something and in their thank-you letters mentioned what they had forgotten. She presumed that some of the hats stacked into one another and laid on the stone ledge were hats forgotten or thrown away. She had grown quite attached to a green one that had lost its ribbons.

The instructor asked to be brought to the souvenir shop. He bought a glass ornament and a collar for his dog. On the way back a man at the petrol station gave one of the children a bird. They put it in the chapel. Made a nest for it. The servant threw it nest and all into the wastepaper basket. That night at supper the talk was of nothing else. He remembered his fish story and told it to the new people who had come, how one morning he had to abandon his harpoon because the lines got tangled and next day, when he went back, he found the shark had retreated into the cave and had two great lumps of rock in his mouth, where obviously he had bitten himself free. That incident had a profound effect on him.

"Is the boat named after your mother?" she asked of his daughter. Her mother's name was Beth and the boat was called Miss Beth. "He never said," the daughter replied. She always disappeared after lunch. It must have been to accommodate them. Despite the heat they made a point of going to his room. And made a point of inventiveness. She tried a strong green stalk, to excite him, marveling at it, comparing him and it. He watched. He could not endure such competition. With her head upside down and close to the tiled floor she saw all the oils and ointments on his bathroom ledge and tried reading their labels backward. Do I like all this lovemaking? she asked herself. She had to admit that possibly she did not, that it went on too long, that it was involvement she sought, involvement and threat.

They swapped dreams. It was her idea. He was first. Everyone was careful to humor him. He said in a dream a dog was lost and his grief was great. He seemed to want to say more but he didn't, or couldn't. Repeated the same thing, in fact. When it came to her turn, she told a different dream from the one she had meant to tell. A short, uninvolved little dream.

In the night she heard a guest sob. In the morning the same guest wore a flame dressing gown and praised the marmalade, which she ate sparingly.

She asked for the number of lessons to be increased. She had three a day and she did not go on the boat with the others. Between lessons she would walk along the shore. The pine trunks were white, as if a lathe had been put to them. The winds of winter the lathe. In winter they would move; to catch up with friends, business meetings, art exhibitions, to buy presents, to shop. He hated suitcases, he liked clothes to be waiting wherever he went, and they were. She saw a wardrobe with his winter clothes neatly stacked, she saw his frieze cloak with the black astrakhan collar, and she experienced such a longing for that impossible season, that impossible city, and his bulk inside the cloak as they set out in the cold to go to a theater. Walking along the shore, she did the swimming movements in her head.

It had got into all her thinking. Invaded her dreams. Atrocious dreams about her mother, her father, and one where lion cubs surrounded her as she lay on a hammock. The cubs were waiting to pounce the second she moved. The hammock, of course, was unsteady. Each time she wakened from one of those dreams she felt certain that her cries were the repeated cries of infancy, and it was then she helped herself to the figs she had brought up.

He put a handkerchief, folded like a letter, before her plate at table. On opening it she found some sprays of fresh mint, wide-leafed and cold. He had obviously put it in the refrigerator first. She smelled it and passed it around. Then on impulse she got up to kiss him and on her journey back nearly bumped into the servant with a tureen of soup, so excited was she.

Her instructor was her friend. "We're winning, we're winning," he said. He walked from dawn onward, walked the hills and saw the earth with dew on it. He wore a handkerchief on his head that he knotted over the ears, but as he approached the house, he removed this headdress. She met him on one of these morning walks. As it got nearer the time, she could neither sleep nor make love. "We're winning, we're winning." He always said it no matter where they met.

They set out to buy finger bowls. In the glass factory there were thin boys with very white skin who secured pieces of glass with pokers and thrust them into the stoves. The whole place smelled of wood. There was chopped wood in piles, in corners.

Circular holes were cut along the top of the wall between the square grated windows. The roof was high and yet the place was a furnace. Five kittens with tails like rats lay bunched immobile in a heap. A boy, having washed himself in one of the available buckets of water, took the kittens one by one and dipped them in. She took it to be an act of kindness. Later he bore a hot blue bubble at the end of a poker and laid it before her. As the flame subsided it became mauve, and as it cooled more, it was almost colorless. It had the shape of a sea serpent and an unnaturally long tail. Its color and its finished appearance were an accident, but the gift was clearly intentioned. There was nothing she could do but smile. As they were leaving she saw him waiting near the motorcar, and as she got in, she waved wanly. That night they had asparagus, which is why they went to the trouble to get finger bowls. These were blue with small bubbles throughout, and though the bubbles may have been a defect, they gave to the thick glass an illusion of frost.

There was a new dog, a mongrel, in whom he took no interest. He said the servants got new dogs simply because he allotted money for that. But as they were not willing to feed more than one animal, the previous year's dog was either murdered or put on the mountain. All these dogs were of the same breed, part wolf; she wondered if when left on the mountain they reverted to being wolves. He said solemnly to the table at large that he would never allow himself to become attached to another dog. She said to him directly, "Is it possible to know beforehand?" He said, "Yes." She could see that she had irritated him.

He came three times and afterward coughed badly. She sat with him and stroked his back, but when the coughing took command he moved her away. He leaned forward, holding a pillow to his mouth. She saw a film of his lungs, orange shapes with insets of dark that boded ill. She wanted to do some simple domestic thing like give him medicine, but he sent her away. Going back along the terrace, she could hear the birds. The birds were busy with their song. She met the fat woman. "You have been derouted," the woman said, "and so have I." And they bowed mockingly.

An archaeologist had been on a dig where a wooden temple was discovered. "Tell me about your temple," she said.

"I would say it's 400 B.C.," he said, nothing more. Dry, dry.

A boy who called himself Jasper and wore mauve shirts received letters under the name of John. The letters were arranged on the hall table, each person's under a separate stone. Her mother wrote to say they were anxiously awaiting the good news. She said she hoped they would get engaged first but admitted that she was quite prepared to be told that the marriage had actually taken place. She knew how unpredictable he was. Her mother managed a poultry farm in England and was a compulsive eater.

Young people came to ask if Clay Sickle was staying at the house. They were in rags, but it looked as if they were rags worn on purpose and for effect. Their shoes were bits of motor tire held up with string. They all got out of the car, though the question could have been asked by any one of them. He was on his way back from the pool, and after two minutes' conversation he invited them for supper. He throve on new people. That night they were the ones in the limelight—the three unkempt boys and the long-haired girl. The girl had very striking eyes, which she fixed on one man and then another. She was determined to compromise one of them. The boys described their holiday, being broke, the trouble they had with the car, which was owned by a hire purchase firm in London. After dinner an incident occurred. The girl followed one of the men into the bathroom. "Want to see what you've got there," she said, and insisted on watching while the man peed. She said they would do any kind of fucking he wanted. She said he would be a slob not to try. It was too late to send them away, because earlier on they'd been invited to spend the night and beds were put up, down in the linen room. The girl was the last to go over there. She started a song, "All around his cock he wears a tricolored rash-eo," and she went on yelling it as she crossed the courtyard and went down the steps, brandishing a bottle.

In the morning, she determined to swim by herself. It was not that she mistrusted her instructor, but the time was getting closer and she was desperate. As she went to the pool, one of the youths appeared in borrowed white shorts, eating a banana. She greeted him with faltering gaiety. He said it was fun to be out before the others. He had a big head with closely cropped hair, a short neck, and a very large nose.

"Beaches are where I most want to be, where it all began,"

he said. She thought he was referring to creation, and upon hearing such a thing he laughed profanely. "Let's suppose there's a bunch of kids and you're all horsing around with a ball and all your sensory dimensions are working..."

"What?" she said.

"A hard-on..."

"Oh..."

"Now the ball goes into the sea and I follow and she follows me and takes the ball from my hand and a dense rain of energy, call it love, from me to her and vice versa, reciprocity in other words..."

Sententious idiot. She thought, Why do people like that have to be kept under his roof? Where is his judgment, where? She walked back to the house, furious at having to miss her chance to swim.

> *Dear Mother: It's not that kind of relationship. Being unmarried installs me as positively as being married, and neither installs me with any certainty. It is a beautiful house, but staying here is quite a strain. You could easily get filleted. Friends do it to friends. The food is good. Others cook it, but I am responsible for each day's menu. Shopping takes hours. The shops have a special smell that is impossible to describe. They are all dark, so that the foodstuffs won't perish. An old woman goes along the street in a cart selling fish. She has a very penetrating cry. It is like the commencement of a song. There are always six or seven little girls with her, they all have pierced ears and wear fine gold sleepers. Flies swarm around the cart even when it is upright in the square. Living off scraps and fish scales, I expect. We do not buy from*

her, we go to the harbor and buy directly from the fishermen. The guests—all but one woman—eat small portions. You would hate it. All platinum people. They have a canny sense of self-preservation; they know how much to eat, how much to drink, how far to go; you would think they invented somebody like Shakespeare, so proprietary are they about his talent. They are not fools—not by any means. There is a chessboard of ivory and it is so large it stands on the floor. Seats of the right height are stationed around it.

Far back—in my most distant childhood, Mother—I remember your nightly cough; it was a lament really and I hated it. At the time I had no idea that I hated it, which goes to show how unreliable feelings are. We do not know what we feel at the time and that is very perplexing. Forgive me for mentioning the cough, it is simply that I think it is high time we spoke our minds on all matters. But don't worry. You are centuries ahead of the people here. In a nutshell, they brand you as idiot if you are harmless. There are jungle laws which you never taught me; you couldn't, you never knew them. Ah well!

I will bring you a present. Probably something suede. He says the needlework here is appalling and that things fall to pieces, but you can always have it remade. We had some nice china jelly molds when I was young. Whatever happened to them? Love.

Like the letter to the doctor, it was not posted. She didn't tear it up or anything, it just lay in an envelope and she omitted to post it from one day to the next. This new tendency disturbed her. This habit of postponing everything. It was as if something vital had first to be gone through. She blamed the swimming.

The day the pool was emptied she missed her three lessons. She could hear the men scrubbing, and from time to time she walked down and stood over them as if her presence could hurry the proceedings and make the water flow in, in one miracle burst. He saw how she fretted, he said they should have had two pools built. He asked her to come with them on the boat. The books and the suntan oil were as she had last seen them. The cliffs as intriguing as ever. "Hello, cliff, can I fall off you?" She waved merrily. In a small harbor they saw another millionaire with his girl. They were alone, without even a crew. And for some reason it went straight to her heart. At dinner the men took bets as to who the girl was. They commented on her prettiness though they had hardly seen her. The water filling the pool sounded like a stream from a faraway hill. He said it would be full by morning.

Other houses had beautiful objects, but theirs was in the best taste. The thing she liked most was the dull brass chandelier from Portugal. In the evenings when it was lit, the cones of light tapered toward the rafters and she thought of woodsmoke and the wings of birds endlessly fluttering. Votive. To please her he had a fire lit in a far-off room simply to have the smell of woodsmoke in the air.

The watercress soup that was to be a specialty tasted like salt water. Nobody blamed her, but afterward she sat at the table and wondered how it had gone wrong. She felt defeated. On request he brought another bottle of red wine, but asked if she was sure she ought to have more. She thought, He does not understand the workings of my mind. But then, neither did she. She was drunk. She held the glass out. Watching the meniscus, letting it tilt from side to side, she wondered how drunk she would be when she stood up. "Tell me," she said, "what interests you?" It was the first blunt question she had ever put to him.

"Why, everything," he said.

"But deep down," she said.

"Discovery," he said, and walked away.

But not self-discovery, she thought, not that.

A neurologist got drunk and played jazz on the chapel organ. He said he could not resist it, there were so many things to press. The organ was stiff from not being used.

She retired early. Next day she was due to swim for them. She thought he would come to visit her. If he did they would lie in one another's arms and talk. She would knead his poor worn scrotum and ask questions about the world beneath the sea where he delved each day, ask about those depths and if there were flowers of some sort down there, and in the telling he would be bound to tell her about himself. She kept wishing for the organ player to fall asleep. She knew he would not come until each guest had retired, because he was strangely reticent about his loving.

But the playing went on. If anything, the player gathered strength and momentum. When at last he did fall asleep, she opened the shutters. The terrace lights were all on. The night breathlessly still. Across the fields came the lap from the sea and then the sound of a sheep bell, tentative and intercepted. Even a sheep recognized the dead of night. The lighthouse worked faithfully as a heartbeat.

The dog lay in the chair, asleep, but with his ears raised. On other chairs were sweaters and books and towels, the remains of the day's activities. She watched and she waited. He did not come. She lamented that she could not go to him on the night she needed him most.

For the first time she thought about cramp.

In the morning she took three headache pills and swallowed them with hot coffee. They disintegrated in her mouth. Afterward she washed them down with soda water. There was no lesson because the actual swimming performance was to be soon after breakfast. She tried on one bathing suit, then another; then, realizing how senseless this was, she put the first one back on and stayed in her room until it was almost time.

When she came down to the pool they were all there ahead of her. They formed quite an audience: the twenty house guests and the six complaining children who had been obliged to quit the pool. Even the housekeeper stood on the stone seat under the tree, to get a view. Some smiled, some were a trifle embarrassed. The pregnant woman gave her a medal for good luck. It was attached to a pin. So they were friends. Her instructor stood near the front, the rope coiled around his wrist just in case. The children gave to the occasion its only levity. She went down the ladder backward and looked at no face in particular. She crouched until the water covered her shoulders, then she gave a short leap and delivered herself to it. Almost at once she knew that she was going to do it. Her hands, no longer loath to delve deep, scooped the water away, and she kicked with a ferocity she had not known to be possible. She was aware of cheering but it did not matter about that. She swam, as she had promised, across the width of the pool in the shallow end. It was pathetically short, but it was what she had vouched to do. Afterward one of the children said that her face was tortured. The rubber flowers had long since come off her bathing cap, and she pulled it off as she stood up and held on to the ladder. They clapped. They said it called for a celebration. He said nothing, but she could see that he was pleased. Her instructor was the happiest person there.

When planning the party they went to the study, where they could sit and make lists. He said they would order gypsies and flowers and guests and caviar and swans of ice to put the caviar in. None of it would be her duty. They would get people to do it. In all, they wrote out twenty telegrams. He asked how she felt. She admitted that being able to swim bore little relation to not being able. They were two unreconcilable feelings. The true thrill, she said, was the moment when she knew she would master it but had not yet achieved it with her body. He said he looked forward to the day when she went in and out of the water like a knife. He did the movement deftly with his hand. He said next thing she would learn was riding. He would teach her himself or he would have her taught. She remembered the chestnut mare with head raised, nostrils searching the air, and she herself unable to stroke it, unable to stand next to it without exuding fear.

"Are you afraid of nothing?" she asked, too afraid to tell him specifically about the encounter with the mare, which took place in his stable.

"Sure, sure."

"You never reveal it."

"At the time I'm too scared."

"But afterward, afterward..." she said.

"You try to live it down," he said, and looked at her and hurriedly took her in his arms. She thought, Probably he is as near to me as he has been to any living person and that is not very near, not very near at all. She knew that if he chose her they would not go in the deep end, the deep end that she dreaded and dreamed of. When it came to matters inside himself, he took no risks.

She was tired. Tired of the life she had elected to go into and disappointed with the man she had put pillars around. The tiredness came from inside, and like a deep breath going out slowly, it tore at her gut. She was sick of her own predilection for tyranny. It seemed to her that she always held people to her ear, the way her mother held eggs, shaking them to guess at their rottenness, but unlike her mother she chose the very ones that she would have been wise to throw away. He seemed to sense her sadness, but he said nothing; he held her and squeezed her from time to time in reassurance.

Her dress—his gift—was laid out on the bed, its wide white sleeves hanging down at either side. It was of openwork and it looked uncannily like a corpse. There was a shawl to go with it, and shoes and a bag. The servant was waiting. Beside the bath her book, an ashtray, cigarettes, and a little book of soft matches that were hard to strike. She lit a cigarette and drew on it heartily. She regretted not having brought up a drink. She felt like a drink at that moment, and in her mind she sampled the drink she might have had. The servant knelt down to put in the stopper. She asked that the bath should not be run just yet. Then she took the biggest towel and put it over her bathing suit and went along the corridor and down by the back stairs. She did not have to turn on the lights; she would have known her way blindfolded to that pool. All the toys were on the water, like farm animals just put to bed. She picked them out one by one and laid them at the side near the pile of empty chlorine bottles. She went down the ladder backward.

She swam in the shallow end and allowed the dreadful thought to surface. She thought, I shall do it or I shall not do it, and the fact that she was of two minds about it seemed to confirm her view of the unimportance of the whole thing. Anyone, even the youngest child, could have persuaded her not to, because her mind was without conviction. It just seemed easier, that was all, easier than the strain and the incomplete loving and the excursions that lay ahead.

"This is what I want, this is where I want to go," she said, restraining that part of herself that might scream. Once she went deep, and she submitted to it, the water gathered all around in a great beautiful bountiful baptism. As she went down to the cold and thrilling region she thought, They will never know, they will never, ever know, for sure.

At some point she began to fight and thresh about, and she cried, though she could not know the extent of those cries.

She came to her senses on the ground at the side of the pool, all muffled up and retching. There was an agonizing pain in her chest, as if a shears were snipping at her guts. The servants were with her and two of the guests and him. The floodlights were on around the pool. She put her hands to her breast to make sure; yes, she was naked under the blanket. They would have ripped her bathing suit off. He had obviously been the one to give respiration, because he was breathing quickly and his sleeves were rolled up. She looked at him. He did not smile. There was the sound of music, loud, ridiculous, and hearty. She remembered first the party, then everything. The nice vagueness quit her and she looked at him with shame. She looked at all of them. What things had she shouted as they brought her back to life? What thoughts had they spoken in those crucial moments? How long did it take? Her immediate concern was that they must not carry her to the house, she must not allow that last episode of indignity. But they did. As she was borne along by him and the gardener, she could see the flowers and the oysters and the jellied dishes and the small roast piglets all along the tables, a feast as in a dream, except that she was dreadfully clearheaded. Once alone in her room she vomited.

For two days she did not appear downstairs. He sent up a pile of books, and when he visited her he always brought someone. He professed a great interest in the novels she had read and asked how the plots were. When she did come down, the guests were polite and offhand and still specious, but along with that they were cautious now and deeply disapproving. Their manner told her that it had been a stupid and ghastly thing to do, and had she succeeded she would have involved all of them in her stupid and ghastly mess. She wished she could go home, without any farewells. The children looked at her and from time to time laughed out loud. One boy told her that his brother had once tried to drown him in the bath. Apart from that and the inevitable letter to the gardener, it was never mentioned. The gardener had been the one to hear her cry and raise the alarm. In their eyes he would be a hero.

People swam less. They made plans to leave. They had ready-made excuses—work, the change in the weather, airplane bookings. He told her that they would stay until all the guests had gone and then they would leave immediately. His secretary was traveling with them. He asked each day how she felt, but when they were alone, he either read or played patience. He appeared to be calm except that his eyes blazed as with fever. They were young eyes. The blue seemed to sharpen in color once the anger in him was resurrected. He was snappy with the servants. She knew that when they got back to London there would be separate cars waiting for them at the airport. It was only natural. The house, the warm flagstones, the shimmer of the water would sometimes, no doubt, reoccur to her; but she would forget him and he would live somewhere in the attic of her mind, the place where failure is consigned.

THE SWIMMERS *by* JOYCE CAROL OATES

JOYCE CAROL OATES (b. 1938) has more than 100 books, including We Were the Mulvaneys *and the National Book Award–winner* them, *to her credit. "The Swimmers" first appeared in* Playboy *in 1989, and later in her collection* Heat. *In a story seen through the innocent eyes of a young observer, two exceedingly private individuals meet at a small-town YMCA. Unfortunately, the simplicity of swimming laps is no match for the complexity of adult passion.*

THERE ARE STORIES that go unaccountably wrong and become impermeable to the imagination. They lodge in the memory like an old wound never entirely healed. This story of my father's younger brother Clyde Farrell, my uncle, and a woman named Joan Lunt, with whom he fell in love, years ago, in 1959, is one of those stories.

Some of it I was a part of, aged 13. But much of it I have to imagine.

It must have been a pale, wintry, unflattering light he first saw her in, swimming laps in the early morning in the local Y.M.C.A. pool, but that initial sight of Joan Lunt—not her face, which was obscured from him, but the movement of her strong, supple, creamy-pale body through the water, and the sureness of her strokes—never faded from Clyde Farrell's mind.

He'd been told of her; in fact, he'd come to the pool that morning to observe her, but still you didn't expect to see such serious swimming, 7:45 A.M. of a weekday, in the antiquated white-tiled "Y" pool, light slating down from the wired glass skylight overhead, a sharp medicinal smell of chlorine and disinfectant pinching your nostrils. There were a few other swimmers in the pool, ordinary swimmers, one of them an acquaintance of Clyde's who waved at him, called out his name when Clyde appeared in his swim trunks on the deck, climbed up onto the diving board, then paused to watch Joan Lunt swimming toward the far end of the pool...just stood watching her, not rudely but with a frank, childlike interest, smiling with the spontaneous pleasure of seeing another person doing something well, with so little waste motion. Joan Lunt in her yellow bathing suit with the crossed straps in back and her white rubber cap that gleamed and sparked in the miniature waves: an attractive woman in her mid-30s, though she looked younger, with an air of total absorption in the task at hand, swimming to the limit of her capacity, maintaining a pace and a rhythm Clyde Farrell would have been challenged to maintain himself, and Clyde was a good swimmer, known locally as a very good swimmer, a winner, years before, when he was in his teens, of county and state competitions. Joan Lunt wasn't aware of him standing on the diving board watching her, or so it appeared. Just swimming, counting laps. How many she'd done already he couldn't imagine. He saw that she knew to cup the water when she stroked back, not to let it thread through her fingers like most people do; she knew as if by instinct how to take advantage of the element she was in, propelling herself forward like an otter or a seal, power in her shoulder muscles and upper arms, and the swift scissors kick of her legs, feet flashing white through the chemical-turquoise glitter of the water. When Joan Lunt reached the end of the pool, she ducked immediately down into the water in a well-practiced maneuver, turned, used the tile side to kick off from, in a single graceful motion that took her a considerable distance, and Clyde Farrell's heart contracted when, emerging from the water, head and shoulders and flashing arms, the woman didn't miss a beat, just continued as if she hadn't been confronted with any limit or impediment, any boundary. It was just water, and her in it, water that might go on forever, and her in it, swimming, sealed off and invulnerable.

Clyde Farrell dived into the pool, and swam vigorously, keeping to his own lane, energetic and single-minded, too, and when, after some minutes, he glanced around for the woman in the yellow bathing suit, the woman I'd told him of meeting, Joan Lunt, he saw, to his disappointment, that she was gone.

His vanity was wounded. He thought, She never once looked at me.

My father and my uncle Clyde were farm boys who left the farm as soon as they were of age: joined the U.S. Navy out of high school, went away, came back and lived and worked in town, my father in a small sign shop and Clyde in a succession of jobs. He drove a truck for a gravel company, he was a foreman in a local tool factory, he managed a sporting-goods store; he owned property at Wolf's Head Lake, 20 miles to the north, and spoke with vague enthusiasm of developing it someday. He wasn't a practical man and he never saved money. He liked to gamble at cards and horses. In the Navy, he'd learned to box and for a while after being discharged, he considered a professional career as a welterweight, but that meant signing contracts, traveling around the country, taking orders from other men. Not Clyde Farrell's temperament.

He was good-looking, not tall, about 5'9", compact and quick on his feet, a natural athlete, with well-defined shoulder and arm muscles, strong sinewy legs. His hair was the color of damp sand, his eyes a warm liquid brown, all iris. There was a gap between his two front teeth that gave him a childlike look and was misleading.

No one ever expected Clyde Farrell to get married, or even to fall seriously in love. That capacity in him seemed missing, somehow: a small but self-proclaimed absence, like the gap between his teeth.

But Clyde was powerfully attracted to women, and after watching Joan Lunt swim that morning, he drifted by later in the day to Kress's, Yewville's largest department store, where he knew she'd recently started to work. Kress's was a store of some distinction, the merchandise was of high quality, the counters made of solid, burnished oak; the overhead lighting was muted and flattering to women customers. Behind the counter displaying gloves and leather handbags, Joan Lunt struck the eye as an ordinarily pretty woman, composed, intelligent, feminine, brunette, with a brunette's waxy-pale skin, carefully made up, even glamourous, but not a woman Clyde Farrell would have noticed, much. He was 32 years old, in many ways much younger. This woman was too mature for him, wasn't she? Probably married or divorced, very likely with children. Clyde thought, In her clothes, she's just another one of them.

So Clyde walked out of Kress's, a store he didn't like anyway, and wasn't going to think about Joan Lunt, but one morning a

few days later, there he was, unaccountably, back at the Y.M.C.A., 7:30 A.M. of a weekday in March 1959, and there, too, was Joan Lunt in her satiny-yellow bathing suit and gleaming white cap. Swimming laps, arm over strong, slender arm, stroke following stroke, oblivious of Clyde Farrell and of her surroundings, so Clyde was forced to see how her presence in the old, tacky, harshly chlorinated pool made of the place something extraordinary that lifted his heart.

That morning, Clyde swam in the pool for only about ten minutes, then left and hastily showered and dressed and was waiting for Joan Lunt out in the lobby. Clyde wasn't a shy man, but he could give that impression when it suited him. When Joan Lunt appeared, he stepped forward and smiled and introduced himself, saying, "Miss Lunt? I guess you know my niece Sylvie? She told me about meeting you." Joan Lunt hesitated, then shook hands with Clyde and said in that way of hers that suggested that she was giving information meant to be clear and unequivocal, "My first name is Joan." She didn't smile but seemed prepared to smile.

Joan Lunt was a good-looking woman with shrewd dark eyes, straight dark eyebrows, an expertly reddened mouth. There was an inch-long white scar at the left corner of her mouth like a sliver of glass. Her thick, shoulder-length dark-brown hair was carefully waved, but the ends were damp; although her face was pale, it appeared heated, invigorated by exercise.

Joan Lunt and Clyde Farrell were nearly of a height, and comfortable together.

Leaving the Y.M.C.A., descending the old granite steps to Main Street that were worn smooth in the centers, nearly hollow with decades of feet, Clyde said to Joan, "You're a beautiful swimmer—I couldn't help admiring you in there," and Joan Lunt laughed and said, "And so are you—I was admiring you, too," and Clyde said, surprised, "Really? You saw me?" and Joan Lunt said, "Both times."

It was Friday. They arranged to meet for drinks that afternoon, and spent the next two days together.

In Yewville, no one knew who Joan Lunt was except as she presented herself: a woman in her mid-30s, solitary, very private, seemingly unattached, with no relatives or friends in the area. No one knew where exactly she'd come from, or why; why here of all places, Yewville, New York, a small city of fewer than 30,000 people, built on the banks of the Eden River, in the southwestern foothills of the Chautauqua Mountains. She had arrived in early February, in a dented rusted 1956 Chevrolet with New York State license plates, the rear of the car piled with suitcases, cartons, clothes. She spent two nights in Yewville's single good hotel, The Mohawk, then moved into a tiny furnished apartment on Chambers Street. She spent several days interviewing for jobs downtown, all of which you might call jobs for women specifically, and was hired at Kress's, and started work promptly on the first Monday morning following her arrival. If it was sheerly good luck, the job at Kress's, the most prestigious store in town, Joan Lunt seemed to take it in stride, the way a person would who felt she deserved as much. Or better.

The other saleswomen at Kress's, other tenants in the Chambers Street building, men who approached her—no one could get to know her. It was impossible to get beyond the woman's quick, just slightly edgy smile, her resolute cheeriness, her purposefully vague manner. Asked where she was from, she would say, "Nowhere

you'd know." Asked was she married, did she have a family, she would say, "Oh, I'm an independent woman, I'm well over eighteen." She'd laugh to suggest that this was a joke, of a kind, the thin scar beside her mouth white with anger.

It was observed that her fingers were entirely ringless.

But the nails were perfectly manicured, polished an enamel-hard red.

It was observed that, for a solitary woman, Joan Lunt had curious habits.

For instance, swimming. Very few women swam in the Y.M.C.A. pool in those days. Sometimes Joan Lunt swam in the early morning, and sometimes, Saturdays, in the late morning; she swam only once in the afternoon, after work, but the pool was disagreeably crowded, and too many people approached her. A well-intentioned woman asked, "Who taught you to swim like *that*?" and Joan Lunt said quietly, "I taught myself." She didn't smile and the conversation was not continued.

It was observed that, for a woman in her presumed circumstances, Joan Lunt was remarkably arrogant.

It seemed curious, too, that she went to the Methodist church Sunday mornings, sitting in a pew at the very rear, holding an opened hymnbook in her hand but not singing with the congregation; and that she slipped away afterward without speaking to anyone. Each time, she left a neatly folded dollar bill in the collection basket.

She wasn't explicitly unfriendly, but she wasn't friendly. At church, the minister and his wife tried to speak with her, tried to make her feel welcome, *did* make her feel welcome, but nothing came of it, she'd hurry off in her car, disappear. In time, people began to murmur that there was something strange about that woman, something not right, yes, maybe even something wrong; for instance, wasn't she behaving suspiciously? Like a runaway wife, for instance? A bad mother? A sinner fleeing Christ?

Another of Joan Lunt's curious habits was to drink, alone, in the early evening, in the Yewville Bar & Grill, or the White Owl Tavern, or the restaurant-bar adjoining the Greyhound Bus Station. If possible, she sat in a booth at the very rear of these taverns where she could observe the front entrances without being seen herself. For an hour or more she'd drink bourbon and water, slowly, very slowly, with an elaborate slowness, her face perfectly composed but her eyes alert. In the Yewville Bar & Grill, there was an enormous sectioned mirror stretching the length of the taproom, and in this mirror, muted by arabesques of frosted glass, Joan Lunt was reflected as beautiful and mysterious. Now and then, men approached her to ask if she were alone. Did she want company? How's about another drink? But she responded coolly to them and never invited anyone to join her. Had my uncle Clyde approached her in such a fashion, she would very likely have been cool to him, too, but my uncle Clyde wasn't the kind of man to set himself up for any sort of public rejection.

One evening in March, before Joan Lunt met up with Clyde Farrell, patrons at the Yewville Bar & Grill, one of them my father, reported with amusement hearing an exchange between Joan Lunt and a local farmer who, mildly drunk, offered to sit with her and buy her a drink, which ended with Joan Lunt's saying, in a loud, sharp voice, "You don't want trouble, mister. Believe me, you don't."

Rumors spread, delicious and censorious, that Joan Lunt was a man-hater. That she carried a razor in her purse. Or an ice pick. Or a lady's-sized revolver.

It was at the Y.M.C.A. pool that I became acquainted with Joan Lunt, on Saturday mornings. She saw that I was alone, that I was a good swimmer, might have mistaken me for younger than I was (I was 13), and befriended me, casually and cheerfully, the way an adult woman might befriend a young girl to whom she isn't related. Her remarks were often exclamations, called across the slapping little waves of the turquoise-tinted water, "*Isn't* it heavenly!"—meaning the pool, the prospect of swimming, the icy rain pelting the skylight overhead while we, in our bathing suits, were snug and safe below.

Another time, in the changing room, she said almost rapturously, "There's nothing like swimming, is there? Your mind just *dissolves*."

She asked my name, and when I told her, she stared at me and said, "*Sylvie*—I had a close friend once named Sylvie, a long time ago. I loved that name, and I loved *her*."

I was embarrassed, but pleased. It astonished me that an adult woman, a woman my mother's age, might be so certain of her feelings and so direct in expressing them to a stranger. I fantasized that Joan Lunt came from a part of the world where people knew what they thought and announced their thoughts importantly to others. This struck me with the force of a radically new idea.

I watched Joan Lunt covertly, and I didn't even envy her in the pool—she was so far beyond me. Her face that seemed to me strong and rare and beautiful and her body that was a fully developed woman's body—prominent breasts, shapely hips, long firm legs—all beyond me. I saw how the swiftness and skill with which Joan Lunt swam made other swimmers, especially the adults, appear slow by contrast; clumsy, ill-coordinated, without style.

One day, Joan Lunt was waiting for me in the lobby, hair damp at the ends, face carefully made up, her lipstick seemingly brighter than usual. "Sylvie," she said, smiling, "let's walk out together."

So we walked outside into the snow-glaring, windy sunshine, and she said, "Are you going in this direction? Good, let's walk together." She addressed me as if I were much younger than I was, and her manner was nervous, quick, alert. As we walked up Main Street, she asked questions of me of a kind she'd never asked before, about my family, about my "interests," about school, not listening to the answers and offering no information about herself. At the corner of Chambers and Main, she asked eagerly if I would like to come back to her apartment to visit for a few minutes, and although out of shyness I wanted to say "No, thank you," I said "Yes" instead, because it was clear that Joan Lunt was frightened about something, and I didn't want to leave her.

Her apartment building was shabby and weather-worn, as modest a place as even the poorest of my relatives lived in, but it had about it a sort of makeshift glamour, up the street from the White Owl Tavern and the Shamrock Diner, where motorcyclists hung out, close by the railroad yards on the river. I felt excited and pleased to enter the building and to climb with Joan Lunt—who was chatting briskly all the while—to the fourth floor. On each floor, Joan would pause, breathless, glancing around, listening, and I wanted to ask if someone might be following her, waiting for her. But, of course, I didn't say a thing. When she unlocked the door to her apartment, stepped inside and whispered, "Come in, Sylvie," I seemed to understand that no one else had ever been invited in.

The apartment was really just one room with a tiny kitchen alcove, a tiny bathroom, a doorless closet and a curtainless window with stained, injured-looking Venetian blinds. Joan Lunt said with an apologetic little laugh, "Those blinds—I tried to wash them, but the dirt turned to a sort of paste." I was standing at the window peering down into a weedy back yard of tilting clotheslines and wind-blown trash, curious to see what the view was from Joan Lunt's window, and she came over and drew the blinds, saying, "The sunshine is too bright, it hurts my eyes."

She hung up our coats and asked if I would like some coffee or fresh-squeezed orange juice. "It's my half day off from Kress's," she said. "I don't have to be there until one." It was shortly after 11 o'clock.

We sat at a worn dinette table, and Joan Lunt chatted animatedly and plied me with questions, as I drank orange juice in a tall glass, and she drank black coffee, and an alarm clock on the window sill ticked the minutes briskly by. Few rooms in which I've lived even for considerable periods of time are as vividly imprinted in my memory as that room of Joan Lunt's, with its spare, battered-looking furniture (including a sofa bed and a chest of drawers), its wanly wallpapered walls bare of any hangings, even a mirror, and its badly faded shag rug laid upon painted floor boards. There was a mixture of smells—talcum powder, perfume, cooking odors, insect spray, general mustiness. Two opened suitcases were on the floor beside the sofa bed, apparently unpacked, containing underwear, toiletries, neatly folded sweaters and blouses, several pairs of shoes.

A single dress hung in the closet, and a shiny black raincoat, and our two coats Joan had hung on wire hangers. I stared at the suitcases thinking how strange, she'd been living here for weeks but hadn't had time yet to unpack.

So this was where the mysterious Joan Lunt lived! The woman of whom people in Yewville spoke with such suspicion and disapproval! She was far more interesting to me, and in a way more real, than I was to myself; shortly, the story of the lovers Clyde Farrell and Joan Lunt, as I imagined it, would be infinitely more interesting, and infinitely more real, than any story with Sylvie Farrell at its core. (I was a fiercely introspective child, in some ways perhaps a strange child, and the solace of my life would be to grow, not away from but ever more deeply and fruitfully into my strangeness, the way a child with an idiosyncratic, homely face often grows into that face and emerges, in adulthood, as "striking," "distinctive," sometimes even "beautiful.") It turned out that Joan liked poetry, and so we talked about poetry, and about love, and Joan asked me in that searching way of hers if I were "happy in my life," if I were "loved and prized" by my family, and I said, "Yes—I guess so," though these were not issues I had ever considered before, and would not have known to consider if she hadn't asked. For some reason, my eyes filled with tears.

Joan said, "The crucial thing, Sylvie, is to have precious memories." She spoke almost vehemently, laying her hand on mine. "That's even more important than Jesus Christ in your heart, do you know why? Because Jesus Christ can fade out of your heart, but precious memories never do."

We talked like that. Like I'd never talked with anyone before.

I was nervy enough to ask Joan how she'd gotten the little scar beside her mouth, and she touched it, quickly, and said, "In a way I'm not proud of, Sylvie." I sat staring, stupid. The scar wasn't disfiguring in my eyes but enhancing. "A man hit me once," Joan said. "Don't ever let a man hit you, Sylvie."

Weakly, I said, "No, I won't."

No man in our family had ever struck a woman that I knew of, but it happened sometimes in families we knew. I recalled how a ninth-grade girl had come to school that winter with a blackened eye, and she'd seemed proud of it, in a way, and everyone had stared—and the boys just drifted to her, staring. Like they couldn't wait to get their hands on her themselves. And she knew precisely what they were thinking.

I told Joan Lunt that I wished I lived in a place like hers, by myself, and she said, laughing, "No you don't, Sylvie, you're too young." I asked where she was from and she shrugged, "Oh—nowhere," and I persisted, "But is it north of here, or south? Is it the country? Or a city?" and she said, running her fingers nervously through her hair, fingering the damp ends, "My only home is *here, now,* in this room, and, sweetie, that's more than enough for me to think about."

It was time to leave. The danger had passed, or Joan had passed out of thinking there was danger.

She walked with me to the stairs, smiling, cheerful, and squeezed my hand when we said goodbye. She called down after me, "See you next Saturday at the pool, maybe—" but it would be weeks before I saw Joan Lunt again. She was to meet my uncle Clyde the following week and her life in Yewville that seemed to me so orderly and lonely and wonderful would be altered forever.

Clyde had a bachelor's place (that was how the women in our family spoke of it) to which he brought his women friends. It was a row house made of brick and cheap stucco, on the west side of town, near the old, now defunct tanning factories on the river. With the money he made working for a small Yewville construction company, and his occasional gambling wins, Clyde could have afforded to live in a better place, but he hadn't much mind for his surroundings and spent most of his spare time out. He brought Joan Lunt home with him because, for all the slapdash clutter of his house, it was more private than her apartment on Chambers Street, and they wanted privacy, badly.

The first time they were alone together, Clyde laid his hands on Joan's shoulders and kissed her, and she held herself steady, rising to the kiss, putting pressure against the mouth of this man who was virtually a stranger to her so that it was like an exchange, a handshake, between equals. Then, stepping back from the kiss, they both laughed—they were breathless, like people caught short, taken by surprise. Joan Lunt said faintly, "I—I do things sometimes without meaning them," and Clyde said, "Good. So do I."

Through the spring, they were often seen together in Yewville; and when, weekends, they weren't seen, it was supposed they were at Clyde's cabin at Wolf's Head Lake (where he was teaching Joan Lunt to fish) or at the Scholharie Downs race track (where Clyde gambled on the standardbreds). They were an attractive, eye-catching couple. They were frequent patrons of local bars and restaurants, and they turned up regularly at parties given by friends of Clyde's, and at all-night poker parties in the upstairs, rear, of the

Iroquois Hotel—Joan Lunt didn't play cards, but she took an interest in Clyde's playing, and, as Clyde told my father, admiringly, she never criticized a move of his, never chided or teased or second-guessed him. "But the woman has me figured out completely," Clyde said. "Almost from the first, when she saw the way I was winning, and the way I kept on, she said, 'Clyde, you're the kind of gambler who won't quit, because, when he's losing, he has to get back to winning, and when he's winning, he has to give his friends a chance to catch up.' "

In May, Clyde brought Joan to a Sunday gathering at our house, a large, noisy affair, and we saw how when Clyde and Joan were separated, in different rooms, they'd drift back together until they were touching, literally touching, without seeming to know what they did, still less that they were being observed. So that was what love was! Always a quickness of a kind was passing between them, a glance, a hand squeeze, a light pinch, a caress, Clyde's lazy fingers on Joan's neck beneath her hair, Joan's arm slipped around Clyde's waist, fingers hooked through his belt loop. I wasn't jealous, but I watched them covertly. My heart yearned for them, though I didn't know what I wanted of them, or for them.

At 13, I was more of a child still than an adolescent girl: thin, long-limbed, eyes too large and naked-seeming for my face and an imagination that rarely flew off into unknown territory but turned, and turned, and turned, upon what was close at hand and known, but not altogether known. Imagination, says Aristotle, begins in desire: But what *is* desire? I could not, nor did I want to, possess my uncle Clyde and Joan Lunt. I wasn't jealous of them, I loved them both. I wanted them to *be*. For this, too, was a radically new idea to me, that a man and a woman might be nearly strangers to each other, yet lovers; lovers, yet nearly strangers; and the love passing between them, charged like electricity, might be visible, without their knowing. Could they know how I dreamt of them!

After Clyde and Joan left our house, my mother complained irritably that she couldn't get to know Joan Lunt. "She's sweet-seeming, and friendly enough, but you know her mind isn't there for you," my mother said. "She's just plain *not there*."

My father said, "As long as the woman's there for Clyde."

He didn't like anyone speaking critically of his younger brother apart from himself.

But sometimes, in fact, Joan Lunt wasn't there for Clyde: He wouldn't speak of it, but she'd disappear in her car for a day or two or three, without explaining very satisfactorily where she'd gone, or why. Clyde could see by her manner that wherever Joan had gone had, perhaps, not been a choice of hers, and that her disappearances, or flights, left her tired and depressed; but still he was annoyed, he felt betrayed. Clyde Farrell wasn't the kind of man to disguise his feelings. Once, on a Friday afternoon in June before a weekend they'd planned at Wolf's Head Lake, Clyde returned to the construction office at 5:30 P.M. to be handed a message hastily telephoned in by Joan Lunt an hour before: CAN'T MAKE IT THIS WEEKEND. SORRY. LOVE, JOAN. Clyde believed himself humiliated in front of others, vowed he'd never forgive Joan Lunt and that very night, drunk and mean-spirited, he took up again with a former girlfriend...and so it went.

But in time they made up, as naturally they would, and Clyde said, "I'm thinking maybe we should get married, to stop this sort of thing," and Joan, surprised, said, "Oh, that isn't necessary, darling—I mean, for you to offer that."

Clyde believed, as others did, that Joan Lunt was having difficulties with a former man friend or husband, but Joan refused to speak of it; just acknowledged that, yes, there was a man, yes, of course he was an ex in her life, but she resented so much as speaking of him; she refused to allow him re-entry into her life. Clyde asked, "What's his name?" and Joan shook her head, mutely, just no; no, she would not say, would not utter that name. Clyde asked, "Is he threatening you? Now? Has he ever shown up in Yewville?" and Joan, as agitated as he'd ever seen her, said, "He does what he does, and I do what I do. And I don't talk about it."

But later that summer, at Wolf's Head Lake, in Clyde's bed in Clyde's hand-hewn log cabin on the bluff above the lake, overlooking wooded land that was Clyde Farrell's property for a mile in either direction, Joan Lunt wept bitterly, weakened in the aftermath of love, and said, "If I tell you, Clyde, it will make you feel too bound to me. It will seem to be begging a favor of a kind, and I'm not begging."

Clyde said, "I know you're not."

"I don't beg favors from anyone."

"I know you don't."

"I went through a long spell in my life when I did beg favors, because I believed that was how women made their way, and I was hurt because of it, but not more hurt than I deserved. I'm older now. I know better. The meek don't inherit the earth and they surely don't deserve to."

Clyde laughed sadly and said, "Nobody's likely to take you for meek, Joan honey."

Making love, they were like two swimmers deep in each other, plunging hard. Wherever they were when they made love, it wasn't the place they found themselves in when they returned, and whatever the time, it wasn't the same time.

The trouble came in September: A cousin of mine, another niece of Clyde's, was married, and the wedding party was held in the Nautauga Inn, on Lake Nautauga, about ten miles east of Yewville. Clyde knew the inn's owner, and it happened that he and Joan Lunt, handsomely dressed, were in the large public cocktail lounge adjacent to the banquet room reserved for our party, talking with the owner-bartender, when Clyde saw an expression on Joan's

face of a kind he'd never seen on her face before—fear, and more than fear, a sudden sick terror—and he turned to see a stranger approaching them, not slowly, exactly, but with a restrained sort of haste: a man of about 40, unshaven, in a blue seersucker sports jacket now badly rumpled, tieless, a muscled but soft-looking man with a blunt, rough, ruined-handsome face, complexion like an emery board, and this man's eyes were too bleached a color for his skin, unless there was a strange light rising in them. And this same light rose in Clyde Farrell's eyes, in that instant.

Joan Lunt was whispering, "Oh, no—*no*," pulling at Clyde's arm to turn him away, but naturally, Clyde Farrell wasn't going to step away from a confrontation, and the stranger, who would turn out to be named Robert Waxman, Rob Waxman, Joan Lunt's former husband, divorced from her 15 months before, co-owner of a failing meat-supplying company in Kingston, advanced upon Clyde and

Joan smiling as if he knew them both, saying loudly, in a slurred but vibrating voice, "Hello, hello, hello!" and when Joan tried to escape, Waxman leapt after her, cursing, and Clyde naturally intervened, and suddenly, the two men were scuffling, and voices were raised, and before anyone could separate them, there was the astonishing sight of Waxman, with his gravelly face and hot eyes, crouched, holding a pistol in his hand, striking Clyde clumsily about the head and shoulders with the butt and crying, enraged, "Didn't ask to be born! Goddamn you! I didn't ask to be born!" And "I'm no different from you! Any of you! *You*! In my heart!" There were screams as Waxman fired the pistol point-blank at Clyde, a popping sound like a firecracker, and Waxman stepped back to get a better aim—he'd hit his man in the fleshy part of a shoulder—and Clyde Farrell, desperate, infuriated, scrambled forward in his wedding-party finery, baboon style, not on his hands and knees but on his hands and feet, bent double, face contorted, teeth bared, and managed to throw himself on Waxman, who outweighed him by perhaps 40 pounds, and the men fell heavily to the floor, and there was Clyde Farrell straddling his man, striking him blow after blow in the face, even with his weakened left hand, until Waxman's nose was broken and his nostrils streamed blood, and his mouth, too, was broken and bloody, and someone risked being struck by Clyde's wild fists and pulled him away.

And there on the floor of the breezy screened-in barroom of the Nautauga Inn lay a man, unconscious, breathing erratically, bleeding from his face, whom no one except Joan Lunt knew was Joan Lunt's former husband; and there, panting, hot-eyed, stood Clyde Farrell over him, bleeding, too, from a shoulder wound he was to claim he'd never felt.

Said Joan Lunt repeatedly, "Clyde, I'm sorry. I'm so sorry."

Said Joan Lunt carefully, "I just don't know if I can keep on seeing you. Or keep on living here in Yewville."

And my uncle Clyde was trying hard, trying very hard, to understand.

"You don't love me, then?" he asked several times.

He was baffled, he wasn't angry. It was the following week and by this time he wasn't angry, nor was he proud of what he'd done, though everyone was speaking of it, and would speak of it, in awe, for years. He wasn't proud because, in fact, he couldn't remember clearly what he'd done, what sort of lightning-swift action he'd performed; no conscious decision had been made that he could recall. Just the light dancing up in a stranger's eyes, and its immediate reflection in his own.

Now Joan Lunt was saying this strange, unexpected thing, this thing he couldn't comprehend. Wiping her eyes, and, yes, her voice was shaky, but he recognized the steely stubbornness in it, the resolute will. She said, "I do love you. I've told you. But I can't live like that any longer."

"You're still in love with *him*."

"Of course I'm not in love with him. But I can't live like that any longer."

"Like what? What I did? I'm not *like* that."

"I'm thirty-six years old. I can't take it any longer."

"Joan, I was only protecting you."

"Men fighting each other, men trying to kill each other—I can't take it any longer."

"I was only protecting you. He might have killed you."

"I know. I know you were protecting me. I know you'd do it again if you had to."

Clyde said, suddenly furious, "You're damned right I would. If that son of a bitch ever—"

Waxman was out on bail and returned to Kingston. Like Clyde Farrell, he'd been treated in the emergency room at Yewville General Hospital; then he'd been taken to the county sheriff's headquarters and booked on charges of assault with a deadly weapon and reckless endangerment of life. In time, Waxman would be sentenced to a year's probation: He had no prior record except for traffic violations; he was to impress the judge with his air of sincere remorse and repentance. Clyde Farrell, after giving testimony and hearing the sentencing, would never see the man again.

Joan Lunt was saying, "I know I should thank you, Clyde. But I can't."

Clyde splashed more bourbon into Joan's glass and into his own. They were sitting at Joan's dinette table beside a window whose grimy and cracked Venetian blinds were tightly closed. Clyde smiled and said, "Never mind thanking me, honey: Just let's forget it."

Joan said softly, "Yes, but I can't forget it."

"It's just something you're saying. Telling yourself. Maybe you'd better stop."

"I want to thank you, Clyde, and I can't. You risked your life for me. I know that. And I can't thank you."

So they discussed it, like this. For hours. For much of a night. Sharing a bottle of bourbon Clyde had brought over. And eventually, they made love, in Joan Lunt's narrow sofa bed that smelled of talcum powder, perfume and the ingrained dust of years, and their lovemaking was tentative and cautious but as sweet as ever, and driving back to his place early in the morning, at dawn, Clyde thought surely things were changed; yes, he was convinced that things were changed. Hadn't he Joan's promise that she would think it all over, not make any decision, they'd see each other that evening and talk it over then? She'd kissed his lips in goodbye, and walked him to the stairs, and watched him descend to the street.

But Clyde never saw Joan Lunt again.

That evening, she was gone, moved out of the apartment, like that, no warning, not even a telephone call, and she'd left only a brief letter behind with CLYDE FARRELL written on the envelope. Which Clyde never showed to anyone and probably, in fact, ripped up immediately.

It was believed that Clyde spent some time, days, then weeks, into the early winter of that year, looking for Joan Lunt; but no one, not even my father, knew exactly what he did, where he drove, whom he questioned, the depth of his desperation or his yearning or his rage, for Clyde wasn't, of course, the kind of man to speak of such things.

Joan Lunt's young friend Sylvie never saw her again, either, nor heard of her. And this hurt me, too, more than I might have anticipated.

And over the years, once I left Yewville to go to college in another state, then to begin my own adult life, I saw less and less of my uncle Clyde. He never married; for a few years, he continued the life he'd been leading before meeting Joan Lunt—a typical "bachelor" life, of its place and time; then he began to spend more and more time at Wolf's Head Lake, developing his property, building small wood-frame summer cottages and renting them out to vacationers, and acting as caretaker for them, an increasingly solitary life no one would have predicted for Clyde Farrell.

He stopped gambling, too, abruptly. His luck had turned, he said.

I saw my uncle Clyde only at family occasions, primarily weddings and funerals. The last time we spoke together in a way that might be called forthright was in 1971, at my grandmother's funeral: I looked up and saw through a haze of tears a man of youthful middle age moving in my general direction, Clyde, who seemed shorter than I recalled, not stocky but compact, with a look of furious compression, in a dark suit that fitted him tightly about the shoulders. His hair had turned not silver but an eerie metallic blond, with faint tarnished streaks, and it was combed down flat and damp on his head, a look here, too, of furious constraint. Clyde's face was familiar to me as my own, yet altered: The skin had a grainy texture, roughened from years of outdoor living, like dried earth, and the creases and dents in it resembled animal tracks; his eyes were narrow, damp, restless; the eyelids looked swollen. He was walking with a slight limp that he tried, in his vanity, to disguise; I learned later that he'd had knee surgery. And the gunshot wound to his left shoulder he'd insisted at the time had not given him much, or any, pain gave him pain now, an arthritic sort of pain, agonizing in cold weather. I stared at my uncle thinking, *Oh, why? Why?* I didn't know if I were seeing the man Joan Lunt had fled from or the man her flight had made.

But Clyde sighted me and hurried over to embrace me, his favorite niece, still. If he associated me with Joan Lunt—and I had the idea he did—he'd forgiven me long ago.

Death gives to life, to the survivors' shared life, that is, an insubstantial quality. It's like an image of absolute clarity reflected in water—then disturbed, shattered into ripples, revealed as mere surface. Its clarity, even its beauty, can resume, but you can't any longer trust in its reality.

So my uncle Clyde and I regarded each other, stricken in that instant with grief. But, being a man, *he* didn't cry.

We drifted off to one side, away from the other mourners, and I saw it was all right between us, it was all right to ask, so I asked if he had ever heard from Joan Lunt after that day. Had he ever heard of her? He said, "I never go where I am not welcome, honey," as if this were the answer to my question. Then added, seeing my look of distress, "I stopped thinking of her years ago. We don't need each other the way we think we do when we're younger."

I couldn't bear to look at my uncle. *Oh, why? Why?* Somehow, I must have believed all along that there was a story, a story unknown to me, that had worked itself out without my knowing, like a stream tunneling its way underground. I would not have minded not knowing this story could I only know that it *was*.

Clyde said, roughly, "*You* didn't hear from her, did you? The two of you were so close."

He wants me to lie, I thought. But I said only, sadly, "No, I never hear from her. And we weren't close."

Said Clyde, "Sure you were."

The last I saw of Clyde that day, it was after dark and he and my father were having a disagreement just outside the back door of our house. My father insisted that Clyde, who'd been drinking, wasn't in condition to drive his pickup truck back to the lake, and Clyde was insisting he was, and my father said, "Maybe yes, Clyde, and maybe no," but he didn't want to take a chance, why didn't *he* drive Clyde home, and Clyde pointed out truculently that, if my father drove him home, how in hell would he get back here except by taking Clyde's only means of transportation? So the brothers discussed their predicament, as dark came on.

SUMMER PEOPLE *by* ERNEST HEMINGWAY

ERNEST HEMINGWAY (1899–1961) wrote "Summer People" in 1926, the same year he wrote The Sun Also Rises, *but it was not published until after his death. The story describes—in uncharacteristically explicit fashion—an illicit warm-weather tryst by the lake, and is the earliest installment of more than thirty semi-autobiographical stories featuring young Nick Adams, Papa's alter ego.*

HALFWAY DOWN THE GRAVEL ROAD from Hortons Bay, the town, to the lake there was a spring. The water came up in a tile sunk beside the road, lipping over the cracked edge of the tile and flowing away through the close growing mint into the swamp. In the dark Nick put his arm down into the spring but could not hold it there because of the cold. He felt the featherings of the sand spouting up from the spring cones at the bottom against his fingers. Nick thought, I wish I could put all of myself in there. I bet that would fix me. He pulled his arm out and sat down at the edge of the road. It was a hot night.

Down the road through the trees he could see the white of the Bean house on its piles over the water. He did not want to go down to the dock. Everybody was down there swimming.

He did not want Kate with Odgar around. He could see the car on the road beside the warehouse. Odgar and Kate were down there. Odgar with that fried-fish look in his eye every time he looked at Kate. Didn't Odgar know anything? Kate wouldn't ever marry him. She wouldn't ever marry anybody that didn't make her. And if they tried to make her she would curl up inside of herself and be hard and slip away. He could make her do it all right. Instead of curling up hard and slipping away she would open out smoothly, relaxing, untightening, easy to hold. Odgar thought it was love that did it. His eyes got walleyed and red at the edges of the lids. She couldn't bear to have him touch her. It was all in his eyes. Then Odgar would want them to be just the same friends as ever. Play in the sand. Make mud images. Take all-day trips in the boat together. Kate always in her bathing suit. Odgar looking at her.

Odgar was thirty-two and had been twice operated on for varicocele. He was ugly to look at and everybody liked his face. Odgar could never get it and it meant everything in the world to him. Every summer he was worse about it. It was pitiful. Odgar was awfully nice. He had been nicer to Nick than anybody ever had. Now Nick could get it if he wanted it. Odgar would kill himself, Nick thought, if he knew it. I wonder how he'd kill himself. He couldn't think of Odgar dead. He probably wouldn't do it. Still people did. It wasn't just love. Odgar thought just love would do it. Odgar loved her enough, God knows. It was liking, and liking the body, and introducing the body, and persuading, and taking chances, and never frightening, and assuming about the other person, and always taking never asking, and gentleness and liking, and making liking and happiness, and joking and making people not afraid. And making it all right afterwards. It wasn't loving. Loving was frightening. He, Nicholas Adams, could have what he wanted because of something in him. Maybe it did not last. Maybe he would lose it. He wished he could give it to Odgar, or tell Odgar about it. You couldn't ever tell anybody about anything. Especially Odgar. No not especially Odgar. Anybody, anywhere. That had always been his first mistake, talking. He had talked himself out of too many things. There ought to be something you could do for the Princeton, Yale and Harvard virgins, though. Why weren't there any virgins in state universities? Coeducation maybe. They met girls who were out to marry and the girls helped them along and married them. What would become of fellows like Odgar and Harvey and Mike and all the rest? He didn't know. He hadn't lived long enough. They were the best people in the world. What became of them? How the hell could he know. How could he write like Hardy and Hamsun when he only knew ten years of life. He couldn't. Wait till he was fifty.

In the dark he kneeled down and took a drink from the spring. He felt all right. He knew he was going to be a great writer. He knew things and they couldn't touch him. Nobody could. Only he did not know enough things. That would come all right. He knew. The water was cold and made his eyes ache. He had swallowed too big a gulp. Like ice cream. That's the way with drinking with your nose underwater. He'd better go swimming. Thinking was no good. It started and went on so. He walked down the road, past the car and the big warehouse on the left where apples and potatoes were loaded onto the boats in the fall, past the white-painted Bean house where they danced by lantern light sometimes on the hardwood floor, out on the dock to where they were swimming.

They were all swimming off the end of the dock. As Nick walked along the rough boards high above the water he heard the double protest of the long springboard and a splash. The water lapped below in the piles. That must be the Ghee, he thought. Kate came up out of the water like a seal and pulled herself up the ladder.

"It's Wemedge," she shouted to the others. "Come on in, Wemedge. It's wonderful."

"Hi, Wemedge," said Odgar. "Boy it's great."

"Where's Wemedge?" It was the Ghee, swimming far out.

"Is this man Wemedge a nonswimmer?" Bill's voice very deep and bass over the water.

Nick felt good. It was fun to have people yell at you like that. He scuffed off his canvas shoes, pulled his shirt over his head and stepped out of his trousers. His bare feet felt the sandy planks of the dock. He ran very quickly out the yielding plank of the springboard, his toes shoved against the end of the board, he tightened and he was in the water, smoothly and deeply, with no consciousness of the dive. He had breathed in deeply as he took off and now went on and on through the water, holding his back arched, feet straight and trailing. Then he was on the surface, floating face down. He rolled over and opened his eyes. He did not care anything about swimming, only to dive and be underwater.

"How is it, Wemedge?" The Ghee was just behind him.

"Warm as piss," Nick said.

He took a deep breath, took hold of his ankles with his hands, his knees under his chin, and sank slowly down into the water. It was warm at the top but he dropped quickly into the cool, then cold. As he neared the bottom it was quite cold. Nick floated down gently against the bottom. It was marly and his toes hated it as he uncurled and shoved hard against it to come up to the air. It was strange coming up from underwater into the dark. Nick rested in the water, barely paddling and comfortable. Odgar and Kate were talking together up on the dock.

"Have you ever swum in a sea where it was phosphorescent, Carl?"

"No." Odgar's voice was unnatural talking to Kate.

We might rub ourselves all over with matches, Nick thought. He took a deep breath, drew his knees up, clasped tight and sank, this time with his eyes open. He sank gently, first going off to one side, then sinking head first. It was no good. He could not see underwater in the dark. He was right to keep his eyes shut when he first dove in. It was funny about reactions like that. They weren't always right, though. He did not go all the way down but straightened out and swam along and up through the cool, keeping just below the warm surface water. It was funny how much fun it was to swim underwater and how little fun there was in plain swimming. It was fun to swim on the surface in the ocean. That was the buoyancy. But there was the taste of the brine and the way it made you thirsty. Fresh water was better. Just like this on a hot night. He came up for air just under the projecting edge of the dock and climbed up the ladder.

"Oh, dive, Wemedge, will you?" Kate said. "Do a good dive." They were sitting together on the dock leaning back against one of the big piles.

"Do a noiseless one, Wemedge," Odgar said.

"All right."

Nick, dripping, walked out on the springboard, remembering how to do the dive. Odgar and Kate watched him, black in the dark, standing at the end of the board, poise and dive as he had learned from watching a sea otter. In the water as he turned to come up to the air Nick thought, Gosh, if I could only have Kate down here. He came up in a rush to the surface, feeling water in his eyes and ears. He must have started to take a breath.

"It was perfect. Absolutely perfect," Kate shouted from the dock.

Nick came up the ladder.

"Where are the men?" he asked.

"They're swimming way out in the bay," Odgar said.

Nick lay down on the dock beside Kate and Odgar. He could hear the Ghee and Bill swimming way out in the dark.

"You're the most wonderful diver, Wemedge," Kate said, touching his back with her foot. Nick tightened under the contact.

"No," he said.

"You're a wonder, Wemedge," Odgar said.

"Nope," Nick said. He was thinking, thinking if it was possible to be with somebody underwater, he could hold his breath three minutes, against the sand on the bottom, they could float up together, take a breath and go down, it was easy to sink if you knew how. He had once drunk a bottle of milk and peeled and eaten a banana underwater to show off, had to have weights, though, to hold him down, if there was a ring at the bottom, something he could get his arm through, he could do it all right. Gee, how it would be, you couldn't ever get a girl though, a girl couldn't go through with it, she'd swallow water, it would drown Kate, Kate wasn't really any good underwater, he wished there was a girl like that, maybe he'd get a girl like that, probably never, there wasn't anybody but him that was that way underwater. Swimmers, hell, swimmers were slobs, nobody knew about the water but him, there was a fellow up at Evanston that could hold his breath six minutes but he was crazy. He wished he was a fish, no he didn't. He laughed.

"What's the joke, Wemedge?" Odgar said in his husky, near-to-Kate voice.

"I wished I was a fish," Nick said.

"That's a good joke," said Odgar.

"Sure," said Nick.

"Don't be an ass, Wemedge," said Kate.

"Would you like to be a fish, Butstein?" he said, lying with his head on the planks, facing away from them.

"No," said Kate. "Not tonight."

Nick pressed his back hard against her foot.

"What animal would you like to be, Odgar?" Nick said.

"J.P. Morgan," Odgar said.

"You're nice, Odgar," Kate said. Nick felt Odgar glow.

'I'd like to be Wemedge," Kate said.

"You could always be Mrs. Wemedge," Odgar said.

"There isn't going to be any Mrs. Wemedge," Nick said. He tightened his back muscles. Kate had both her legs stretched out against his back as though she were resting them on a log in front of a fire.

"Don't be too sure," Odgar said.

"I'm awful sure," Nick said. "I'm going to marry a mermaid."

"She'd be Mrs. Wemedge," Kate said.

"No she wouldn't," Nick said. "I wouldn't let her."

"How would you stop her?"

"I'd stop her all right. Just let her try it."

"Mermaids don't marry," Kate said.

"That'd be all right with me," Nick said.

"The Mann Act would get you," said Odgar.

"We'd stay outside the four-mile limit," Nick said. "We'd get food from the rumrunners. You could get a diving suit and come and visit us, Odgar. Bring Butstein if she wants to come. We'll be at home every Thursday afternoon."

"What are we going to do tomorrow?" Odgar said, his voice becoming husky, near to Kate again.

"Oh, hell, let's not talk about tomorrow," Nick said. "Let's talk about my mermaid."

"We're through with your mermaid."

"All right," Nick said. "You and Odgar go and talk. I'm going to think about her."

"You're immoral, Wemedge. You're disgustingly immoral."

"No, I'm not. I'm honest." Then, lying with his eyes shut, he said, "Don't bother me. I'm thinking about her."

He lay there thinking of his mermaid while Kate's insteps pressed against his back and she and Odgar talked.

Odgar and Kate talked but he did not hear them. He lay, no longer thinking, quite happy.

Bill and the Ghee had come out of the water farther down the shore, walked down the beach up to the car and then backed it out onto the dock. Nick stood up and put on his clothes. Bill and the Ghee were in the front seat, tired from the long swim. Nick got in behind with Kate and Odgar. They leaned back. Bill drove roaring up the hill and turned onto the main road. On the main highway Nick could see the lights of other cars up ahead, going out of sight, then blinding as they mounted a hill, blinking as they came near, then dimmed as Bill passed. The road was high along the shore of the lake. Big cars out from Charlevoix, rich slobs riding behind their chauffeurs, came up and passed, hogging the road and not dimming their lights. They passed like railway trains. Bill flashed the spotlights on cars alongside the road in the trees, making the occupants change their positions. Nobody passed Bill from behind, although a spotlight played on the back of their heads for some time until Bill drew away. Bill slowed, then turned abruptly onto the sandy road that ran up through the orchard to the farmhouse. The car, in low gear, moved steadily up through the orchard. Kate put her lips to Nick's ear.

"In about an hour, Wemedge," she said. Nick pressed his thigh hard against hers. The car circled at the top of the hill above the orchard and stopped in front of the house.

"Aunty's asleep. We've got to be quiet," Kate said.

"Good night, men." Bill whispered. "We'll stop by in the morning."

"Good night, Smith," whispered the Ghee. "Good night, Butstein."

"Good night, Ghee," Kate said.

Odgar was staying at the house.

"Good night, men," Nick said. "See you, *Morgen*."

"Night, Wemedge," Odgar said from the porch.

Nick and the Ghee walked down the road into the orchard. Nick reached up and took an apple from one of the Duchess trees. It was still green but he sucked the acid juice from the bite and spat out the pulp.

"You and the Bird took a long swim, Ghee," he said.

"Not so long, Wemedge," the Ghee answered.

They came out from the orchard past the mailbox onto the hard state highway. There was a cold mist in the hollow where the road crossed the creek. Nick stopped on the bridge.

"Come on, Wemedge," the Ghee said.

"All right," Nick agreed.

They went on up the hill to where the road turned into the grove of trees around the church. There were no lights in any of the houses they passed. Hortons Bay was asleep. No motor cars had passed them.

"I don't feel like turning in yet," Nick said.

"Want me to walk with you?"

"No, Ghee. Don't bother."

"All right."

"I'll walk up as far as the cottage with you," Nick said. They unhooked the screen door and went into the kitchen. Nick opened the meat safe and looked around.

"Want some of this, Ghee?" he said.

"I want a piece of pie," the Ghee said.

"So do I," Nick said. He wrapped up some fried chicken and two pieces of cherry pie in oiled paper from the top of the icebox.

"I'll take this with me," he said. The Ghee washed down his pie with a dipper full of water from the bucket.

"If you want anything to read, Ghee, get it out of my room," Nick said. The Ghee had been looking at the lunch Nick had wrapped up.

"Don't be a damn fool, Wemedge," he said.

"That's all right, Ghee."

"All right. Only don't be a damn fool," the Ghee said. He opened the screen door and went out across the grass to the cottage. Nick turned off the light and went out, hooking the screen door shut. He had the lunch wrapped up in a newspaper and crossed the wet grass, climbed the fence and went up the road through the town under the big elm trees, past the last cluster of R.F.D. mailboxes at the crossroads and out onto the

Charlevoix highway. After crossing the creek he cut across a field, skirted the edge of the orchard, keeping to the edge of the clearing, and climbed the tall fence into the wood lot. In the center of the wood lot four hemlock trees grew close together. The ground was soft with pine needles and there was no dew. The wood lot had never been cut over and the forest floor was dry and warm without underbrush. Nick put the package of lunch by the base of one of the hemlocks and lay down to wait. He saw Kate coming through the trees in the dark but did not move. She did not see him and stood a moment, holding the two blankets in her arms. In the dark it looked like some enormous pregnancy. Nick was shocked. Then it was funny.

"Hello, Butstein," he said. She dropped the blankets.

"Oh, Wemedge. You shouldn't have frightened me like that. I was afraid you hadn't come."

"Dear Butstein," Nick said. He held her close against him, feeling her body against his, all the sweet body against his body. She pressed close against him.

"I love you so, Wemedge."

"Dear, dear old Butstein," Nick said.

They spread the blankets, Kate smoothing them flat.

"It was awfully dangerous to bring the blankets," Kate said.

"I know," Nick said. "Let's undress."

"Oh, Wemedge."

"It's more fun." They undressed sitting on the blankets. Nick was a little embarrassed to sit there like that.

"Do you like me with my clothes off, Wemedge?"

"Gee, let's get under," Nick said. They lay between the

rough blankets. He was hot against her cool body, hunting for it, then it was all right.

"Is it all right?"

Kate pressed all the way up for answer.

"Is it fun?"

"Oh, Wemedge. I've wanted it so. I've needed it so."

They lay together in the blankets. Wemedge slid his head down, his nose touching along the line of the neck, down between her breasts. It was like piano keys.

"You smell so cool," he said.

He touched one of her small breasts with his lips gently. It came alive between his lips, his tongue pressing against it. He felt the whole feeling coming back again and, sliding his hands down, moved Kate over. He slid down and she fitted close in against him. She pressed tight in against the curve of his abdomen. She felt wonderful there. He searched, a little awkwardly, then found it. He put both hands over her breasts and held her to him. Nick kissed hard against her back. Kate's head dropped forward.

"Is it good this way?" he said.

"I love it. I love it. I love it. Oh, come, Wemedge. Please come. Come, come. Please, Wemedge. Please, please, Wemedge."

"There it is," Nick said.

He was suddenly conscious of the blanket rough against his bare body.

"Was I bad, Wemedge?" Kate said.

"No, you were good," Nick said. His mind was working

very hard and clear. He saw everything very sharp and clear. "I'm hungry," he said.

"I wish we could sleep here all night." Kate cuddled against him.

"It would be swell," Nick said. "But we can't. You've got to get back to the house."

"I don't want to go," Kate said.

Nick stood up, a little wind blowing on his body. He pulled on his shirt and was glad to have it on. He put on his trousers and shoes.

"You've got to get dressed, Stut," he said. She lay there, the blankets pulled over her head.

"Just a minute," she said. Nick got the lunch from over the hemlock. He opened it up.

"Come on, get dressed, Stut," he said.

"I don't want to," Kate said. "I'm going to sleep here all night." She sat up in the blankets. "Hand me those things, Wemedge."

Nick gave her the clothes.

"I've just thought of it," Kate said. "If I sleep out here they'll just think that I'm an idiot and came out here with the blankets and it will be all right."

"You won't be comfortable," Nick said.

"If I'm uncomfortable I'll go in."

"Let's eat before I have to go," Nick said.

"I'll put something on," Kate said.

They sat together and ate the fried chicken and each ate a piece of cherry pie.

Nick stood up, then kneeled down and kissed Kate.

He came through the wet grass to the cottage and upstairs to his room, walking carefully not to creak. It was good to be in bed, sheets, stretching out full length, dipping his head in the pillow. Good in bed, comfortable, happy, fishing tomorrow, he prayed as he always prayed when he remembered it, for the family, himself, to be a great writer, Kate, the men, Odgar, for good fishing, poor old Odgar, poor old Odgar, sleeping up there at the cottage, maybe not fishing, maybe not sleeping all night. Still there wasn't anything you could do, not a thing.

THE SIGHT OF YOU *by* AMY BLOOM

Compassion and acuity are found in equal shares in the stories of AMY BLOOM (b. 1953), the novelist and essayist who is also a practicing psychotherapist. In this story from her National Book Award–finalist collection Come to Me, *a dissatisfied wife decides—one sweltering day at the club pool—that she is capable of leaving her husband.*

IT WAS NINETY-SEVEN DEGREES and I took my kids to the club for a swim. Everybody was there, including my lover, Henry, his wife, Marie, and their two boys, whose names I forget. My husband, David, stayed home to mow the lawn and read the *Times*.

Henry and I didn't really see each other that much during the two years we were lovers. We could have, I think. I'm a musician; I could have practiced a little less. Henry ran a construction company; he was his own boss. All of our time together was shaved off something bigger, slivered into pieces so thin you could look right at them and never even see. Those two winters I would look out my window at dawn and see his crew plowing driveways. They were like angels in the snow, their little white and yellow lights turning softly in the storm, right into my bedroom.

I was watching Henry from the clubhouse deck as he showed

the youngest boy how to swim, his big arms carving runnels in the water, clearing a path for the littler arms to move in. I wore huge sunglasses so I could watch him. That was all I really wanted, just to watch Henry, forever. I grew up on the Plains and didn't know how I'd longed for the ocean until my foot felt the first wave's edge. And I hadn't known the wordless, leaping power of beauty until I saw Henry.

Marie walked past my chaise looking the other way, and I tried not to blame her for her bad manners and tight red face. Grief made her ugly, and I know that she was not always ugly.

I lay back, calculating whether I had time to talk to Henry while Marie was wherever she was. I thought so and dove in from the pool's edge, surfacing next to him. Under his little boy's splashing, he put his hand on my waist, watching for Marie, who seemed to have a sixth sense about us. She worried that we were having an affair and complained, obliquely, about my presence. She never saw anything between us. I could have kissed him on the mouth that day, in front of all the neighbors, and everything would have been different.

He stood close to me and smiled. We could both look down and see his erection, even in the cold water. Marie came zipping out of the snack area, a bag of chips in one hand and a racket in the other.

"Hank, we've got a court. Go dry off and I'll get your sneakers." Among the club set, she was a serious tennis player. She stood there, looking down on us, her hands on her hips. She didn't move until Henry headed for the wall. Then she smiled at me and walked toward the court.

I followed him to the wall, watching the small drops quiver down his back. I didn't know I was about to speak. "Henry, I don't think this is working. What about our time together?" We were both surprised. "If you still want me to leave him, I will."

I swam across the pool and went back to my chaise. Henry was still standing in the water, looking dazed. He hoisted himself out, emerging smoothly like a big dark dolphin, all muscle and flex, no visible bones. He glanced at me and then headed for the court, his tennis shirt clinging to his wide wet back. I put my chin on the deck's redwood railing and watched them play.

I always felt powerful with Henry, powerful and grateful. That day, I felt like God Almighty, holding a crowd of tiny people in one huge hand. I had wanted to hold just Henry, but somehow another six had climbed aboard. David had given me the only home I'd ever had, but like the little mermaid in the fairy tale, I was prepared to cut my true self in two and walk in pain and artifice just to dance with Henry, dazzled by all that unfamiliar light.

I thought about the girls and hoped they'd be all right. The three of us had been a team, and that wouldn't have to change. David had been a good father, better than most I've seen; he played Scrabble with them, went to their concerts, picked them up from swim team when I was touring, hugged them every day, and knew how to braid their hair. I thought Henry would help out the way he did with his boys, and nothing would keep David from Rose and Violet. I used to think the girls were like my arms, I didn't need anyone's help growing them or taking care of them. When Rose was an infant, she would sleep through my practicing but wake up as soon as I started to vacuum. I stopped vacuuming. And Violet, my baby, used to help the ushers at my concerts, tripping over her Mary Janes and her lavender organdy skirt, but knowing where every seat in the hall was. I took them most everywhere I went; we all loved music and new places and hotel rooms. David usually stayed home; he's a psychiatrist and never likes to leave his patients for too long.

I didn't know what would happen when Henry finished playing tennis. We would have to talk on the phone, work out details. The girls would go to music camp for a month, and I could move then if David wanted the house. Or maybe he'd move out. The house didn't matter much to me as long as I had my piano and a bedroom for the girls. I have to force myself to sleep in a bed, even now.

When I got home, I sat down at the piano and stared at the keys, waiting for a wave of guilt or panic that would tell me to stop.

Henry loved me the way I was taught Indians loved Nature; I was everywhere for him, in the air, in the light, seeping right into his skin. It scared me a little, how much he loved me, handing over everything he had. He would kneel in front of me, big man, putting his hands around my waist as though to snap me in two, and he'd say, "There is nothing I wouldn't do for you." And I would rest my hands in his black curly hair.

"Nothing," he'd say again.

And I said, "I know," and he'd relax and lay me on the bed.

It was like nothing else in my life, that river of love that I could dip into and leave and return to once more and find it still flowing, undisturbed by my comings and goings. And when we made love, it was the same. He would wash over me and into me and he didn't need me to smile, or cry out, or move. I lay there, like the riverbed.

I was orphaned at sixteen, by two lonely, curdled people who had hoped to divorce without too much scandal when I finished high school. Instead, their car hit a tree. I was sent off to boarding school by a committee of relatives and came home to visit Mrs. Wallace (the one my father hoped to marry) and Dr. Davidson (the one my mother had in the wings). I went on being their memorial tribute to thwarted love and bad planning until I turned eighteen. I escaped to Juilliard and didn't answer their letters. Being an orphan didn't bother me.

While I was at Juilliard, I met David. He was finishing his residency in psychiatry, and I was one of his guinea pigs. I was nineteen, he was twenty-nine. My faculty adviser had noticed that I never went away for holidays, never had family in the audience, never had trouble paying my tuition. I told her the highlights of my personal history, and she turned her face away and suggested that I "talk to someone" at the Washington Square Clinic. I thought it had something to do with piano playing, so I went.

It was April, and the big waiting room was still wintry. All the chairs were gray plastic. As I put my feet up on one of them, I saw two men talking on the far side of the room. My hearing is acute, and I eavesdropped.

"I'll take her," said the tall, chubby one.

"No," said the other one, David. "You're full up this week, and anyway, you couldn't handle your countertransference."

"My countertransference? Please. All right, you take her. Take her."

I was smiling when David invited me into his cubicle.

"You have a lovely smile," he said, and then he frowned.

"Thank you. Why are you frowning?"

"I'm not...I'm Dr. Silverstein and you're...Galen Nichols?"

"Yes."

"Well." He arched his fingertips together the way they must have taught him in Practical Psychiatry. "What can I do for you?"

"I don't know," I said, and I didn't say anything else.

We had three sessions like that, and at the end of the third I got up and shook his hand.

"Thanks for your time," I said. I liked him, he acted just like me.

Two weeks later, he called and asked how I was doing. A few weeks after that, he invited me to go for coffee. I went, and we sat in the Big Apple Coffee Shoppe for two hours while he told me that he was married but just couldn't stop thinking about me. I thanked him for the coffee and went home and listened to my most recent performance tapes.

After two more coffee dates, he asked me to have dinner with him.

"I can't take a break for dinner these days, we're rehearsing. But if you want to get something for yourself and come listen, you're welcome to."

David sat at the back of the auditorium until 1:00 A.M., and he walked me home.

"You play so beautifully. May I please come in?"

"Sure."

By then, I had figured out that he wasn't really like me at all, but he was a gentle, sweet man, not like the cowboys at home. He touched me as if I were made of glass and gold dust. At about 3:00 A.M. he jumped out of bed and into his jeans, mumbling how sorry he was. I was too tired to walk him to the door, so I blew him a kiss and told him to take the extra key.

"I'll call you," he said.

"All right."

When he called, though, I couldn't see him because I'd gotten a grant to study in Paris for the rest of the summer. I gave him my address at the pension and told him to take care. Three weeks later, Madame Laverre whispered that I had a visitor waiting in the courtyard. There was David, unshaven, an enormous bouquet of flowers in his shaking hands. I was glad to see him.

He said that he'd asked his wife for a separation and that she'd agreed. I didn't want to talk about it. We found a couple of jars for the flowers and walked along the river. He took a room down the hall and stayed for ten days. I'd practice or go to class during the day, and he'd visit museums and read. At night, we'd eat in the café and then have sex in his room. I slept in my own room. We had a nice time, and when he was leaving I said I'd call him in September.

I remember how he smiled then. "You've never called me."

"I will."

"Okay, I'll be in my own place by then, and I'll list the new number with Information right away so you can get it." He was swinging my hand back and forth. "Coming to Paris was the best thing I could have done. I love you, you know."

"I'm glad you came," I said. "Don't miss your plane." And he stroked my hair and cried for a minute before he left.

When I got back I did call him, and we spent most of our evenings together. For a year he asked me to marry him and I ignored him. I thought I'd be dead by the time I was twenty-five, I couldn't see getting married. One morning David started banging his fists on my kitchen table and said, "You are killing me. All I want is to love you, and you won't let me."

I got dressed and left him sitting in the kitchen. I bought a white silk shirt to go with my white jeans and called him from Macy's to meet me for a blood test. Ten years later, we had two girls, quiet, like me, but friendly. David is a good person, and I knew that women would be lining up six-deep, with casseroles, the minute I left him.

I walked into the kitchen, still thinking about the nice, normal woman who would become David's next wife, and watched him carry a plate of chicken to the grill, balancing tongs and a fork and a bottle of barbecue sauce. He had sent the girls to get out of their wet suits, and while I chopped red peppers and hulled strawberries I kept my head down, wondering if it'd be better to leave a note. He watched me putter, and after he had washed and dried his hands carefully, he rested them on my shoulders for just a second. Then he went into the living room and put on Vivaldi while I set the table.

After dinner, we let the girls bike around the neighborhood and we washed the dishes together. David went to work on an article, and I sat in the bedroom, in the bent willow rocking chair that we bought when I was pregnant with Rose, and waited for the phone to ring.

"Hi, it's Hank DiMartino." We were always very careful, in case a spouse picked up simultaneously.

"Hi, David's in his study." The study didn't have a phone, so that he wouldn't be disturbed. "How'd the tennis game go?"

"Not bad, considering that I was out of my mind. You looked so beautiful today, and you've made me so happy. You did mean it? You'll leave?"

"Yes."

"I can't believe that I'm going to wake up every morning for the rest of my life and look at your face on the pillow next to mine. I want to marry you, as soon as we can."

I was picking dead leaves off the fig tree in our bedroom. "I'll be yours until the stars fall from the sky, Henry. I don't have any thoughts about marriage." I also had some doubts about sleeping in the same bed. David was used to my slipping onto the floor during the night.

"I want us to belong to each other."

"That doesn't make any sense. You belonged to Marie, and you're ready to divorce her. I belonged to David, and before that, he belonged to Nina. It's really silly, the whole idea."

"Gae, honey, I want to be with you and I want it to be forever."

"I want to be with you too, Henry." And I did.

David came into the bedroom. He mouthed, "For me?" and I shook my head. He stood in the middle of the bedroom, looking at me, before he went back to his study.

"I have to go. David's wandering around. I'll drive by the construction site tomorrow. Columbine Lane, right?"

"Right. That'll be great. I love you, you."

"I know. See you tomorrow."

David came to bed a little earlier than usual, and he laid his hand on my breast. After a while, he put his hand on my thigh, his sign, and I shifted my legs to let him enter me. It wasn't as nice as cooking to the Vivaldi, but it was really all right. I awoke on the floor. David had put a quilt over me and tucked his sweater under my head.

I put the sweater on and practiced for about three hours after the girls went out to play and David went downtown to see patients. This was one of my favorite times, and I didn't want to cut it short. I practiced some performance pieces I was having trouble with and threw in a little jazz at the end. My fingers were getting stiffer as I got older. I showered and went to meet Henry, wearing a shapeless blue shift that he hated. I drove over to Columbine Lane, where he was building a house.

His crew was there, taking a coffee break. Most of the guys knew me, or my car, by sight. Henry and I counted on the fact that most people, especially men, don't like to get into other people's business. I came and went freely, undisguised. Usually, I'd just pull over onto the ridge near his trailer and sit in the car waiting. Henry would come out after a few minutes and scrunch down by the window to talk to me about our schedules and try to work his plans around mine. Once in a while, if we had a chunk of time during the day, we'd go to a hotel. I would have gone to a motel, or even to the park, but Henry felt we deserved better. I didn't think it had much to do with what we deserved.

He saw me right away and hopped down from the unfinished patio. I could watch him run toward me and never tire of the sight, his right leg slightly stiff at the knee from an old baseball injury, his muscles flowing beneath his clothes. I wanted that ease, that perfect unconsciousness, to transform me so that I would never again find myself in the middle of traffic, paralyzed by the risk and complexity of the next step.

Once, the summer before, I'd been watching him from the clubhouse as he did his laps. He felt my eyes on him and he got out of the water, face turned to me, and came up the stairs to the deck, dripping water through the building. No one else was around.

"I can't not come to you," he said. "I just don't have any choice about it." And he gathered up my hair into little bunches and pressed them against his wet face, like flowers. After Rose and Violet, I loved that kind of love the most.

It wasn't his wanting me that got to me. That was nice, but not so rare in my life. Men see something in me, or something missing, that they like. It's that he didn't fight the feeling; a lot of times men want you and then they get mad about wanting you, whether they have you or not. He had never been angry with me, or disappointed, or blamed me for what I couldn't do. And more than that, it was that he was so beautiful and that beauty belonged to me.

When he got to my car, I swung the door open and he knelt in front of me, I put my hand on his arm, breaking our public display rules, which now seemed irrelevant. He smiled down at my hand, a sunny, white smile that was like nothing I'd ever seen in my mirror.

"Ready to take the plunge?" he asked.

"I'm ready to tell David, after the girls go to camp. I can move out then, or he'll move out, and we can get started."

"Started? Galen, we're a lot further along than 'getting started.' I really do want to marry you, and I want us to try and get custody of the boys."

Shit, I thought. First of all, Marie does a perfectly fine job with the boys, it's not like they need to be rescued, and second of all, I could just see myself spending the next five years of my life trying to win over the older one. Making hot dogs and burgers when I've trained my girls to eat French, Thai, Indian, and whatever's put in front of them; having to wear a robe when I take a shower; going to tennis matches every weekend; stepping over GoBots and pieces of GI Joe.

"Henry, let's wait and see. Let's give ourselves a chance to enjoy ourselves, just be together and see how it goes."

He got very dark and his brows drew down. I didn't know what else to say.

"I don't have much choice, do I? If you don't want to take what I want to give you, I can't make you. But I'm going to keep asking you, and one of these days you're going to say yes. It's meant to be, sweetheart." He was smiling again; he believed everything he was saying.

Like hell, I thought. I was touched, of course, but I could never answer the same question over and over. And I don't believe that anything's written for us, certainly nothing good. I slept on the floor, I lost track of time, and love and death had always looked pretty much the same to me. David needed to marry someone crazy; Henry had mistaken me for someone interesting.

He put his big hand over mine, and I watched a little cloud of plaster dust settle on us.

"I have to go. I'll talk to you tomorrow." I slammed the car door and drove off, watching him shrink in the rearview mirror.

My arms and legs were cold, driving home through the woods, and I thought about what I was going home to. I pulled the car off the road, picturing Henry and his boys, and his kids with my kids, and Marie bitching about money, and Henry sitting in a studio apartment with mismatched plates, waiting for me to make his divorce meaningful, valuable, decent. Waiting for me to make his life beautiful. And when I'd finally get up to leave, he'd watch me go, letting me know that I was supposed to stay with him, that I was hurting him.

I got home about ten of twelve and called David between appointments. He picked up on the first ring.

"Dr. Silverstein here."

"Ms. Nichols here."

He sounded surprised and he laughed. I didn't call him often, since he was calling home once or twice a day at this point. I used to hate that when we were first married, and he finally stopped, but that year he had started again and I didn't say anything about it. He was right to be afraid.

"I could call Mrs. Stevenson for the girls and we could go to the Siam, just the two of us," I said.

"Okay, that would be fine. That would be nice."

I hadn't expected more than that. "Good. See you at home."

"Okay. I'm glad you called."

"See you at home."

"I love you," he said.

"I know. See you soon."

I practiced for another hour, and when the girls came in we took turns playing duets for a while, and then I had to go lie down. I fell asleep for about an hour, and when David woke me up I tried to focus and made the girls stir-fry vegetables and fried dumplings.

Our own dinner was pretty nice, smooth white platters of dark, peppery food, cold beer, and enough room for me to lie back against the cold vinyl seats. David kept reaching forward, touching my temples and my wrists, where my veins are big and blue.

"How do you keep so cool?" he asked. It was an old joke between us.

"No heart," I said.

He smiled, and I thought, I cannot do this again. I smiled back at him.

I drove down to see Henry the next day, and the guys waved to me. I got out of the car and went over to Henry and kissed him on the mouth, and then on both cheeks, and then at the corner of each perfect eye. He didn't smile.

"You're not going to leave him, are you? You're going to tell me that you can't do it, and I just don't want to hear it. Please, Galen, please, baby. Don't say it."

"I won't say I can't. That's too easy. I have to say that I'm choosing not to. I'm so sorry."

He looked me up and down for a minute, and he put his warm face into my neck. I could feel every bone in his face pressing in, but I stood fast.

"I had an offer for the business, a pretty good offer. I could go down to North Carolina, I could go back into business with my dad. Should I take it?"

"Do you want to?" I could see him going, striding loosely down a back road, the sun shining on him, wherever he was.

"No, goddamnit, I don't want to. I want to stay here and marry you and have a child with you, that's what I want. That's all I've wanted for two years, and if I can't have that, I don't even know what to want."

"I don't know what you should do. Does Marie want to move?"

"Of course. I haven't even told her about the offer. You know Marie, she'll have us packed before the ink's dry on the contract. Getting me away from you will make her very happy."

We smiled; Marie had been suspicious long before there had

been anything between us, and somehow that had left us feeling slightly less guilty.

"I know." And I thought about having him near and him looking at me like he had a splinter in his heart and Marie looking at me the same way, only without the love.

"Take the offer," I said. "Move."

"Okay," he said, like a threat.

"Okay," I said, and I kissed him, just one quick time, and I closed my eyes until he walked away.

FOREVER OVERHEAD

by DAVID FOSTER WALLACE

DAVID FOSTER WALLACE (b. 1962) is the author of the acclaimed novel Infinite Jest. *From* Brief Interviews with Hideous Men, *"Forever Overhead" tells of a boy who confronts the vertigo of puberty atop a high diving board at a Tucson, Arizona public pool.*

HAPPY BIRTHDAY. Your thirteenth is important. Maybe your first really public day. Your thirteenth is the chance for people to recognize that important things are happening to you.

Things have been happening to you for the past half year. You have seven hairs in your left armpit now. Twelve in your right. Hard dangerous spirals of brittle black hair. Crunchy, animal hair. There are now more of the hard curled hairs around your privates than you can count without losing track. Other things. Your voice is rich and scratchy and moves between octaves without any warning. Your face has begun to get shiny when you don't wash it. And two weeks of a deep and frightening ache this past spring left you with something dropped down from inside: your sack is now full and vulnerable, a commodity to be protected. Hefted and strapped in tight supporters that stripe your buttocks red. You have grown into a new fragility.

And dreams. For months there have been dreams like nothing before: moist and busy and distant, full of yielding curves, frantic pistons, warmth and a great falling; and you have awakened through fluttering lids to a rush and a gush and a toe-curling scalp-snapping jolt of feeling from an inside deeper than you knew you had, spasms of a deep sweet hurt, the streetlights through your window blinds cracking into sharp stars against the black bedroom ceiling, and on you a dense white jam that lisps between legs, trickles and sticks, cools on you, hardens and clears until there is nothing but gnarled knots of pale solid animal hair in the morning shower, and in the wet tangle a clean sweet smell you can't believe comes from anything you made inside you.

The smell is, more than anything, like this swimming pool: a bleached sweet salt, a flower with chemical petals. The pool has a strong clear blue smell, though you know the smell is never as strong when you are actually in the blue water, as you are now, all swum out, resting back along the shallow end, the hip-high water lapping at where it's all changed.

Around the deck of this old public pool on the western edge of Tucson is a Cyclone fence the color of pewter, decorated with a bright tangle of locked bicycles. Beyond this is a hot black parking lot full of white lines and glittering cars. A dull field of dry grass and hard weeds, old dandelions' downy heads exploding and snowing up in a rising wind. And past all this, reddened by a round slow September sun, are mountains, jagged, their tops' sharp angles darkening into definition against a deep red tired light. Against the red their sharp connected tops form a spiked line, an EKG of the dying day.

The clouds are taking on color by the rim of the sky. The water is spangles of soft blue, five-o'clock warm, and the pool's smell, like the other smell, connects with a chemical haze inside you, an interior dimness that bends light to its own ends, softens the difference between what leaves off and what begins.

Your party is tonight. This afternoon, on your birthday, you have asked to come to the pool. You wanted to come alone, but a birthday is a family day, your family wants to be with you. This is nice, and you can't talk about why you wanted to come alone, and really truly maybe you didn't want to come alone, so they are here. Sunning. Both your parents sun. Their deck chairs have been marking time all afternoon, rotating, tracking the sun's curve across a desert sky heated to an eggy film. Your sister plays Marco Polo near you in the shallows with a group of thin girls from her grade. She is being blind now, her Marco's being Polo'd. She is shut-eyed and twirling to different cries, spinning at the hub of a wheel of shrill girls in bathing caps. Her cap has raised rubber flowers. There are limp old pink petals that shake as she lunges at blind sound.

There at the other end of the pool is the diving tank and the high board's tower. Back on the deck behind is the SN CK BAR, and on either side, bolted above the cement entrances to dark wet showers and lockers, are gray metal bullhorn speakers that send out the pool's radio music, the jangle flat and tinny thin.

Your family likes you. You are bright and quiet, respectful to elders—though you are not without spine. You are largely good. You look out for your little sister. You are her ally. You were six when she was zero and you had the mumps when they brought her home in a very soft yellow blanket; you kissed her hello on her feet out of concern that she not catch your mumps. Your parents say that this augured well. That it set the tone. They now feel they were right. In all things they are proud of you, satisfied, and they have retreated to the warm distance from which pride and satisfaction travel. You all get along well.

Happy Birthday. It is a big day, big as the roof of the whole southwest sky. You have thought it over. There is the high board. They will want to leave soon. Climb out and do the thing.

Shake off the blue clean. You're half-bleached, loose and soft, tenderized, pads of fingers wrinkled. The mist of the pool's too-clean smell is in your eyes; it breaks light into gentle color. Knock your head with the heel of your hand. One side has a flabby echo. Cock your head to the side and hop—sudden heat in your ear, delicious, and brain-warmed water turns cold on the nautilus of your ear's outside. You can hear harder tinnier music, closer shouts, much movement in much water.

The pool is crowded for this late. Here are thin children, hairy animal men. Disproportionate boys, all necks and legs and knobby joints, shallow-chested, vaguely birdlike. Like you. Here are old people moving tentatively through shallows on stick legs, feeling at the water with their hands, out of every element at once.

And girl-women, women, curved like instruments or fruit, skin burnished brown-bright, suit tops held by delicate knots of fragile colored string against the pull of mysterious weights, suit bottoms riding low over the gentle juts of hips totally unlike your own, immoderate swells and swivels that melt in light into a surrounding space that cups and accommodates the soft curves as things precious. You almost understand.

The pool is a system of movement. Here now there are: laps, splash fights, dives, corner tag, cannonballs, Sharks and Minnows, high fallings, Marco Polo (your sister still It, halfway to tears, too long to be It, the game teetering on the edge of cruelty, not your business to save or embarrass). Two clean little bright-white boys caped in cotton towels run along the poolside until the guard stops them dead with a shout through his bullhorn. The guard is brown as a tree, blond hair in a vertical line on his stomach, his head in a jungle explorer hat, his nose a white triangle of cream. A girl has an arm around a leg of his little tower. He's bored.

Get out now and go past your parents, who are sunning and reading, not looking up. Forget your towel. Stopping for the towel means talking and talking means thinking. You have decided being scared is caused mostly by thinking. Go right by, toward the tank at the deep end. Over the tank is a great iron tower of dirty white. A board protrudes from the top of the tower like a tongue. The pool's concrete deck is rough and hot against your bleached feet. Each of your footprints is thinner and fainter. Each shrinks behind you on the hot stone and disappears.

Lines of plastic wieners bob around the tank, which is entirely its own thing, empty of the rest of the pool's convulsive ballet of heads and arms. The tank is blue as energy, small and deep and perfectly square, flanked by lap lanes and SN CK BAR and rough hot deck and the bent late shadow of the tower and board. The tank is quiet and still and healed smooth between fallings.

There is a rhythm to it. Like breathing. Like a machine. The line for the board curves back from the tower's ladder. The line moves in its curve, straightens as it nears the ladder. One by one, people reach the ladder and climb. One by one, spaced by the beat of hearts, they reach the tongue of the board at the top. And once on the board, they pause, each exactly the same tiny heartbeat pause. And their legs take them to the end, where they all give the same sort of stomping hop, arms curving out as if to describe something circular, total; they come down heavy on the edge of the board and make it throw them up and out.

It's a swooping machine, lines of stuttered movement in a sweet late bleach mist. You can watch from the deck as they hit the cold blue sheet of the tank. Each fall makes a white that plumes and falls into itself and spreads and fizzes. Then blue clean comes up in the middle of the white and spreads like pudding, making it all new. The tank heals itself. Three times as you go by.

You are in line. Look around. Look bored. Few talk in the line. Everyone seems by himself. Most look at the ladder, look bored. You almost all have crossed arms, chilled by a late dry rising wind on the constellations of blue-clean chlorine beads that cover your backs and shoulders. It seems impossible that everybody could really be this bored. Beside you is the edge of the tower's shadow, the tilted black tongue of the board's image. The system of shadow is huge, long, off to the side, joined to the tower's base at a sharp late angle.

Almost everyone in line for the board watches the ladder. Older boys watch older girls' bottoms as they go up. The bottoms are in soft thin cloth, tight nylon stretch. The good bottoms move up the ladder like pendulums in liquid, a gentle uncrackable code. The girls' legs make you think of deer. Look bored.

Look out past it. Look across. You can see so well. Your mother is in her deck chair, reading, squinting, her face tilted up to get light on her cheeks. She hasn't looked to see where you are. She sips something sweet out of a bright can. Your father is on his big stomach, back like the hint of a hump of a whale, shoulders curling with animal spirals, skin oiled and soaked red-brown with too much sun. Your towel is hanging off your chair and a corner of the cloth now moves—your mother hit it as she waved away a sweat bee that likes what she has in the can. The bee is back right away, seeming to hang motionless over the can in a sweet blur. Your towel is one big face of Yogi Bear.

At some point there has gotten to be more line behind you than in front of you. Now no one in front except three on the slender ladder. The woman right before you is on the low rungs, looking up, wearing a tight black nylon suit that is all one piece. She climbs. From above there is a rumble, then a great falling, then a plume and the tank reheals. Now two on the ladder. The pool rules say one on the ladder at a time, but the guard never shouts about it. The guard makes the real rules by shouting or not shouting.

This woman above you should not wear a suit as tight as the suit she is wearing. She is as old as your mother, and as big. She is too big and too white. Her suit is full of her. The backs of her thighs are squeezed by the suit and look like cheese. Her legs have abrupt little squiggles of cold blue shattered vein under the white skin, as if something were broken, hurt, in her legs. Her legs look like they hurt to be squeezed, full of curled Arabic lines of cold broken blue. Her legs make you feel like your own legs hurt.

The rungs are very thin. It's unexpected. Thin round

iron rungs laced in slick wet Safe-T felt. You taste metal from the smell of wet iron in shadow. Each rung presses into the bottoms of your feet and dents them. The dents feel deep and they hurt. You feel heavy. How the big woman over you must feel. The handrails along the ladder's sides are also very thin. It's like you might not hold on. You've got to hope the woman holds on, too. And of course it looked like fewer rungs from far away. You are not stupid.

Get halfway up, up in the open, big woman placed above you, a solid bald muscular man on the ladder underneath your feet. The board is still high overhead, invisible from here. But it rumbles and makes a heavy flapping sound, and a boy you can see for a few contained feet through the thin rungs falls in a flash of a line, a knee held to his chest, doing a splasher. There is a huge exclamation point of foam up into your field of sight, then scattered claps into a great fizzing. Then the silent sound of the tank healing to new blue all over again.

More thin rungs. Hold on tight. The radio is loudest here, one speaker at ear-level over a concrete locker room entrance. A cool dank whiff of the locker room inside. Grab the iron bars tight and twist and look down behind you and you can see people buying snacks and refreshments below. You can see down into it: the clean white top of the vendor's cap, tubs of ice cream, streaming brass freezers, scuba tanks of soft drink syrup, snakes of soda hose, bulging boxes of salty popcorn kept hot in the sun. Now that you're overhead you can see the whole thing.

There's wind. It's windier the higher you get. The wind is thin; through the shadow it's cold on your wet skin. On the ladder in the shadow your skin looks very white. The wind makes a thin whistle in your ears. Four more rungs to the top of the tower. The rungs hurt your feet. They are thin and let you know just how much you weigh. You have real weight on the ladder. The ground wants you back.

Now you can see just over the top of the ladder. You can see the board. The woman is there. There are two ridges of red, hurt-looking callus on the backs of her ankles. She stands at the start of the board, your eyes on her ankles. Now you're up above the tower's shadow. The solid man under you is looking through the rungs into the contained space the woman's fall will pass through.

She pauses for just that beat of a pause. There's nothing slow about it at all. It makes you cold. In no time she's at the end of the board, up, down on it, it bends low like it doesn't want her. Then it nods and flaps and throws her violently up and out, her arms opening out to inscribe that circle, and gone. She disappears in a dark blink. And there's time before you hear the hit below.

Listen. It does not seem good, the way she disappears into a time that passes before she sounds. Like a stone down a well. But you think she did not think so. She was part of a rhythm that excludes thinking. And now you have made yourself part of it, too. The rhythm seems blind. Like ants. Like a machine.

You decide this needs to be thought about. It may, after

all, be all right to do something scary without thinking, but not when the scariness is the not thinking itself. Not when not thinking turns out to be wrong. At some point the wrongnesses have piled up blind: pretend-boredom, weight, thin rungs, hurt feet, space cut into laddered parts that melt together only in a disappearance that takes time. The wind on the ladder not what anyone would have expected. The way the board protrudes from shadow into light and you can't see past the end. When it all turns out to be different you should get to think. It should be required.

The ladder is full beneath you. Stacked up, everyone a few rungs apart. The ladder is fed by a solid line that stretches back and curves into the dark of the tower's canted shadow. People's arms are crossed in the line. Those on the ladder's feet hurt and they are all looking up. It is a machine that moves only forward.

Climb up onto the tower's tongue. The board turns out to be long. As long as the time you stand there. Time slows. It thickens around you as your heart gets more and more beats out of every second, every movement in the system of the pool below.

The board is long. From where you stand it seems to stretch off into nothing. It's going to send you someplace which its own length keeps you from seeing, which seems wrong to submit to without even thinking.

Looked at another way, the same board is just a long thin flat thing covered with a rough white plastic stuff. The white surface is very rough and is freckled and lined with a pale watered red that is nevertheless still red and not yet pink—drops of old pool water that are catching the light of the late sun over sharp mountains. The rough white stuff of the board is wet. And cold. Your feet are hurt from the thin rungs and have a great ability to feel. They feel your weight. There are handrails running above the beginning of the board. They are not like the ladder's handrails just were. They are thick and set very low, so you almost have to bend over to hold on to them. They are just for show, no one holds them. Holding on takes time and alters the rhythm of the machine.

It is a long cold rough white plastic or fiberglass board, veined with the sad near-pink color of bad candy.

But at the end of the white board, the edge, where you'll come down with your weight to make it send you off, there are two areas of darkness. Two flat shadows in the broad light. Two vague black ovals. The end of the board has two dirty spots.

They are from all the people who've gone before you. Your feet as you stand here are tender and dented, hurt by the rough wet surface, and you see that the two dark spots are from people's skin. They are skin abraded from feet by the violence of the disappearance of people with real weight. More people than you could count without losing track. The weight and abrasion of their disappearance leaves little bits of soft tender feet behind, bits and shards and curls of skin that dirty and darken and tan as they lie tiny and smeared in the sun at the end of the board. They pile up and get smeared and mixed together. They darken in two circles.

No time is passing outside you at all. It is amazing. The late ballet below is slow motion, the overboard movements of mimes in blue jelly. If you wanted you could really stay here forever, vibrating inside so fast you float motionless in time, like a bee over something sweet.

But they should clean the board. Anybody who thought about it for even a second would see that they should clean the end of the board of people's skin, of two black collections of what's left of before, spots that from back here look like eyes, like blind and cross-eyed eyes.

Where you are now is still and quiet. Wind radio shouting splashing not here. No time and no real sound but your blood squeaking in your head.

Overhead here means sight and smell. The smells are intimate, newly clear. The smell of bleach's special flower, but out of it other things rise to you like a weed's seeded snow. You smell deep yellow popcorn. Sweet tan oil like hot coconut. Either hot dogs or corn dogs. A thin cruel hint of very dark Pepsi in paper cups. And the special smell of tons of water coming off tons of skin, rising like steam off a new bath. Animal heat. From overhead it is more real than anything.

Look at it. You can see the whole complicated thing, blue and white and brown and white, soaked in a watery spangle of deepening red. Everybody. This is what people call a view. And you knew that from below you wouldn't look nearly so high overhead. You see now how high overhead you are. You knew from down there no one could tell.

He says it behind you, his eyes on your ankles, the solid bald man, Hey kid. They want to know. Do your plans up here involve the whole day or what exactly is the story. Hey kid are you okay.

There's been time this whole time. You can't kill time with your heart. Everything takes time. Bees have to move very fast to stay still.

Hey kid he says Hey kid are you okay.

Metal flowers bloom on your tongue. No more time for thinking. Now that there is time you don't have time.

Hey.

Slowly now, out across everything, there's a watching that spreads like hit water's rings. Watch it spread out from the ladder. Your sighted sister and her thin white pack, pointing. Your mother looks to the shallows where you used to be, then makes a visor of her hand. The whale stirs and jiggles. The guard looks up, the girl around his leg looks up, he reaches for his horn.

Forever below is rough deck, snacks, thin metal music, down where you once used to be; the line is solid and has no reverse gear; and the water, of course, is only soft when you're inside it. Look down. Now it moves in the sun, full of hard coins of light that shimmer red as they stretch away into a mist that is your own sweet salt. The coins crack into new moons, long shards of light from the hearts of sad stars. The square tank is a cold blue sheet. Cold is just a kind of hard. A kind of blind. You have been taken off guard. Happy Birthday. Did you think it over. Yes and no. Hey kid.

Two black spots, violence, and disappear into a well of time. Height is not the problem. It all changes when you get back down. When you hit, with your weight.

So which is the lie? Hard or soft? Silence or time?

The lie is that it's one or the other. A still, floating bee is moving faster than it can think. From overhead the sweetness drives it crazy.

The board will nod and you will go, and eyes of skin can cross blind into a cloud-blotched sky, punctured light emptying behind sharp stone that is forever. That is forever. Step into the skin and disappear.

Hello.

A PUBLIC POOL *by* ALICE ADAMS

ALICE ADAMS (1923–1999) made San Francisco her adoptive home after moving there as a young woman. In this quiet, Bay Area tale of self-renewal, the local public pool has become a refuge for unemployed Maxine, surrounded by walls of her own making. To her surprise, as her stroke grows more confident, so does she. Originally published in Adams's 1985 collection Return Trips, *"A Public Pool" shows a young woman—and her city—in transition.*

WIMMING

Reaching, pulling, gliding through the warm blue chlorinated water, I am strong and lithe: I am not oversized, not six feet tall, weighing one eighty-five. I am not myself, not Maxine.

I am fleet, possessed of powerful, deep energy. I could swim all day, swim anywhere. Sometimes I even wonder if I should try the San Francisco Bay, that treacherous cold tide-wracked water. People do swim there, they call themselves Polar Bears. Maybe I should, although by now I like it here in the Rossi Pool, swimming back and forth, doing laps in the Fast Lane, stretching and pulling my forceful, invisible body.

Actually the lane where I swim is not really Fast. I swim during Recreational Swimming, and during Rec. hours what was Fast during Laps is roped off for anyone to use who does laps—Slow, Medium, or genuinely Fast, which I am not.

Last summer I started off in Slow, and then I could not do many lengths at a time, 16 or 18 at most, and only sidestroke. But I liked it, the swimming and the calm, rested way it seemed to make me feel. And I thought that maybe, eventually I might get thinner, swimming. Also, it takes up a certain amount of time, which for an out-of-work living-at-home person is a great advantage. I have been laid off twice in the past five years, both times by companies going out of business. I have a real knack, my mother says. And how many hours a day can a young woman read? That is a question my mother often asks. She is a downtown saleslady, old but blonde, and very thin.

So—swimming.

After a month or so I realized that I was swimming faster than most of the people in Slow, and that some people who could barely swim at all were in my way. For another two or three weeks I watched Medium, wondering if I dare try to swim in there. One day I forced myself, jumping into Medium, the middle lane. I felt very anxious, but that was hardly an unfamiliar or unusual sort of emotion; sometimes shopping for groceries can have the same effect. And actually Medium turned out to be okay. There were a few hotshots who probably belonged in Fast but were too chicken to try it there, but quite a few people swam about the same as I did, and some swam slower.

Sometime during the fall—still warm outside, big dry yellow sycamore leaves falling down to the sidewalks—the pool schedule changed so that all the lap swimming was geared to people with jobs: Laps at noon and after five. Discouraging: I knew that all those people would be eager, pushy aggressive swimmers, kicking big splashes into my face as they swam past, almost shoving me aside in their hurry to get back to their wonderful jobs.

However, I found out that during Rec. there is always a lane roped off for laps, and the Rec. hours looked much better: mid to late afternoon, and those can be sort of cold hours at home, a sad end of daytime, with nothing accomplished.

In any case, that is why I now swim my laps during Rec., in the Fast lane. In the rest of the pool some little kids cavort around, and some grownups, some quite fat, some hardly able to swim at all. Sometimes a lot of school kids, mostly girls, mostly black, or Asian. A reflection of this neighborhood, I guess.

TO MEET SOMEONE

Of course I did not begin swimming with any specific idea that I might meet someone, any more than meeting someone is in my mind when I go out to the Ninth Avenue Library. Still, there is always that possibility: the idea of someone is always there, in a way, wherever I go. Maybe everywhere everyone goes, even if most people don't think of it that way?

For one thing, the area of the Rossi Recreation Center, where the pool is, has certain romantic associations for me: a long time ago, in the sixties when I was only in junior high (and still thin!), that was where all the peace marches started; everyone gathered there on the Rossi playing field, behind the pool house, with their placards and flags and banners, in their costumes or just plain clothes. I went to all the marches; I loved them, and I hated LBJ, and I knew that his war was crazy, wicked, killing off kids and poor people, mostly blacks, was how it looked to me. Anyway, one Saturday in May, I fell in with a group of kids from another school, and we spent the rest of that day together, just messing around, walking almost all over town—eating pizza in North Beach and smoking a little dope in the park. Sort of making out, that night, at one of their houses, over on Lincoln Way. Three guys and a couple of girls, all really nice. I kept hoping that I would run into them somewhere again, but I never did. Or else they, too, underwent sudden changes, the way I did, and grew out-of-sight tall, and then fat. But I still think of them sometimes, walking in the direction of Rossi.

Swimming, though: even if you met someone it would be hard to tell anything about them, beyond the most obvious physical facts. For one thing almost no one says anything, except for a few superpolite people who say Sorry when they bump into you, passing in a lane. Or, there is one really mean-looking black woman, tall, and a very fast swimmer, who one day told me, "You ought to get over closer to the side." She ought to have been in Fast, is what I would like to have said, but did not.

The men all swim very fast, and hard, except for a couple of really fat ones; most men somersault backward at the end of each length, so as not to waste any time. A few women do that, too, including the big mean black one. There is one especially objectionable guy, tall and blond (but not as tall as I am), with a little blond beard; I used to watch him zip past, ploughing the water with his violent crawl, in Fast, when I was still pushing along in Medium. Unfortunately, now he, too, comes to swim in Rec., and mostly at the same times that I do. He swims so fast, so roughly cutting through the water; he doesn't even know I am there, nor probably anyone else. He is just the kind of guy who used to act as though I was air, along the corridors at Washington High.

I have noticed that very few old people come to swim at Rossi. And if they do you can watch them trying to hide their old bodies, slipping down into the water. Maybe for that reason, body shyness, they don't come back; the very old never come more than once to swim, which is a great pity, I think. The exercise would be really good for them, and personally I like very old people, very much. For a while I had a job in a home for old people, a rehabilitation center, so-called, and although in many ways it was a terrible job, really exhausting and sometimes very depressing, I got to like a lot of them very much. They have a lot to say that's interesting, and if they like you it's more flattering, I think, since they have more people to compare you with. I like real old people, who look their age.

People seem to come and go, though, at Rossi. You can see someone there regularly for weeks, or months, and then suddenly never again, and you don't know what has happened to that person. They could have switched over to the regular lap hours, or maybe found a job so that now they come very late, or early in the morning. Or they could have died, had a heart attack, or been run down by some car. There is no way you could ever know, and their sudden absences can seem very mysterious, a little spooky.

GARLIC FOR LUNCH

Since my mother has to stay very thin to keep her job (she has to look much younger than she is), and since God knows I should lose some weight, we usually don't eat much for dinner. Also, most of my mother's money goes for all the clothes she has to have for work, not to mention the rent and the horrible utility bills. We eat a lot of eggs.

However, sometimes I get a powerful craving for something really good, like a pizza, or some pasta, my favorite. I like just plain spaghetti, with scallions and garlic and butter and some Parmesan, mostly stuff we have already in the house. Which makes it all the harder not to yield to that violent urge for pasta, occasionally.

One night there was nothing much else around to eat, and so I gave in to my lust, so to speak. I made a big steaming bowl of oniony, garlicky, buttery spaghetti, which my mother, in a worse than usual mood, ate very little of. Which meant that the next day there was a lot left over, and at noontime, I was unable not to eat quite a lot of it for lunch. I brushed my teeth before I went off to swim, but of course that doesn't help a lot, with garlic. However, since I almost never talk to anyone at Rossi it didn't much matter, I thought.

130

I have worked out how to spend the least possible time undressed in the locker room: I put my bathing suit on at home, then sweatshirt and jeans, and I bring along underthings wrapped up in a towel. That way I just zip off my clothes to swim, and afterward I can rush back into them, only naked for an instant; no one has to see me. While I am swimming I leave the towel with the understuff wrapped up in it on the long bench at one side of the pool, and sometimes I have horrible fantasies of someone walking off with it; however, it is comforting to think that no one would know whose it was, probably.

I don't think very much while swimming, not about my old bra and panties, nor about the fact that I ate all that garlic for lunch. I swim fast and freely, going up to the end with a crawl, back to Shallow with my backstroke, reaching wide, stretching everything.

Tired, momentarily winded, I pause in Shallow, still crouched down in the water and ready to go, but resting.

Just then, startlingly, someone speaks to me, a man's conversational voice. "It's nice today," he says. "Not too many people, right?"

Standing up, I see that I am next to the blond-bearded man, the violent swimmer. Who has spoken.

Very surprised, I say, "Oh yes, it's really terrific, isn't it. Monday it was awful, so many people I could hardly move, really terrible. I hate it when it's crowded like that, hardly worth coming at all on those days, but how can you tell until you get here?" I could hear myself saying all that; I couldn't stop.

He looks up at me in—amazement? disgust? great fear, that I will say even more. It is hard to read the expression in his small blue bloodshot eyes, and he only mutters, "That's right," before plunging back into the water.

Was it my garlic breath or simply my height, my incredible size that drove him off like that? In a heavy way I wondered, as I continued to swim, all the rest of my laps, which seemed laborious. It could have been either, easily, or in fact anything about me could have turned him off, off and away, for good; I knew that he would never speak to me again. A pain which is close to and no doubt akin to lust lay heavily in my body's lower quadrant, hurtful and implacable.

SEX

The atmosphere in the pool is not exactly sexy, generally, although you might think that it would be, with everyone so stripped down, wearing next to nothing, and some of the women looking really great, so slim and trim, high-breasted, in their thin brief bathing suits.

Once, just as I was getting in I overheard what looked like the start of a romance between a young man, fairly good-looking, who was talking to a very pretty Mexican girl.

The girl said, "You're Brad?"

"No. Gregory."

"Well, Greg, I'll try to make it. Later."

But with brief smiles they then both plunged back into doing their laps, seeming not to have made any significant (sexual) contact.

I have concluded that swimming is not a very sexual activity. I think very infrequently of sex while actually swimming. Well, all sports are supposed to take your mind off sex, aren't they? They are supposed to make you miss it less?

The lifeguards, during swimming hours, usually just sit up on their high wooden lifeguard chairs, looking bored. A couple of youngish, not very attractive guys. Every now and then one of the guys will walk around the pool very slowly, probably just to break his own monotony, but trying to look like a person on patrol.

One afternoon I watched one of those guys stop at Shallow, and stare down for a long time at a little red-haired girl who was swimming there. She was a beautiful child, with narrow blue eyes and long wet red hair, a white little body, as lithe as a fish, as she laughed and slipped around. The lifeguard stared and stared, and I knew—I could tell that sex was on his mind. Could he be a potential child molester?

I myself think of sex more often, in spite of swimming, since the day Blond Beard spoke to me, the day I'd had all that garlic for lunch. I hate to admit this.

THE SHRINK

An interesting fact that I have gradually noticed as I come to Rossi, to swim my laps, is that actually there is more variety among the men's trunks than among the bathing suits the women wear. The men's range from cheap, too-tight Lastex to the khaki shorts with thin blue side stripes that they advertise at Brooks, or Robert Kirk. Whereas, I noted early on, all the women wear quite similar-looking dark suits. Do the men who are rich, or at least getting along okay in the world, not bother to hide it when they come to a cheap public pool, while the women do? A puzzle. I cannot quite work it out. Blond Beard wears new navy Lastex trunks, which might mean anything at all.

Most people, including a lot of the men, but not Blond Beard, wear bathing caps, which makes it even harder to tell people apart, and would make it almost impossible, even, to recognize someone you knew. It is not surprising that from time to time I see someone I think I know, or have just met somewhere or other. At first, remembering the peace march kids, I imagined that I saw one or all of them, but that could have been just hope, a wishful thought. I thought I saw my old gym teacher, also from junior-high days. And one day I saw a man who looked like my father, which was a little crazy, since he split for Seattle when I was about five years old; I probably wouldn't know him if I did see him somewhere, much less in a pool with a bathing cap on.

But one day I saw an old woman with short white hair, swimming very fast, who I really thought was the shrink I went to once in high school, as a joke.

Or, going to the shrink started out to be a joke. The school had a list of ones that you could go to, if you had really "serious problems," and to me and my girlfriend, then, Betty, who was black, it seemed such a ludicrous idea, paying another person just to listen, telling them about your sex life, all like that, that we dreamed up the idea of inventing some really serious problems, and going off to some fool doctor and really putting him on, and at the same time finding out what it was like, seeing shrinks.

Betty, who was in most ways a lot smarter than me, much faster to catch on to things, chickened out early on; but she kept saying that I should go; Betty would just help me make up some stuff to say. And we did; we spent some hilarious afternoons at Betty's place in the project, making up lists of "serious problems"; heavy drugs, of course, and dealers. And stepfathers or even fathers doing bad sex things to you, and boys trying to get you to trick. All those things were all around Betty's life, and I think they scared her, really, but she laughed along with me, turning it into one big joke between us.

I made the appointment through the guidance office, with a Dr. Sheinbaum, and I went to the address, on Steiner Street. And that is where the joke stopped being a joke.

A nice-looking white-haired lady (a surprise right there; I had expected some man) led me into a really nice-looking living room, all books and pictures and big soft comfortable leather furniture. And the lady, the doctor, asked me to sit down, to try to tell her about some of the things that upset me.

I sat down in a soft pale-colored chair, and all of the funny made-up stuff went totally out of my mind—and I burst into tears. It was horrible, great wracking sobs that I absolutely could not stop. Every now and then I would look up at the doctor, and see that gentle face, that intelligent look of caring, and for some reason that made me cry much harder, even.

Of course I did not tell Betty—or anyone—about crying like that. All I said about going to the shrink was that it was all right, no big deal. And I said about the good-looking furniture. Betty was interested in things like that.

But could the fast-swimming older woman be that shrink? Well, she could be; it seemed the kind of thing that she might do, not caring what anyone thought, or who might see her. But she would never remember or recognize me—or would she?

LOOKING FOR WORK

The job search is something that I try not to think about, along with sex, general deprivation. It is what I should be doing, naturally; and in theory that is what I do all day, look for work. However, these days I seldom get much further than the want ads in the paper, those columns and columns of people saying they want secretaries, or sales people. And no one, not in a million years, would think of hiring me for either of those slots. Secretaries are all about the same size, very trim and tidy-looking, very normal, and so are people in sales—just ask my mother.

Sometimes an ad for a waitress sounds possible, and that is something I've done; I had a part-time waitress job the summer I got out of Washington High. But in those days I was thinner, and just now my confidence is pretty low. In my imagination, prospective employers, restaurant owners take one look at me and they start to sneer: "We don't even have the space for a person your size," or some such snub.

Instead I swim, and swim, swim—for as long as I can, every day.

I can feel my muscles stretching, pulling, getting longer, in the warm strong water.

HELLO

An odd coincidence: on a Tuesday afternoon—short Rec. hours, one-thirty to three—both Blond Beard and the big black woman who told me to swim closer to the side, so crossly—both those people on that same day said Hello to me, very pleasantly.

First, I had just jumped down into the pool, the shallow end of the lap section, when Blond Beard swam up and stood beside me for a minute. Looking up at me, he said Hello, and he smiled. However, his small pale eyes were vague; very likely he did not remember that we sort of talked before (hopefully, he did not remember the garlic).

I concentrated on not making too much of that encounter.

Later, when I had finished swimming and was drying off and dressing in the locker room, I was half aware that someone else was in there, too, on the other side of a row of lockers. Hurrying, not wanting to see anyone (or anyone to see me!), I was about to rush out of the room when at the exit door I almost bumped into the big black woman. In fact, it was a little funny, we are so nearly the exact same size. We both smiled; maybe she saw the humor in it, too? And then she said, "Say, your stroke's coming along real good."

"Oh. Uh, thanks."

"You're a real speeder these days."

I felt a deep pleasure in my chest. It was like praise from a teacher, someone in charge. We walked out of the building together, the black woman going up across the playground, where the peace marches gathered, maybe toward Geary Boulevard. And I walked down Arguello, out into the avenues. Home.

WARMTH

The water in the pool is warm. In our cold apartment, where my mother screams over the higher and higher utility bills and keeps the heat down, I only have to think about that receiving warmness, touching all my skin, to force myself out into the cold and rain, to walk the long blocks to Rossi Pool, where quickly undressed I will slip down into it.

And swim.

In January, though, the weather got suddenly warmer. The temperature in the pool also seemed to have suddenly changed; it was suddenly cooler. Distrustful, as I guess I tend to be regarding my perceptions, I wondered if the water only seemed cooler. Or, had they turned it down because of the warmer weather, economizing, as my mother does? In any case it was disappointing, and the pool was much less welcoming, no matter how falsely spring-like the outside air had turned.

"Do you think the water's colder?" It was Blond Beard who asked this of me one day; we were standing momentarily in the shallow end. But although I was the person he had chosen to ask, I was still sure that for him I was no one; he remembers nothing of me from one tiny, minor contact to another. I am a large non-person.

I told him, "Yes, it seems a little colder to me" (not wanting to say too much—again).

"They must have turned it down."

SWIMMING

Since the pool is 100 feet long, a half mile is 26 lengths, which is what I try to do every day. "I swim three miles a week," would sound terrific, to anyone, or even, "I swim a little over two miles a week." Anyone would be impressed, except my mother.

On some days, though, I have to trick myself into swimming the whole 26. "I'm tired, didn't sleep too well, 16 lengths is perfectly okay, respectable," I tell myself. And then, having done the 16, I will say (to myself) that I might as well do a couple more, or four more. And if you get to 20 you might as well go on to 26, as I almost always do.

On other, better days I can almost forget what I am doing; that is, I forget to count. I am only aware of a long strong body (mine) pulling through the water, of marvelous muscles, a strong back, and long, long legs.

THE NEIGHBORHOOD

Sometimes, walking around the neighborhood, I see swimmers from the pool—or, people I think I have seen in swimming; in regular clothes it is hard to be sure.

Once, passing a restaurant out on Clement Street I was almost sure that the waitress with her back to the window was the big black woman, formerly cross but now friendly and supportive. Of course I could go in and check it out, even say Hello, but I didn't want to do that, really. But I was pleased with just the idea that she might be there, with a waitress job in such a nice loose-seeming coffee place. I even reasoned that if they hired that woman, big as she is, mightn't someone hire me, about the same size? (I think swimming is making me more optimistic, somehow.)

Maybe I should look harder, not be so shy about applying for waitress jobs?

However, one day in late June, there is no mistaking Blond Beard, who comes up to me on Arguello, near Clement: I am just coming out of the croissant place where I treated myself to a cup of hot chocolate. I am celebrating, in a way: the day before I had pulled all my courage together and went out to a new "rehabilitation place" for old people, out in the Sunset, and they really seemed to like me. I am almost hired, I think. They would give me a place to live—I could leave home!

"Hey! I know you from swimming, don't I? In Rossi?" Blond Beard has come up close to me; he is grinning confidently up into my face. His clothes are very sharp, all clean and new, like from a window at Sears.

"You look so good, all that swimming's really trimmed you down," he tells me. And then, "This is a coincidence, running into you like this when I was needing a cup of coffee. Come on back in and keep me company. My treat."

He is breathing hard up into my face, standing there in the soft new sunlight. I am overwhelmed by the smell of Juicy Fruit—so much, much worse than garlic. I suddenly decide. And I hate sharp clothes.

Stepping back I say, "Thanks, but I have to go home now," and I move as smoothly as though through water.

I leave him standing there.

I swim away.

LEARNING TO SWIM *by* GRAHAM SWIFT

Hailed in his native England as a master of the short story, GRAHAM SWIFT (b. 1949) is also the author of six novels, including Waterland *and the Booker Prize–winner* Last Orders. *The title story from his collection* Learning to Swim *limns the undercurrents of a family holiday at the shore—the kind you wouldn't want to go on. An impromptu swimming lesson turns into a domestic war between narcissistic mother and demanding father, while the young boy struggles to keep his head above water.*

MRS. SINGLETON HAD THREE TIMES thought of leaving her husband. The first time was before they were married, on a charter plane coming back from a holiday in Greece. They were students who had just graduated. They had rucksacks and faded jeans. In Greece they had stayed part of the time by a beach on an island. The island was dry and rocky with great grey and vermilion coloured rocks and when you lay on the beach it seemed that you too became a hot, basking rock. Behind the beach there were eucalyptus trees like dry, leafy bones, old men with mules and gold teeth, a fragrance of thyme, and a café with melon seeds on the floor and a jukebox which played bouzouki music and songs by Cliff Richard. All this Mr. Singleton failed to appreciate. He'd only like the milk-warm, clear blue sea, in which he'd stayed most of the time as if afraid of foreign soil. On the plane she'd thought: He hadn't enjoyed the holiday, hadn't liked Greece at all. All that sunshine. Then she'd thought she ought not to marry him.

Though she had, a year later.

The second time was about a year after Mr. Singleton, who was a civil engineer, had begun his first big job. He became a junior partner in a firm with a growing reputation. She ought to have been pleased by this. It brought money and comfort; it enabled them to move to a house with a large garden, to live well, to think about raising a family. They spent weekends in country hotels. But Mr. Singleton seemed untouched by this. He became withdrawn and incommunicative. He went to his work austere-faced. She thought: He likes his bridges and tunnels better than me.

The third time, which was really a phase, not a single moment, was when she began to calculate how often Mr. Singleton made love to her. When she started this it was about once every fortnight on average. Then it became every three weeks. The interval had been widening for some time. This was not a predicament Mrs. Singleton viewed selfishly. Love-making had been a problem before, in their earliest days together, which, thanks to her patience and initiative, had been overcome. It was Mr. Singleton's unhappiness, not her own, that she saw in their present plight. He was distrustful of happiness as some people fear heights or open spaces. She would reassure him, encourage him again. But the averages seemed to defy her personal effort: once every three weeks, once every month...She thought: Things go back to as they were.

But then, by sheer chance, she became pregnant.

Now she lay on her back, eyes closed, on the coarse sand of the beach in Cornwall. It was hot and, if she opened her eyes, the sky was clear blue. This and the previous summer had been fine enough to make her husband's refusal to go abroad for holidays tolerable. If you kept your eyes closed it could be Greece or Italy or Ibiza. She wore a chocolate-brown bikini, sun-glasses, and her skin, which seldom suffered from sunburn, was already beginning to tan. She let her arms trail idly by her side, scooping up little handfuls of sand. If she turned her head to the right and looked towards the sea she could see Mr. Singleton and their son Paul standing in the shallow water. Mr. Singleton was teaching Paul to swim. "Kick!" he was saying. From here, against the gentle waves, they looked like no more than two rippling silhouettes.

"Kick!" said Mr. Singleton, "Kick!" He was like a punisher, administering lashes.

She turned her head away to face upwards. If you shut your eyes you could imagine you were the only one on the beach; if you held them shut you could be part of the beach. Mrs. Singleton imagined that in order to acquire a tan you had to let the sun make love to you.

She dug her heels in the sand and smiled involuntarily.

When she was a thin, flat-chested, studious girl in a grey school uniform Mrs. Singleton had assuaged her fear and desperation about sex with fantasies which took away from men the brute physicality she expected of them. All her lovers would be artists. Poets would write poems to her, composers would dedicate their works to her. She would even pose, naked and immaculate, for painters, who having committed her true, her eternal form to canvas, would make love to her in an impalpable, ethereal way, under the power of which her bodily and temporal self would melt away, perhaps for ever. These fantasies (for she had never entirely renounced them) had crystallized for her in the image of a sculptor, who from a cold intractable piece of stone would fashion her very essence—which would be vibrant and full of sunlight, like the statues they had seen in Greece.

At university she had worked on the assumption that all men lusted uncontrollably and insatiably after women. She had not yet encountered a man who, whilst prone to the usual instincts, possessing moreover a magnificent body with which to fulfil them, yet had scruples about doing so, seemed ashamed of his own capacities. It did not matter that Mr. Singleton was reading engineering, was scarcely artistic at all, or that his powerful physique was unlike the nebulous creatures of her dreams. She found she loved this solid man-flesh. Mrs. Singleton had thought she was the shy, inexperienced, timid girl. Overnight she discovered that she wasn't this at all. He wore tough denim shirts, spoke and smiled very little and had a way of standing very straight and upright as if he didn't need any help from anyone. She had to educate him into moments of passion, of self-forgetfulness which made her glow with her own achievement. She was happy because she had not thought she was happy and she believed she could make someone else happy. At the university girls were starting to wear jeans, record-players played the Rolling Stones and in the hush of the Modern Languages Library she read Leopardi and Verlaine. She seemed to float with confidence in a swirling, buoyant element she had never suspected would be her own.

"Kick!" she heard again from the water.

Mr. Singleton had twice thought of leaving his wife. Once was after a symphony concert they had gone to in London when they had not known each other very long and she still tried to get him to read books, to listen to music, to take an interest in art. She would buy concert or theatre tickets, and he had to seem pleased. At this concert a visiting orchestra was playing some titanic, large-scale work by a late nineteenth-century composer. A note in the programme said it represented the triumph of life over death. He had sat on his plush seat amidst the swirling barrage of sound. He had no idea what he had to do with it or the triumph of life over death. He had thought the same thought about the rapt girl on his left, the future Mrs. Singleton, who now and then bobbed, swayed or rose in her seat as if the music physically lifted her. There were at least seventy musicians on the platform. As the piece worked to its final crescendo the conductor, whose arms were flailing frantically so that his white shirt back appeared under his flying tails, looked so absurd Mr. Singleton thought he would laugh. When the music stopped and was immediately supplanted by wild cheering and clapping he thought the world had gone mad. He had struck his own hands together so as to appear to be sharing the ecstasy. Then, as they filed out, he had almost wept because he felt like an insect. He even thought she had arranged the whole business so as to humiliate him.

He thought he would not marry her.

The second time was after they had been married some years. He was one of a team of engineers working on a suspension bridge over an estuary in Ireland. They took it in turns to stay on the site and to inspect the construction work personally. Once he had to go to the very top of one of the two piers of the bridge to examine work on the bearings and housing for the main overhead cables. A lift ran up between the twin towers of the pier amidst a network of scaffolding and power cables to where a working platform was positioned. The engineer, with the supervisor and the foreman, had only to stay on the platform from where all the main features of construction were visible. The men at work on the upper sections of the towers, specialists in their trade, earning up to two hundred pounds a week—who balanced on precarious cat-walks and walked along exposed reinforcing girders—often jibed at the engineers who never left the platform. He thought he would show them. He walked out on to one of the cat-walks on the outer face of the pier where they were fitting huge grip-bolts. This was quite safe if you held on to the rails but still took some nerve. He wore a check cheesecloth shirt and his white safety helmet. It was a grey, humid August day. The cat-walk hung over greyness. The water of the estuary was the colour of dead fish. A dredger was chugging near the base of the pier. He thought, I could swim the estuary; but there is a bridge. Below him the yellow helmets of workers moved over the girders for the roadway like beetles. He took his hands from the rail. He wasn't at all afraid. He had been away from his wife all week. He thought: She knows nothing of this. If he were to step out now into the grey air he would be quite by himself, no harm would come to him...

Now Mr. Singleton stood in the water, teaching his son to swim. They were doing the water-wings exercise. The boy wore a pair of water-wings, red underneath, yellow on top, which ballooned up under his arms and chin. With this to support him, he would splutter and splash towards his father who stood facing him some feet away. After a while at this they would try the same procedure, his father moving a little nearer, but without the water-wings, and this the boy dreaded. "Kick!" said Mr. Singleton. "Use your legs!" He watched his son draw painfully towards him. The boy had not yet grasped that the body naturally floated and that if you added to this certain mechanical effects, you swam.

He thought that in order to swim you had to make as much frantic movement as possible. As he struggled towards Mr. Singleton his head, which was too high out of the water, jerked messily from side to side, and his eyes which were half closed swivelled in every direction but straight ahead. "Towards me!" shouted Mr. Singleton. He held out his arms in front of him for Paul to grasp. As his son was on the point of clutching them he would step back a little, pulling his hands away, in the hope that the last desperate lunge to reach his father might really teach the boy the art of propelling himself in water. But he sometimes wondered if this were his only motive.

"Good boy. Now again."

At school Mr. Singleton had been an excellent swimmer. He had won various school titles, broken numerous records and competed successfully in ASA championships. There was a period between the ages of about thirteen and seventeen which he remembered as the happiest in his life. It wasn't the medals and trophies that made him glad, but the knowledge that he didn't have to bother about anything else. Swimming vindicated him. He would get up every morning at six and train for two hours in the baths, and again before lunch; and when he fell asleep, exhausted, in French and English periods in the afternoon, he didn't have to bother about the indignation of the masters—lank, ill-conditioned creatures—for he had his excuse. He didn't have to bother about the physics teacher who complained to the headmaster that he would never get the exam results he needed if he didn't cut down his swimming, for the headmaster (who was an advocate of sport) came to his aid and told the physics teacher not to interfere with a boy who was a credit to the school. Nor did he have to bother about a host of other things which were supposed to be going on inside him, which made the question of what to do in the evening, at week-ends, fraught and tantalizing, which drove other boys to moodiness and recklessness. For once in the cool water of the baths, his arms reaching, his eyes fixed on the blue marker line on the bottom, his ears full so that he could hear nothing around him, he would feel quite by himself, quite sufficient. At the end of races, when for one brief instant he clung panting alone like a survivor to the finishing rail which his rivals had yet to touch, he felt an infinite peace. He went to bed early, slept soundly, kept to his training regimen; and he enjoyed this Spartan purity which disdained pleasure and disorder. Some of his school mates mocked him—for not going to dances on Saturdays or to pubs, under age, or the Expresso after school. But he did not mind. He didn't need them. He knew they were weak. None of them could hold out, depend upon themselves, spurn comfort if they had to. Some of them would go under in life. And none of them could cleave the water as he did or possessed a hard, stream-lined, perfectly tuned body as he did.

Then, when he was nearly seventeen all this changed.

His father, who was an engineer, though proud of his son's trophies, suddenly pressed him to different forms of success. The headmaster no longer shielded him from the physics master. He said: "You can't swim into your future." Out of spite perhaps or an odd consistency of self-denial, he dropped swimming altogether rather than cut it down. For a year and a half he worked at his maths and physics with the same single-mindedness with which he had perfected his sport. He knew about mechanics and engineering because he knew how to make his body move through water. His work was not merely competent but good. He got to university where he might have had the leisure, if he wished, to resume his swimming. But he did not. Two years are a long gap in a swimmer's training; two years when you are near your peak can mean you will never get back to your true form. Sometimes he went for a dip in the university pool and swam slowly up and down amongst practising members of the university team, whom perhaps he could still have beaten, as a kind of relief.

Often, Mr. Singleton dreamt about swimming. He would be moving through vast expanses of water, an ocean. As he moved it did not require any effort at all. Sometimes he would go for long distances under water, but he did not have to bother about breathing. The water would be silvery-grey. And as always it seemed that as he swam he was really trying to get beyond the water, to put it behind him, as if it were a veil he were parting and he would emerge on the other side of it at last, on to some pristine shore, where he would step where no one else had stepped before.

When he made love to his wife her body got in the way; he wanted to swim through her.

Mrs. Singleton raised herself, pushed her sun-glasses up over her dark hair and sat with her arms stretched straight behind her back. A trickle of sweat ran between her breasts. They had developed to a good size since her schoolgirl days. Her skinniness in youth had stood her in good stead against the filling out of middle age, and her body was probably more mellow, more lithe and better proportioned now than it had ever been. She looked at Paul and Mr. Singleton half immersed in the shallows. It seemed to her that her husband was the real boy, standing stubbornly upright with his hands before him, and that Paul was some toy being pulled and swung relentlessly around him and towards him as though on some string. They had seen her sit up. Her husband waved, holding the boy's hand, as though for the two of them. Paul did not wave; he seemed more concerned with the water in his eyes. Mrs. Singleton did not wave back. She would have done if her son had waved. When they had left for their holiday Mr. Singleton had said to Paul, "You'll learn to swim this time. In salt water, you know, it's easier." Mrs. Singleton hoped her son wouldn't swim; so that she could wrap him, still, in the big yellow towel when he came out, rub him dry and warm, and watch her husband stand apart, his hands empty.

She watched Mr. Singleton drop his arm back to his side. "If you wouldn't splash it wouldn't go in your eyes," she just caught him say.

The night before, in their hotel room, they had argued. They always argued about half way through their holidays. It was symbolic, perhaps, of that first trip to Greece, when he had somehow refused to enjoy himself. They had to incur injuries so that they could then appreciate their leisure, like convalescents. For the first four days or so of their holiday Mr. Singleton would tend to be moody, on edge. He would excuse this as "winding down," the not-to-be-hurried process of dispelling the pressures of work. Mrs. Singleton would be patient. On about the fifth day Mrs. Singleton would begin to suspect that the winding down would never end and indeed (which she had known all along) that it was not winding down at all—he was clinging, as to a defence, to his bridges and tunnels; and she would show her resentment. At this point Mr. Singleton would retaliate by an attack upon her indolence.

Last night he had called her "flabby." He could not mean, of course, "flabby-bodied" (she could glance down, now, at her still flat belly), though such a sensual attack, would have been simpler, almost heartening, from him. He meant "flabby of attitude." And what he meant by this, or what he wanted to mean, was that *he* was not flabby;

that he worked, facing the real world, erecting great solid things on the face of the land, and that, whilst he worked, he disdained work's rewards—money, pleasure, rich food, holidays abroad—that he hadn't "gone soft," as she had done since they graduated eleven years ago, with their credentials for the future and their plane tickets to Greece. She knew this toughness of her husband was only a cover for his own failure to relax and his need to keep his distance. She knew that he found no particular virtue in his bridges and tunnels (it was the last thing he wanted to do really—build); it didn't matter if they were right or wrong, they were there, he could point to them as if it vindicated him—just as when he made his infrequent, if seismic, love to her it was not a case of enjoyment or satisfaction; he just did it.

It was hot in their hotel room. Mr. Singleton stood in his blue pyjama bottoms, feet apart, like a PT instructor.

"Flabby? What do you mean—'flabby'!?" she had said, looking daunted.

But Mrs. Singleton had the advantage whenever Mr. Singleton accused her in this way of complacency, of weakness. She knew he only did it to hurt her, and so to feel guilty, and so to feel the remorse which would release his own affection for her, his vulnerability, his own need to be loved. Mrs. Singleton was used to this process, to the tenderness that was the tenderness of successively opened and reopened wounds. And she was used to being the nurse who took care of the healing scars. For though Mr. Singleton inflicted the first blow he would always make himself more guilty than he made her suffer, and Mrs. Singleton, though in pain herself, could not resist wanting to clasp and cherish her husband, wanting to wrap him up safe when his own weakness and submissiveness showed and his body became liquid and soft against her; could not resist the old spur that her husband was unhappy and it was for her to make him happy. Mr. Singleton was extraordinarily lovable when he was guilty. She would even have yielded indefinitely, foregoing her own grievance, to this extreme of comforting him for the pain he caused her, had she not discovered, in time, that this only pushed the process a stage further. Her forgiveness of him became only another level of comfort, of softness he must reject. His flesh shrank from her restoring touch.

She thought: Men go round in circles, women don't move.

She kept to her side of the hotel bed, he, with his face turned, to his. He lay like a person washed up on a beach. She reached out her hand and stroked the nape of his neck. She felt him tense. All this was a pattern.

"I'm sorry," he said, "I didn't mean—"

"It's all right, it doesn't matter."

"Doesn't it matter?" he said.

When they reached this point they were like miners racing each other for deeper and deeper seams of guilt and recrimination.

But Mrs. Singleton had given up delving to rock bottom. Perhaps it was five years ago when she had thought for the third time of leaving her husband, perhaps long before that. When they were students she'd made allowances for his constraints, his reluctances. An unhappy childhood perhaps, a strict upbringing. She thought his inhibition might be lifted by the sanction of marriage. She'd thought, after all, it would be a good thing if he married her. She had not thought what would be good for her. They stood outside Gatwick Airport, back from Greece, in the grey, wet August light. Their tanned skin had seemed to glow. Yet she'd known this mood of promise would pass. She watched him kick against contentment, against ease, against the long, glittering life-line she threw to him; and, after a while, she ceased to try to haul him in. She began to imagine her phantom artists. She thought: People slip off the shores of the real world, back into dreams. She hadn't "gone soft," only gone back to herself. Hidden inside her like treasure there were lines of Leopardi, of Verlaine her husband would never appreciate. She thought, he doesn't need me, things run off him, like water. She even thought that her husband's neglect in making love to her was not a problem he had but a deliberate scheme to deny her. When Mrs. Singleton desired her husband she could not help herself. She would stretch back on the bed with the sheets pulled off like a blissful nude in a Modigliani. She thought this ought to gladden a man. Mr. Singleton would stand at the foot of the bed and gaze down at her. He looked like some strong, chaste knight in the legend of the Grail. He would respond to her invitation, but before he did so there would be this expression, half stern, half innocent, in his eyes. It was the sort of expression that good men in books and films are supposed to make to prostitutes. It would ensure that their love-making was marred and that afterward it would seem as if he had performed something out of duty that only she wanted. Her body would feel like stone. It was at such times, when she felt the cold, dead-weight feel of abused happiness, that Mrs. Singleton most thought she was through with Mr. Singleton. She would watch his strong, compact torso already lifting itself off the bed. She would think: He thinks he is tough, contained in himself, but he won't see what I offer him, he doesn't see how it is I who can help him.

Mrs. Singleton lay back on her striped towel on the sand. Once again she became part of the beach. The careless sounds of the seaside, of excited children's voices, of languid grownups', of wooden bats on balls, fluttered over her as she shut her eyes. She thought: It is the sort of day on which someone suddenly shouts, "Someone is drowning."

When Mrs. Singleton became pregnant she felt she had outmanoeuvred her husband. He did not really want a child (it was the last thing he wanted, Mrs. Singleton thought, a child), but he was jealous of her condition, as of some achievement he himself could attain. He was excluded from the little circle of herself and her womb, and, as though to puncture it, he began for the first time to make love to her of a kind where he took the insistent initiative. Mrs. Singleton was not greatly pleased. She seemed buoyed up by her own bigness. She noticed that her husband began to do exercises in the morning, in his underpants, press-ups, squat-jumps, as if he were getting in training for something. He was like a boy. He even became, as the term of her pregnancy drew near its end, resilient and detached again, the virile father waiting to receive the son (Mr. Singleton knew it would be a son, so did Mrs. Singleton) that she, at the appointed time, would deliver him. When the moment arrived he insisted on being present so as to prove he wasn't squeamish and to make sure he wouldn't be tricked in the transaction. Mrs. Singleton was not daunted. When the pains became frequent she wasn't at all afraid. There were big, watery lights clawing down from the ceiling of the delivery room like the lights in dentists' surgeries. She could just see her husband looking down at her. His face was white and clammy. It was his fault for wanting to be there. She had to push, as though away from him. Then she knew it was happening. She stretched back. She was a great surface of warm, splitting rock and Paul was struggling bravely up into the sunlight. She had to coax him with her cries. She felt him emerge like a trapped survivor. The doctor groped with rubber gloves. "There we are," he said. She managed to look at Mr. Singleton. She wanted suddenly to put him back inside for good where Paul had come from. With a fleeting pity she saw that this was what Mr. Singleton wanted too. His eyes were half closed. She kept hers on him. He seemed to wilt under her gaze. All his toughness and control were draining from him and she was glad. She lay back triumphant and glad. The doctor was holding Paul; but she looked, beyond, at Mr. Singleton. He was far away like an insect. She knew he couldn't hold out. He was going to faint. He was looking where her legs were spread. His eyes went out of focus. He was going to faint, keel over, right there on the spot.

Mrs. Singleton grew restless, though she lay unmoving on the beach. Wasps were buzzing close to her head, round their picnic bag. She thought that Mr. Singleton and Paul had been too long at their swimming lesson. They should come out. It never struck her, hot as she was, to get up and join her husband and son in the sea. Whenever Mrs. Singleton wanted a swim she would wait until there was an opportunity to go in by herself; then she would wade out, dip her shoulders under suddenly and paddle about contentedly, keeping her hair dry, as though she were soaking herself in a large bath. They did not bathe as a family; nor did Mrs. Singleton swim with Mr. Singleton—who now and then, too, would get up by himself and enter the sea, swim at once about fifty yards out, then cruise for long stretches, with a powerful crawl or butterfly, back and forth across the bay. When this happened Mrs. Singleton would engage her son in talk so he would not watch his father. Mrs. Singleton did not swim with Paul either. He was too old now to cradle between her knees in the very shallow water, and she was somehow afraid that while Paul splashed and kicked around her he would suddenly learn how to swim. She had this feeling that Paul would only swim while she was in the sea, too. She did not want this to happen, but it reassured her and gave her sufficient confidence to let Mr. Singleton continue his swimming lessons with Paul. These lessons were obsessive, indefatigable. Every Sunday morning at seven, when they were at home, Mr. Singleton would take Paul to the baths for yet another attempt. Part of this, of course, was that Mr. Singleton was determined that his son should swim; but it enabled him also to avoid the Sunday morning languor; extra hours in bed, leisurely love-making.

Once, in a room at college, Mr. Singleton had told Mrs. Singleton about his swimming, about his training sessions, races, about what it felt like when you could swim really well. She had run her fingers over his long, naked back.

Mrs. Singleton sat up and rubbed sun-tan lotion on to her thighs. Down near the water's edge, Mr. Singleton was standing about waist deep, supporting Paul who, gripped by his father's hands, water wings still on, was flailing, face down, at the surface. Mr. Singleton kept saying, "No, keep still." He was trying to get Paul to hold his body straight and relaxed so he would float. But each time as Paul nearly succeeded he would panic, fearing his father would let go, and thrash wildly. When he calmed down and Mr. Singleton held him, Mrs. Singleton could see the water running off his face like tears.

Mrs. Singleton did not alarm herself at this distress of her son. It was a guarantee against Mr. Singleton's influence, an assurance that Paul was not going to swim; nor was he to be imbued with any of his father's sullen hardiness. When Mrs. Singleton saw her son suffer, it pleased her and she felt loving towards him. She felt that an invisible thread ran between her and the boy which commanded him not to swim, and she felt that Mr. Singleton knew that it was because of her that his efforts with Paul were in vain. Even now, as Mr. Singleton prepared for another attempt, the boy was looking at her smoothing the sun-tan oil on to her legs.

"Come on, Paul," said Mr. Singleton. His wet shoulders shone like metal.

When Paul was born it seemed to Mrs. Singleton that her life with her husband was dissolved, as a mirage dissolves, and that she could return again to what she was before she knew him. She let her staved-off hunger for happiness and her old suppressed dreams revive. But then they were not dreams, because they had a physical object and she knew she needed them in order to live. She did not disguise from herself what she needed. She knew that she wanted the kind of close, even erotic relationship with her son that women who have rejected their husbands have been known to have. The kind of relationship in which the son must hurt the mother, the mother the son. But she willed it, as if there would be no pain. Mrs. Singleton waited for her son to grow. She trembled when she thought of him at eighteen or twenty. When he was grown he would be slim and light and slender, like a boy even though he was a man. He would not need a strong body because all his power would be inside. He would be all fire and life in essence. He would become an artist, a sculptor. She would pose for him naked (she would keep her body trim for this), and he would sculpt her. He would hold the chisel. His hands would guide the cold metal over the stone and its blows would strike sunlight.

Mrs. Singleton thought: All the best statues they had seen in Greece seemed to have been dredged up from the sea.

She finished rubbing the lotion on to her insteps and put the cap back on the tube. As she did so she heard something that made her truly alarmed. It was Mr. Singleton saying, "That's it, that's the way! At last! Now keep it going!" She looked up. Paul was in the same position as before but he had learnt to make slower, regular motions with his limbs and his body no longer sagged in the middle. Though he still wore the water-wings he was moving, somewhat laboriously, forward so that Mr. Singleton had to walk along with him; and at one point Mr. Singleton removed one of his hands from under the boy's ribs and simultaneously looked at his wife and smiled. His shoulders flashed. It was not a smile meant for her. She could see that. And it was not one of her husband's usual, infrequent, rather mechanical smiles. It was the smile a person makes about some joy inside, hidden and incommunicable.

"That's enough," thought Mrs. Singleton, getting to her feet, pretending not to have noticed, behind her sun-glasses, what had happened in the water. It *was* enough: They had been in the water for what seemed like an hour. He was only doing it because of their row last night, to make her feel he was not outmatched by using the reserve weapon of Paul. And, she added with relief to herself, Paul still had the water-wings and one hand to support him.

"That's enough now!" she shouted aloud, as if she were slightly, but not ill-humouredly, peeved at being neglected. "Come on in now!" She had picked up her purse as a quickly conceived ruse as she got up, and as she walked towards the water's edge she waved it above her head. "Who wants an ice-cream?"

Mr. Singleton ignored his wife. "Well done, Paul," he said. "Let's try that again."

Mrs. Singleton knew he would do this. She stood on the little ridge of sand just above where the beach, becoming fine shingle, shelved into the sea. She replaced a loose strap of her bikini over her shoulder and with a finger of each hand pulled the bottom half down over her buttocks. She stood feet apart, slightly on her toes, like a gymnast. She knew other eyes on the beach would be on her. It flattered her that she—and her husband, too—received admiring glances from those around. She thought, with relish for the irony: Perhaps they think we are happy, beautiful people. For all her girlhood diffidence, Mrs. Singleton enjoyed displaying her attractions and she liked to see other people's pleasure. When she lay sunbathing she imagined making love to all the moody, pubescent boys on holiday with their parents, with their slim waists and their quick heels.

"See if you can do it without me holding you," said Mr. Singleton. "I'll help you at first." He stooped over Paul. He looked like a mechanic making final adjustments to some prototype machine.

"Don't you want an ice-cream then, Paul?" said Mrs. Singleton. "They've got those chocolate ones."

Paul looked up. His short wet hair stood up in spikes. He looked like a prisoner offered a chance of escape, but the plastic water-wings, like some absurd pillory, kept him fixed.

Mrs. Singleton thought: He crawled out of me, now I have to lure him back with ice-cream.

"Can't you see he was getting the hang of it?" Mr. Singleton said. "If he comes out now he'll—"

"Hang of it! It was you. You were holding him all the time."

She thought: Perhaps I am hurting my son.

Mr. Singleton glared at Mrs. Singleton. He gripped Paul's shoulders. "You don't want to get out now, do you Paul?" He looked suddenly as if he really might drown Paul rather than let him come out.

Mrs. Singleton's heart raced. She wasn't good at rescues, at resuscitations. She knew this because of her life with her husband.

"Come on, you can go back in later," she said.

Paul was a hostage. She was playing for time, not wanting to harm the innocent.

She stood on the sand like a marooned woman watching for ships. The sea, in the sheltered bay, was almost flat calm. A few, glassy waves idled in but were smoothed out before they could break. On the headlands there were outcrops of scaly rocks like basking lizards. The island in Greece had been where Theseus left Ariadne. Out over the blue water, beyond the heads of bobbing swimmers, seagulls flapped like scraps of paper.

Mr. Singleton looked at Mrs. Singleton. She was a fussy mother daubed with Ambre Solaire, trying to bribe her son with silly ice-creams; though if you forgot this she was a beautiful, tanned girl, like the girls men imagine on desert islands. But then, in Mr. Singleton's dreams, there was no one else on the untouched shore he ceaselessly swam to.

He thought, If Paul could swim, then I could leave her.

Mrs. Singleton looked at her husband. She felt afraid. The water's edge was like a dividing line between them which marked off the territory in which each existed. Perhaps they could never cross over.

"Well, I'm getting the ice-creams: you'd better get out."

She turned and paced up the sand. Behind the beach was an ice-cream van painted like a fairground.

Paul Singleton looked at his mother. He thought: She is

deserting me—or I am deserting her. He wanted to get out to follow her. Her feet made puffs of sand which stuck to her ankles, and you could see all her body as she strode up the beach. But he was afraid of his father and his gripping hands. And he was afraid of his mother, too. How she would wrap him, if he came out, in the big yellow towel like egg yolk, how she would want him to get close to her smooth, sticky body, like a mouth that would swallow him. He thought: The yellow towel humiliated him, his father's hands humiliated him. The water-wings humiliated him: You put them on and became a puppet. So much of life is humiliation. It was how you won love. His father was taking off the water-wings like a man unlocking a chastity belt. He said: "Now try the same, coming towards me." His father stood some feet away from him. He was a huge, straight man, like the pier of a bridge. "Try." Paul Singleton was six. He was terrified of water. Every time he entered it he had to fight down fear. His father never realized this. He thought it was simple; you said: "Only water, no need to be afraid." His father did not know what fear was; the same as he did not know what fun was. Paul Singleton hated water. He hated it in his mouth and in his eyes. He hated the chlorine smell of the swimming baths, the wet, slippery tiles, the echoing whoops and screams. He hated it when his father read to him from *The Water Babies*. It was the only story his father read, because, since he didn't know fear or fun, he was really sentimental. His mother read lots of stories. "Come on then. I'll catch you." Paul Singleton held out his arms and raised one leg. This was the worst moment. Perhaps having no help was most humiliating. If you did not swim you sank like a statue. They would drag him out, his skin streaming. His father would say: "I didn't mean..." But if he swam his mother would be forsaken. She would stand on the beach with chocolate ice-cream running down her arm. There was no way out; there were all these things to be afraid of and no weapons. But then, perhaps he was not afraid of his mother nor his father, nor of water, but of something else. He had felt it just now—when he'd struck out with rhythmic, reaching strokes and his feet had come off the bottom and his father's hand had slipped from under his chest: as if he had mistaken what his fear was; as if he had been unconsciously pretending, even to himself, so as to execute some plan. He lowered his chin into the water. "Come on!" said Mr. Singleton. He launched himself forward and felt the sand leave his feet and his legs wriggle like cut ropes. "There," said his father as he realized. "There!" His father stood like a man waiting to clasp a lover; there was a gleam on his face. "Towards me! Towards me!" said his father suddenly. But he kicked and struck, half in panic, half in pride, away from his father, away from the shore, away, in this strange new element that seemed all his own.

LEDA AND THE SWAN *by* FAY WELDON

British novelist, playwright, and short story writer FAY WELDON (b. 1931) has made a career of slyly mining the war between the sexes. In "Leda and the Swan," a domineering husband attempts to shame his wife into abandoning the sport she loves: swimming.

WHEN GOSLING WAS TWO, his body was smooth, plump and bronzed. He ran in and out of the waves at the water's edge and was happy. "He's a real water baby," his mother would say fondly. But she carried his little brother in her arms, and her eyes were even softer and kinder for the baby than they were for the little boy, and Gosling noticed.

She called the older one Gosling in pure affection, and the younger one Duckling, which was even more affectionate. Gosling once pushed Duckling under the bath water, but fortunately help came in time: for Duckling, that is, not Gosling.

"Did your mother hope you'd grow up to be a swan?" asked Gosling's wife, interested.

"I don't know what she thought," was all he said. He would volunteer information about his past, but did not like his wife to be too inquisitive. His past was a private planet, full of unscalable heights and hopeless depths where he alone was brave enough to wander. "Anyway," Gosling added, "it's ugly ducklings, not goslings, who grow up to be swans. My little brother was the one she had hopes for."

"Well, I think you grew up to be a swan," she said. They had been married for a year when she said that. She was proud of him: his fine dark eyes, his smooth skin, his sexual confidence; the gregarious fits which interrupted his more sombre moods. She felt she was very ordinary, compared to him. Her name was Eileen, but he called her Leda, and this gratified her very much.

Eileen met Gosling in a London park at the edge of a swimming pool. He was a Sunday father; he took his little daughter Nadine swimming while, he complained, his ex-wife entertained her lover. Nadine did not share her father's enthusiasm for the water; no, but she endured it with patience and polite smiles. She was a good girl. Eileen, that Sunday afternoon, splashed about in the water happily enough, though she did complain of its coldness. But then her parents kept a hotel in Bermuda: Eileen had spent her youth in warm water, chasing sailboats. English water was hard and bitter with chlorine: why did so many people want to go in it? The pool was crowded.

Gosling and Eileen collided underwater: he had to help her to the surface. His hand, firm upon her arm, seemed to transmit some kind of magnetic current: at any rate his touch acted like an electric shock. She squealed aloud and snatched her arm away in alarm; nearly sank. They touched again, tentatively. Again she let out a little yelp. That made him laugh. "We are seriously attracted to each other," he said as they surfaced, and she had to agree. She was eighteen: he was thirty.

When she pulled herself out of the pool, she felt awkward and unattractive; she regretted her freckled, friendly face, her strong, muscular body: men liked her, but that was all. She worried at once about her epileptic brother: she would have to confess to it. Then who would want her? Her brother's existence spoiled everything. Her eyes were pink and smarting. She wished she were not a swimmer: she would like to be Diana the Huntress, chaste and fair, icy and cool like the moon, not goose-pimpled.

"I like swimming," Gosling said.

"I love it," she said, and forgot about Diana and thought his brown eyes grew troubled for a minute, and then he dived back into the water and swam lazily and confidently up and down the pool, knowing quite well she was waiting for him.

"You could be a champion if you tried," said Eileen, as they drank hot chocolate from the drink-dispenser. Her mother had told her the way to win a man was to flatter him, and Eileen wanted to win Gosling as never before had she wanted to win a man.

"I don't want to be a champion," he said. "I just enjoy the water."

"Oh, so do I!" And so she did: she loved the buoyancy of her body in this murderous liquid, which healed and soothed when it didn't kill. Water was both adversary and friend: it parted in front of her, closed behind her. How powerful she was when she cleaved the water. Eileen cleaved unto Gosling the day they met, and after that they never wanted to part. Not really. She didn't tell him all the things that swimming meant to her, partly because she didn't know she was unusual and thought most people felt the same, and partly because she did not want to love what he only liked. While

Eileen had an intense relationship with water, Gosling just swam. He'd swum, he said, in the Atlantic, the Pacific, the Mediterranean, the Black Sea, the North Sea, the English Channel; even in the Dead Sea.

"But the Dead Sea isn't really water," Gosling said. "It's just a chemical soup." The Dead Sea had brought tears to his eyes. He hadn't liked that. He was an engineer and travelled the world, bringing back to Eileen, who became Leda on their wedding day, all kinds of strange presents.

Leda stayed home and looked after her stepdaughter Nadine, and presently her own baby Europa, and joined swimming club and won a race or two.

Leda told Gosling about her victories when he returned from abroad and he raised an eyebrow. "Swimming is something to enjoy," he said, "it shouldn't be something competitive," and she was obliged to agree. He told her about the ocean rollers of Florida and the surfing there, so they thought about these natural wonders instead of victories at the local swimming club.

The family went for an excursion to the seaside: Gosling and Leda and Nadine and Europa; they pottered about rock-pools and avoided the patches of oil on the sand, and Leda tried not to wonder how far was the coast of France and just how fast she could swim there.

Gosling swam and dived and ducked and lashed about. He was, oh yes he was, the real water baby his mother had defined; he was the gosling who was never quite the duckling who never quite became a swan. He was passed over for promotion. Perhaps he had spent too much time on foreign beaches, and not enough in foreign offices. But he was the man who liked swimming: he thought the world well lost for that. His mother had died of cancer, painfully, when he was a young man, at the time when it seemed important for him to renounce and defy her: at the wrong time.

He felt his mother had given him contrary instructions. She had named him Gosling, in the hope of his becoming a swan: she had called him water baby, and water babies surely did not grow up.

When he was on foreign trips he was unfaithful to Leda. He stayed in hotels where there were swimming pools, and always some girl, who did not swim but splashed about, who would admire Gosling's prowess, his lazy confidence in the water, his wet, rippling muscles which gave promise of excitement to come.

"It doesn't mean anything," Gosling would say to Leda. "I like them, I don't love them." Gosling did not believe in lying. "We must be honest with each other," he'd say.

Leda started training in earnest. Her times startled the trainer at the local swimming club.

"You're four seconds off the Olympic crawl record," he said.

"Four seconds is a long time," said Leda.

But she talked about it to Gosling when he returned from New Zealand, where the beaches are long, white and clean, and the girls likewise.

"Crawl is not a swimmer's stroke," he said. "It's the competitor's stroke. An antagonistic, angry sort of swimming. Nothing to do with water, just with doing down your fellow human beings. At best see crawl as the getting-somewhere stroke, not the being-someone stroke."

Leda thereafter swam breast-stroke instead of crawl, to her trainer's annoyance, but soon excelled in that as well. She swam for the County team and won a cup or two. And then rather a lot of cups. They began to line the walls.

"Of course back-stroke is the one that requires real swimming talent," said Gosling. It was his own best stroke, and Leda's weakest. They swam a jokey sort of race, one day, back-stroke, and he won, and after that they were happy for a time. But she knew she had not really tried to win, just been polite: won time and his favour, just for a little.

Gosling was good company, liked good food, good drink and bad women; he could tell a good story. For some reason, friends who liked sport faded away, or perhaps they were gently mocked out of the house. Presently there was no one to ask exactly what the silver cups on the sideboard were, or to care, or admire. The task of polishing them became oppressive; there was so much else to do. Gosling referred to them in any case as "Leda's ego-trip" and she began to be embarrassed for them, and of them. The cups went into the spare room cupboard in the end; the surfboard came out of it, and they went on family weekends to Cornwall, where they all surfed.

Surfing made Leda impatient: she did not like waiting about for the waves, or the messy rough and tumble of the water in their wake. She wanted to conquer the water, cleave it, and enlist its help to do so: as a man about to be shot might be induced to dig his own grave. It was a horrible simile, but one which came to mind, and made her ashamed.

Gosling loved the surf and the thrashing water. "You have to abandon yourself to the sea," he said. "And then you reap its benefits. How anyone can waste their time in swimming pools, I can't imagine. You know why your eyes hurt when you've been in them? It's other people's piss does the damage—not chlorine, as is commonly supposed."

When Leda came home from the swimming pool her eyes would be pink and swollen. When Gosling admired other women—not unkindly or over-frequently—he would always refer to their bright, wide, young eyes.

Sometimes Leda's heart ached so much she thought she was having some kind of seizure. She could not distinguish physical from mental pain. Still she swam.

One evening, when Leda was eight years married, and within a year or two of being past her swimming prime—which Gosling would mention in passing from time to time—and actually in the running for the English Olympic team—a fact which Leda did not mention to Gosling at all—Leda made her usual excuses and left for the pool. This was the evening when the final Olympic selection was to be made. Evenings were family time and it was Leda's practice to stay home if she possibly could, but tonight she had to go.

As Leda walked out of the house, a young woman walked up to it. "Someone called Gosling live round here?" asked the bright, clear-eyed young girl. "He wrote the number on a cigarette paper, but I lost it. You know what parties are."

"Not really," said Leda. "I'm usually looking after the children."

"God save me from children," observed the girl, "and, after children, from husbands. This one's mother should have called him

Jack Rabbit."

And the girl walked one way and Leda walked the other, and that night Leda knocked two seconds off her best and was selected for the England team. Pain in the muscles alleviated pain in the heart: concentration on the matter in hand lessened the bite of jealousy. There was no pleasure in the victory, the record, the selection, the smiles of those who'd trained her, believed in her, and now saw their faith justified. All Leda felt after the race, as she smiled and chatted, and accepted adulation modestly and graciously, was the return of pain.

When Leda got home that night, the bedroom smelt of someone else's scent, but Gosling made love to her sweetly and powerfully, and the electricity glanced from them and round them and seemed to embrace the universe and she knew he loved her, in spite of everything; in spite of her annoying habit of winning, coming first, competing. "She was only here," he said when Leda commented on the smell of scent, "because you weren't. You were swimming."

The word had become bad, somewhere between sinning and shamming. Gosling hardly ever swam himself, these days. It was as if she had stolen his birthright. He, who should have been a water baby, should have gambolled for ever on the water's edge, was now forced by Leda onto dry, arid land. She was his mother's enemy.

Photographers took pictures of Leda. Her body, once so unluminous, prosaic, now seemed something remarkable and beautiful. With it went the nation's hopes.

"I can't have Europa exposed to this kind of thing," said Gosling. "It's one step up from skin-flicks. Surely the least you could do is allow them to photograph you *clothed*."

"But I'm a swimmer," said Leda. "They have to take me in a swimsuit."

"You hardly have the figure for it," he said.

He looked at her body without affection, without admiration, and raised his eyebrows at the folly of the nation.

But always, when the time came and the flag dropped and the water embraced her in its deathly, lovely clasp, Leda would fight it back with its own weapons; she would make it her servant. She would say, vaguely, when people asked her if she was tired or cold or nervous, that she was used to hardship. No one quite understood what she meant by this, for a friendly engineer husband and a little daughter significantly named Europa could hardly count as hardship.

Oh faster, faster: concentrate the will. In the last resort it is not the muscles, not the training, that counts; not up there at the extremity of physical achievement: no, it is the will; it is the pulling down from the sky of a strength that belongs to someone else, in some other world where fish fly and birds swim and human beings are happy.

Swimming, sinning, shamming. Water blinding eyes, deafening ears, to sights that should not be seen and sounds that should not be heard.

On the night of the European Championships, Leda's mother rang from Bermuda: her brother was dying.

"You must fly out at once," said Gosling. "Not even you, surely, can put a competition above life itself."

But Leda did. At seven forty-five she was not on a Boeing 747 on her way to Bermuda, but at the pool's edge at Wembley. She took half a second off her best time, came in first, and only then did she fly out, and her brother was dead when she arrived.

"Bet you're glad he's dead," observed Gosling when she cried.

"Don't be so hypocritical," and he was right, she was, because the epileptic fits had frightened her when she was a child. The writhing, the jerking, the foaming; somewhere in her mind between sex and swimming; something to be ashamed of: something to be admitted to boyfriends, and be ashamed of being ashamed.

Swimming, sinning, shamming. Something held between the teeth to stop the tongue being bitten off. Or was that boxing?

Leda had loved her brother, all the same, as she loved Gosling. Part of her, part of life.

"And you thought winning a race more important than seeing him alive for the last time!" he marvelled.

"I don't want to win," she said. "I can't help winning. You make me win."

He didn't understand her. Leda cried. The more she cried by night, the faster she swam by day, eyes tightly closed against water out, or water in.

"It must be difficult for Gosling," people began to say, "being married to someone as famous as you."

Famous? Did that count as fame? Her picture on the back page, the sports page, not even the front? The Olympics were coming up. Gosling certainly found that difficult.

"Europa needs a natural life," he'd say. "You should never have had a child."

Leda cried. Naiad, child of tears, creature of mythology. If you wandered round Mount Olympus, you could always find a Naiad weeping in the corner of some pool, half tree, half water, all female: creating the tears that filled the pool, that gave you enough to swim in.

Europa went off to boarding school to be out of the glare of publicity. Gosling insisted. Poor little girl, her mother an Olympic swimmer! How could a child develop normally, in such a home?

Tears gave Leda an ethereal look, added eroticism to her body. Her freckles faded, as if the kisses of the sun were of no avail against the embraces of the night. And how they embraced! Leda and her Gosling, Gosling and his Leda: the music of the spheres sang around their bed. By night, in the forgetful dark, all was well. By day Leda remembered Europa, whom she should never have conceived, and missed her.

"In a way," said Gosling, "I suppose you could see something epileptic about winning swimming races, swimming faster than anyone else. It has to be done in a kind of fit. It certainly lacks grace. A matter of frothing and jerks. I can see it runs in the family." And he laughed. It was a joke. "I hope Europa is spared."

Europa, aged six, home for the holidays, ran a very high temperature on the eve of the next Olympic trials; she had convulsions.

"Of course she doesn't have epilepsy," said the doctor, surprised.

"Of course she has epilepsy," said Gosling. "He's only trying to comfort you. But drugs control it very well, don't worry."

"Next time her temperature gets as high as that," said the doctor, leaving, "sponge her down, don't wrap her up."

Leda was chosen for the final team. Flashbulbs clicked. Gosling shut the door in the face of newspaper people.

"This is unendurable," he said, and slept on his side of the bed, not touching. When she put down an ashtray or a vase of flowers he would move it at once to a different place, as if to signify she did not exist. He would sprinkle condiments lavishly upon the food she cooked, as if to change its nature; or would push away the plate entirely, and say he was not hungry, and go out and come back with fish and chips, and eat them silently. Gosling was increasingly silent. When she went out training, he did not raise his head: nor did he when she returned.

Europa's illness returned. The doctor remained puzzled.

Europa's fever rose. Now it was one hundred and six degrees. Gosling wrapped her in blankets.

"Don't, don't," cried Leda. "We must cool her down, not heat her up."

"That's nonsense," cried Gosling. "When I was ill as a child my mother always wrapped me up well. Don't fuss. It's your fussing makes her ill."

Leda seized Europa up, hailed a taxi, and ran with her into the hospital. Here staff put the burning scrap in ice-packs and her fever fell at once. In the morning she was perfectly well, nor did the fever return. Leda missed an eve-of-tour practice, but that was all. She did not go back to Gosling. She stayed at the hospital that night and the next morning her mother flew in from Bermuda to take care of Europa, and said of course Europa should go to Moscow to watch her mother win a gold medal: anything else was not just absurd but nasty.

The next night they all stayed in a hotel; grandmother, mother and daughter; and laughed and talked and cracked jokes and ate chips while photographers clicked and reporters asked questions which she did not answer. Finally she drove them out, and had her family to herself.

Gosling rang Leda just before she left for Moscow to say he could not face life without Europa; he had taken an overdose of sleeping pills.

"Die then," said Leda, and went on to win the Gold.

INTERESTING WOMEN *by* ANDREA LEE

Set in a Thai luxury resort, "Interesting Women" observes a brief but fierce infatuation between a vacationing mother and an intriguing bohemian adventuress who meet by the hotel pool. ANDREA LEE (b. 1953), an American living in Italy, is the author of Russian Journal, Sarah Phillips, Interesting Women, *and most recently,* Lost Hearts in Italy.

INTERESTING WOMEN—are we ever going to be free of them? I meet them everywhere these days, now that there is no longer such a thing as an interesting man. It's the same for all my girlfriends, whether they're in the States or in Hong Kong, where I'm now living. They come back from vacations or parties and announce proudly—with an air of defiance—that they met the most fascinating woman. What a refreshing change it would be if the new acquaintances were gorgeous lesbians or bisexuals whose intoxicating charm fed straight into hot, wet tumbles between rented sheets! Instead, these encounters are always drearily platonic. More than anything—and I speak from experience—they turn out to be schoolgirl crushes in disguise, instant friendships that last as long as it takes to swap tales of love and desperation. In short, an ephemeral traffic of souls that is about as revolutionary as flowers pressed in rice paper.

My hotel in Thailand is swarming with interesting women. I am probably one of them, though I try not to be. My husband, Simon, metallurgist and tireless *père de famille*, is presently looking over strip mines in Hunan Province, so I'm free to reinvent myself. I plan to occupy six days of Easter vacation with conspicuous idleness—no sightseeing, eating and drinking without compunction, binges of in-room movies with our twelve-year-old daughter, Basia. And, when I sit by the pool, I even bend back the cover of the book I'm reading, so no one can see that it's literature.

This hotel is the kind of place where guests read worthy books: it has, of all things, a library on the beach, where one can come in covered with sand and, under lazily revolving ceiling fans, open a glass case and consult *The Oxford English Dictionary*. It also has a meditation pavilion, and a high-tech gym, and bougainvillea garlands placed on the beds in the bungalows every morning; it has a view of an opalescent bay strewn with distant islands of surpassing beauty, and a chef with California leanings, plus a mad French owner who bestows on each guest a handwritten guide that mingles facts about the medieval kingdoms of Ayutthaya and Sukhothai with information like "The hotel grounds are kept secure at night by dogs trained to bark only at Thai faces."

On my third afternoon here, in a lazy moment, I fall into a conversation from which I sense that I will not be able to extricate myself without relating the usual set pieces of emotional history. I am pulling a kayak up over the sand, after a jaunt on the lagoon with Basia. She is still in her kayak, skimming around the shallow waters inside the reef, and I am huffing and puffing, scratching my feet on broken coral, and exchanging cheerful insults with her. "You're a wuss," she calls. "Go ahead, desert your only daughter!"

A slim shape emerges from the palms behind me, and I see that it belongs to a woman I have been observing idly since I arrived. I've seen her by the pool, drinking gin-and-tonics with a pair of Swiss anthropologists, husband and wife, who live in Bangladesh and are here with their adopted baby son. I eavesdropped on an emotional discussion they had about child prostitution and AIDS in Bangkok, and noted that this woman was demanding some kind of attention, not sexual, from her new acquaintances, which the couple, focused on their gorgeous, dark-skinned baby, couldn't give. And at odd moments of the day, I have been aware of the woman sitting, not reading, in a deck chair pulled into one of the furthest clefts of the elephant-colored rocks that loom over the water. I judge her to be in her early fifties, about ten years older than I am. Looking good without pushing it, still in the game. No matronly straw hats or designer sunglasses. Over various stylish bathing suits she wears a white pareu, expertly tied, and she walks barefoot with the lounging gait that in the Far East often marks members of the great diaspora of Westerners who imagine that they are not tourists.

"Is it hard?" she asks, coming up beside me and indicating the kayak.

"It's easy, as long as you don't go outside the reef."

"I'll do it tomorrow. It's on my list of things that scare me."

She looks at me knowingly. "I was very good at canoeing at camp," she goes on, with a sibylline smile.

An American East Coast accent. Upper-class. The old traveler's game of placing a compatriot arranges itself in my thoughts like a fragment of Anglo-Saxon verse: clearly Caucasian, so Jewish or Gentile? A wandering WASP wastrel, or Irish, Italian? Camp? I imagine her at some posh backwoods establishment with secret midnight hazings and awards inscribed on birch bark. But Maine or Blue Ridge? Up close, she's a funny mix of elegance and uncouthness. Her body has a thoroughbred length of bone, but her limbs look slightly wasted—a tropical bug, perhaps, or simply borderline anorexia. Her armpits and legs are unshaven but her toenails are meticulously manicured, painted a glossy orange-red. She is wearing an Indian nose ring, and bangles around her ankles. Her hair, short and raked back from her face, is orange-red as well, the cheap, untempered henna color one sees in fakirs' beards; and her sun-weathered face with its short, arrogant nose and hooded gray eyes—no surgical work that I can discern—displays a peculiar expression of rueful good humor that reminds me of a street urchin in a thirties movie. It is amusing to see her studying me at the same time.

"Taos," she says. And everything is clear. Of course she wasn't born there, because no one like her is ever born in Taos; people like her are reborn there. A horsey childhood in northern New Jersey and Madrid, where her father owned chewing-gum factories, she tells me. Then twenty years as a banker's wife in London, where she ran a shop that imported South American textiles. Then the divorce and the move to New Mexico, which she initially discovered when she was "doing a Thelma and Louise" with a friend. "After all those years in England, I realized that I didn't want to be buried among the Brits. I got to Taos, and knew I could die there." Now that the kids are grown, she is traveling through the East by herself. Roughing it, mostly—she's at this pricey hotel, which fits her style but not her present budget, for a few days of R and R. She has just finished moving from ashram to ashram in India, and was at Poona, where the faithful live on in the waning rays of the glory of the Maharishi.

We are sitting on the powdery sand, our legs stretched out into transparent water the temperature of amniotic fluid. There is too much information, I worry, moving between us too fast. But I'm on vacation, and after a while, I let myself go. Sitting there in my black bikini, the water from my hair dripping down my shoulders, I describe the fancy Santa Fe wedding I once attended, where aristocratic Florentines and Milanese, wearing spanking-new cowboy boots, boogied with Texas millionaires. I complain about the rootlessness of my life as an expatriate wife blown by multinational winds from Massachusetts to Birmingham, Warsaw, and now Hong Kong. Shamelessly, I lament the superficiality of the travel articles I write for two quite reputable magazines back in the States. Then I get to the hard stuff. Showing off to this adventurous new acquaintance with chitchat about cities and jungles we both know, I touch scornfully on the inability of men to appreciate canopic jars and shaft tombs, to deal with knavish cabdrivers, to tolerate bedbugs. I observe that women are better travelers than men, and superior beings altogether. And then I drop the word ex-husband—that password that functions as a secret handshake in the freemasonry of interesting women.

It is five in the afternoon, the time when it rains for ten minutes every day at this season. Steel gray thunderheads loom over the bay and, as a long-prowed fishing boat motors hastily by, there is a distant flare of lightning under an arcade of black cloud. Basia has beached her kayak and is chasing crabs on the rocks, circling closer and closer as she eavesdrops on us. By now, we're engaged in an orgy of divorce talk, slapping away at the mosquitoes that began attacking us once the shore breeze died down. My new friend is telling me in detail exactly how the Filipina maid was bribed to testify against her. And I respond with the well-worn saga of my perfidious lawyer, a woman who, after helping arrange the official dissolution of my brief first marriage, moved in with my ex-husband. Perched above us on the rocks, Basia gives up any pretense of not listening. "You can come and sit beside us, you beautiful girl," says the woman, whose name I still don't know. She speaks to my daughter with a tender familiarity that sends a wary prickle down my spine.

I have to be careful what I say, I think, as Basia climbs down and settles near me. But it's hard. Impromptu confession can be as irresistible as sex. At least I keep my revelations rigorously in the past, and avoid the slightest spilling of guts about my second husband, Basia's father, Simon. Although at other times I can go on for hours about him and his controlling love, his occasional stupid infidelities, and his still more annoying blind devotion—revealing itself more and more over the years—to a fantasy ideal of a family. Or about my two miscarriages after Basia, and how Simon's prolonged and noisy grief left nearly no room for mine. Of none of this do I speak as I watch Basia sitting in the warm sea, her arms crossed to protect her twelve-year-old breasts, those impertinent brand-new breasts that already, I note, attract attention from old and not-so-old lechers around the hotel pool.

Basia is as tall as I am, and wears a larger shoe; she is one of the new, giant breed of American children created by overnurturing parents, and she has the precocious social aplomb of most expat kids. She goes to an international school where kids have tongue studs and Prada running shoes and get alternating lectures on the importance of getting into the right college and of avoiding STDs. However, when it comes to matters other than sex, ambition, and controlled substances—small matters like distinguishing honest people from charlatans—Basia is still as innocent as custard pie. Now she is openly hoarding the specious information we are exchanging. And I feel a flash of alarm that changes to annoyance at her presence. Later, back at our bungalow, I will scold her unfairly, poor baby, for butting into adult conversations.

The rain comes on, cooler than the water where we are sitting. The three of us raise our arms and turn up our faces to the hard drops that rattle down as if someone were tossing handfuls of coins. Up from the lagoon, as if in response, leap entire schools of tiny silver fish. In a minute, the sun pokes through; the daily rainbow bridges two dark banks of clouds, and, on cue, a fashion shoot appears on the beach in the distance, as it does every morning and evening: photographer, dressers, models, minions, trunks and tripods and diffusers. Tonight it's the two male models in long bathing trunks: a sculptural blond with a strange, chopped haircut, and a black guy with a shaved head and a body that makes one realize that sometimes just a body is enough. "Look at that," I say.

"Don't stare at him, Mom!" begs Basia.

"Oh, he doesn't mind being stared at," says our new friend. "He's used to it. It's an element. You learn to breathe in it, and then, if you're not careful, you have to have it. It used to be part of my life," she goes on after a pause. "People turning around to look. Now that phase is over. It's not important anymore."

Basia looks so inclined to take this statement as a pearl of wisdom that I rise abruptly from the water and say that I'm chilled to the bone. I grab my reluctant daughter, and we head off to shower, leaving our new acquaintance reclining in the sea. Before departing, I introduce myself and ask her name. "Silver," she says.

"Is that your real name?" I blurt rudely.

"One of my real names." The voice drifts out of the darkness, which in tropical style has fallen like a sudden curtain.

At dinner, predictably enough, it is Basia who defends Silver while I roll my eyes over that ridiculous New Age alias. "I think she's cool," says Basia, taking a tiny spray of green peppers out of her milky soup. "She's really, really mysterious." At the tables around us, people with careful, moderate tans are wearing pale clothes and sitting over hurricane lamps whose amber glow makes the dining terrace look vaguely like a shrine. A real shrine sits nearby, under the mango tree, a tiny spirit house that is a replica of the hotel, with candles, fruit, and flowers around it. The hotel, recommended by my editor, has been a disappointment, I think: pretentious; arrogantly overpriced; hardly any kids, and none Basia's age. Instead, it's a perfect hideaway for upscale lovers: without turning around, I can count two honeymoon couples, an enamored pair of Englishmen, and a German businessman with his young mistress.

"Mysterious? Oh, please, sweetheart," I say. "She's the classic kind of woman who is very beautiful and lives for that, and then the beauty fades, and she goes and gets spiritual. Like Bianca Jagger."

"Who?"

"Bianca Jagger was one of the most beautiful women back in the seventies. Way back before you were born. Now she's not so beautiful, so she's involved in saving humanity."

"Silver doesn't want to save humanity."

"She wants to save her soul. Same difference."

Basia giggles and crunches the ice from her Diet Coke. "But I thought you liked her. Why are you trashing her?"

"I am not trashing her," I say untruthfully, and I wonder why I am bothering to be malicious about a woman I've just met, who seems more like than unlike me. That's it, of course. That and the fact that I revealed a great many intimate facts of my past to a complete stranger down on the beach. Why, I wonder? Am I becoming an embittered woman of a certain age, maddened at the sight of romantic couples, and driven into serial episodes of pathetic self-revelation as my daughter flowers into maidenhood? For a second, I wallow in gloomy speculation.

Basia stares across the candlelight at me. She is wearing a green tie-dyed dress and her round, seraphic face is deeply tanned, an irritating fact that reminds me of our daily battles over sunscreen and hats. It is Simon's face, but my eyes look out of it, and whenever she turns those eyes directly on me I experience an eerie jolt of total recognition. "Mom? Are you missing Daddy?" she asks.

"Not right this second," I reply, with bravado. But suddenly I do miss Simon. He would have added a bit of male ballast to the unbearable lightness of this female vacation. He would have fussed about the price of drinks and worried about hepatitis and bilharzia and insisted on renting mopeds for horrible family excursions. He'd have insisted on daily screwing at siesta time—not such a bad idea, that—and at least once he would have attempted to amuse both of his girls by turning on MTV and dancing around in a pareu, imitating Cher. He would have laughed at Silver. I take a forkful of rice and try to think of something wise and maternal to say, but Basia has stolen most of my lines. "We'll call him tonight," I mutter.

One of my weak points, as Simon continually tells me, is my untrammeled curiosity. The next morning, when I should be horizontal under a palm tree, reading disguised literature, I agree, in a moment of wild perversity, to share a taxi into town for a morning's shopping with Silver. At breakfast, with

Basia out having a half-day diving lesson, my new acquaintance looked interesting to me again.

I have misgivings already, when I have to wait in the taxi for fifteen minutes, as Silver, at the front desk, calls the States to shout endearments to her boyfriend, who, it seems, is a retired oil-field engineer. Flies swarm sociably into the rear end of the taxi, which is a rump-sprung *tuk-tuk* with aluminum seats. The driver, one of the few fat Thai men I've ever seen, occasionally turns to regard me with lazy amusement. Finally Silver appears, with a crisp white Indian *kurta* pulled over her pareu, and asks me whether I mind making an extra excursion. Before she moves on to the other islands she wants to visit—Bali, Lombok, the Moluccas—there is something she wants to do here. A program of meditation and yoga coupled with high-colonic irrigation.

"Enemas! You're crazy!" I say. I say it in the downright tone of an old Methodist churchwoman.

Silver looks thoughtful. "One thing I really got to understand in India is that the body can't be separated from the spirit," she says. "You can't make any real progress toward enlightenment unless your body is clean. You don't know how much toxic stuff you've been carrying around with you for years."

And then, as the driver heads toward town, she tells me about a man she knows who did colonic irrigation and found that the encrustations in his guts had included a dozen little round pellets of metal, slightly bigger than buckshot. It turned out that when he was six he used to bite the heads off his toy soldiers, and they'd stayed with him.

"Excuse me if I'm too blunt, but the whole thing has always

sounded to me like getting buggered for your health," I say. "People talk about the benefits but why doesn't anybody talk about the erotic part of it?"

It's impossible to offend Silver. She simply smiles, takes back her hennaed hair, revealing a narrow band of white at the roots, and shakes her head at me with a tinge of pity. Then she tells me that in Goa she heard of two places on this island, health centers where one can go on retreats for mediation and purification of both ends of the body. She wants to find them—and this, I discover, is the main purpose of our shared outing. "Come on," she says. "We can get our shopping done, and then set off and look. One of the places is over by the caves. I heard it used to be good, but the owner, a German guy, has turned into an alcoholic, and it may have gone downhill. If it doesn't look promising, we can always go find Cornelia, the American woman who runs a retreat in the bush. They say she's the best, if you can find her."

She looks at me with her urchin's smile, and I recall wondering earlier how this frail-seeming woman had managed to travel alone but unscathed through the backwaters of half of Asia. Now I see how: an exuberant opportunism protects her as absolutely as angels guard saints and children. Already I know that I'm going with her and that I'll probably get stuck with the taxi fare, too.

Silver pats my shoulder as we rattle along. "Come on. It'll be an adventure." She's astute enough not to press any spiritual points. "Cornelia went to Wellesley," she adds brightly.

In the port town, a fat, naked baby with brass anklets crawls around, laughing, on the floor of a shop that sells cheap viscose pants, sundresses, and cotton bathing suits from Bali. The baby's parents are eating noodles in the back of the shop, and keeping a weather eye on Silver, who is going through the racks of clothes and pulling out things with magisterial gestures as if she were shopping at Saks. I catch sight of a black-and-white pair of pants which I immediately know will look good, and buy them. "You move fast," Silver observes.

A pronouncement on my entire uncontemplative life. But part of my haste is due to a suspicion that I might end up paying for her purchases as well. "Yes," I say, and move on to the next shop, arranging to meet her afterward at a café on the waterfront. Wandering through a market past heaps of coriander, lichees, and jackfruit, I ponder whether I should simply escape back to the hotel in one of the many bush taxis that pass me, crammed with country people. But I'm held there by my curiosity, which seems to grow stronger in the heat, like a kind of jungle itch. I wait for Silver in the café, which looks out on two long, decayed jetties that stretch into the flat dazzle of the straits. Around me, waiting for ferries, killing time, sit golden Australian boys with dive gear and many large, ugly foreign men looking like assorted Calibans beside tiny, beautiful Thai prostitutes. A jeep pulls up and a tattooed American girl jumps out and hands around invitations to a full-moon beach party on a far island: live music, magic mushrooms. I stare out over the blazing sea that is as motionless as gelatin, and punish myself by rereading a Chinese poem I found in a book borrowed from the hotel library:

How sad it is to be a woman!
Nothing on earth is held so cheap.
Boys stand leaning at the door
Like gods fallen out of heaven.
No one is glad when a girl is born.

Silver appears, and we get back in the taxi and race toward the first of our anal destinations. We drive along the bay, away from the stylish south of the island, where the good beaches and fancy hotels are. Soon our taxi stops in a palm grove gray with fallen, withered fronds. A large, faded signboard reads EMERALD CAVE HEALTH SPA. Below is a list: "Thai Massage; Yoga Classes; Vegetarian Cuisine; Detoxification Cures; Pranotherapy; Gymnastics." Nine or ten thatched bungalows form a semicircle around a larger bungalow, and beyond gleams the incorruptible sea. After the green-velvet lawns and manicured hibiscus of the hotel where we are staying, the place looks ominously neglected.

Silver disappears into the office, and I walk down a path toward the beach. A small outdoor restaurant with white-plastic tables and chairs is deserted. A Thai woman with square-cut hair and a scowl uncharacteristic of the friendly islanders peers out at me from behind the bamboo bar, and then vanishes. Nearby, three cats are sleeping under a Ping-Pong table with a broken net, and on a deck chair outside an open-air cubicle containing a treadmill and a few barbells sits an enameled tin bowl that once held someone's lunch and is now black with flies.

Music fills the air—a Chopin nocturne. For a minute, I think it is live, produced by the German gone to seed. But then the music shifts to Peruvian flutes, and I realize that it's a cassette, broadcast through speakers wired to the palms. A man, a Westerner, brown-haired and pasty-skinned, is snoring in a hammock at the edge of the beach. I turn and walk quietly back to the car.

Silver comes back with her hands full of papers describing what Emerald Cave can offer. On one is a list of health products with names like Hatha Purge, on another a Xeroxed diagram showing rolls of tubing and a kind of plastic-and-metal table for attaching over a toilet.

I look at it all. "Don't do this," I say to her, overturning my vow not to get involved. "At least, don't do it here."

"It's very cheap," she says stoutly. "My funds aren't what they were."

"Don't."

She looks at me as Basia does when I get tough. "Well, then, we'll go find Cornelia," she says.

Locating Cornelia involves a return to town and a stop at a bakery popular with trekkers, where we look for a notice posted on a bulletin board, and a dive with the taxi down a path into the bush past a huge, unpacific-looking water buffalo. Hours pass, as we jolt over red mud roads. All spirit of independence withers within me. Desperately thirsty, flapping my hands feebly at the mosquitoes that billow into the back of the truck at every stop, I realize that I've undergone a minor conversion to a vaguely Eastern worldview: sweat and fatalism. At one point, the taxi bounces over a bridge across a vine-filled gorge where water is falling among clouds of orchids, a paradise I know I visited in dreams all through my childhood. "Please stop for a minute," I say in a faint voice, but the place is past, never to be found again in this incarnation. And we head onward toward Cornelia.

It is late afternoon, and the taxi driver has begun to give us ominous glances over his shoulder, when we pull into a clearing in the middle of a huge palm grove. Before us is a modest concrete house with a heap of coconuts against one wall. ISLAND WELLNESS CENTER is written on a small sign posted on a tree trunk. A thin, deeply tanned woman in a plum-colored leotard and a pair of loose batik pants comes out on the veranda and looks at us.

"Are you Cornelia?" calls Silver, clambering nimbly out of the truck and advancing with the triumphant air of Stanley sighting Livingstone.

The woman acknowledges her with a spare, formal nod. I instantly dislike her.

In a matter of minutes, Silver and Cornelia have clasped hands like long-lost friends, gazed into each other's eyes, and vanished into an office with screened windows, leaving me on the veranda with a portly, yellow dog, who studies me tranquilly. The reddening sun is level with the tops of the acres of palms surrounding us, and I think with a pang of Basia, who must be fretting because I've run off and left her. Beside the heap of coconuts, our driver, who has plainly given up hope of an early dinner, squats companionably to smoke with a couple of young men who drove up behind us in a truck full of gas canisters. From inside, where the two women are sitting, comes a murmur of excited voices. The door opens and Cornelia beckons me. "You can come in," she says, as if she were speaking to a small child.

I tiptoe inside and settle on a low rattan stool in a corner of the room beside an overflowing bookcase, where I see Castaneda's *Journey to Ixtlan*, and *Back to Eden* by Jethro Kloss. More books crowd the desk where Cornelia sits, and on the wall behind her hangs a Thai anatomy chart, dense with notations in green ink.

"We do a lot of work in the sea," Cornelia is telling Silver. "Breathing and movement. You live in one of our huts down by the beach. They are very basic, of course. No hot water. You'll be fasting and doing the high colonics every morning and evening, before meditation. The results of the colonics can be amazing. People reexperience fragments of past lives."

Cornelia has a phenomenally narrow torso, and breasts with sharp nipples that show clearly through her leotard. Her frizzy, sandy hair is dusted with gray. She has a penetrating voice, and a look in her pale eyes which I recognize as subtle orneriness. She, I see immediately, is another interesting woman. She has already made it clear that she speaks fluent Thai, and has given a quick, disdainful sketch of her rejected past life, not omitting Wellesley.

Silver is staring at her, bedazzled. I feel a pang of the kind of jealously I haven't felt since Girl Scouts, when my troop leader—one of those dear, old-fashioned closet lesbians—liked my best friend better than me. Just yesterday Silver was staring at me like that as I rattled on about my ex-husband's shenanigans and the rigors of a writer's life. Evidently I wasn't ethereal enough for her. And besides, getting a taste for these chaste female encounters can lead to incredible promiscuity. Another day, another soul laid bare.

I clear my throat and announce—philistine that I am—that I have to get back to the hotel, and Silver and Cornelia wince with annoyance. They agree that Silver will begin her cure in a day's time, and then they embrace.

"I think you are absolutely beautiful," says Cornelia to Silver.

"You are exactly what I have been looking for," says Silver to Cornelia.

Silver and I ride back to our hotel in silence and arrive there at dusk, just in time to view the underlings of the fashion shoot trudging up from the beach lugging equipment and screens with the weary air of peons returning from the fields. I pay the entire taxi fare without a murmur and run to find Basia. She is lolling under the mosquito net in our bungalow, watching MTV broadcast from Kuala Lumpur and finishing the last of the forbidden M&Ms from the minibar. She is so happy to see me that she forgets her twelve-year-old's dignity and jumps up and hugs me like a much younger child. "I thought you'd never come back!" she tells me. "I thought I was going to be stuck watching 'An Evening with Aerosmith'!"

Her mouth drops open when I describe Silver's quest. "Oh God, Mom—you mean she's going around looking for places to get her ass washed out?"

"Don't use crude words to show off," I say coldly. "And it's her colon, really."

"It's still her butt. Remember that joke: Are there rings around Uranus? Is there intelligent life on Uranus?"

We look at each other and snicker. Then I tell her about the man who swallowed the heads of toy soldiers and we collapse on the bed and sob with laughter. We're still laughing on our way to dinner. Outside the dining room, Basia stops to inspect the spirit house as she always does, touching with the tip of one finger the minute plastic figures set inside it and the fresh offerings of fruit and flowers around them. On our first night at the hotel she read aloud to me from the guidebook a passage explaining that these tiny houses are set up for wandering guardian spirits. In the light of the candles set on the miniature carved veranda, Basia half resembles a little girl looking over her dolls, and half—with her flimsy dress, tumbled hair, and glowing sunburn—a nymphet in a romantic soft-porn photo. A familiar wave of emotion sweeps over me, an even mixture of tenderness, envy, and general terror of the future. At the same time, I wonder how I could have left this angel even for an hour for such a poor substitute as Silver. It occurs to me, as it often does, that I am supposed to be setting an example for Basia. And what a cockup I make of it, sometimes.

Basia turns away from the little house and looks over at the lamp-lit diners at the restaurant tables. "I'm still thinking about those toy soldiers," she says in a dreamy voice. "I wonder what Silver will find." A pause and a giggle. "I wonder what you would find."

Next day, I keep to myself, as one is entitled to do in a hotel that has a library. When Simon calls from Hunan, before breakfast, I don't say a word about my daylong excursion but instead wax lyrical on the joys of solitude until, through the crackling Chinese static, he asks me suspiciously what I've been up to. "Just the usual sex with hotel waiters," I tell him.

From my lounge chair in the shade beside the pool, I observe Silver's movements on the last day before her retreat. After bidding me a cheerful good morning, she breakfasts garrulously with the assistant manager, who dreams of opening a luxury hotel in Rangoon; she meditates on the rocks by the bay; and by late afternoon she is one of three torsos emerging from the water at the far end of the pool, drinking cocktails with the black male model and one of the stylists from the shoot. When she sees me watching, she holds up her glass. "The last gin-and-tonic!" she calls. "*Vive la folie!*"

I don't see Silver again. She goes off to Cornelia and a cleaner life without saying good-bye. Once or twice, she drifts through my thoughts in her white sarong with her cocky grin. But almost immediately I banish her, and for the last part of my vacation I set about being indolent and uninteresting.

Still, it happens that on the day before I leave I find myself in the library, deep in conversation with a woman I have just met. She is younger than I am, twenty-eight or twenty-nine, and English: blond, with a pudgy, tanned body packed into a girlish bikini; entertainingly foulmouthed, with a Geordie accent. She came to the hotel a couple of days ago, with a tall Jordanian husband covered in gold chains; two blond, black-eyed toddlers; and a pair of male attendants in white robes and Arab headdresses, who carried suitcases and looked after the children, even changing diapers. Leaning on a table covered with weeks-old foreign papers in the dim, low-ceilinged library, she looks at me and says, "I envy you, being practically alone on holiday. Sometimes I get so fucking sick of the lot of them—"

Mice scurry in the palm thatch on the roof. *The Oxford English Dictionary* looms behind us, in its glass case, locked away against the ravages of suntan oil and salt air. Across the room, Basia, reading *MAD* magazine in a varnished planter's chair, has stopped turning the pages. In the woman's surly blue eyes I can see skeins of experience poised to unwind, and the password trembles on my lips.

THE ORPHANED SWIMMING POOL

by JOHN UPDIKE

Two-time Pulitzer Prize–winner John Updike (b. 1923) is the author of more than a dozen short story collections and twenty-two novels, most famously the Rabbit *series. In "The Orphaned Swimming Pool," a broken family abandons their backyard pool, but the guests just keep coming. Given that this story was written just six years after Cheever's "The Swimmer," one would be forgiven for believing that, rather than a symbol of status achieved, the mid-century American swimming pool was in fact an albatross.*

MARRIAGES, LIKE CHEMICAL UNIONS, release upon dissolution packets of the energy locked up in their bonding. There is the piano no one wants, the cocker spaniel no one can take care of. Shelves of books suddenly stand revealed as burdensomely dated and unlikely to be reread; indeed, it is difficult to remember who read them in the first place. And what of those old skis in the attic? Or the doll house waiting to be repaired in the basement? The piano goes out of tune, the dog goes mad. The summer that the Turners got their divorce, their swimming pool had neither a master nor a mistress, though the sun beat down day after day, and a state of drought was declared in Connecticut.

It was a young pool, only two years old, of the fragile type fashioned by laying a plastic liner within a carefully carved hole in the ground. The Turners' side yard looked infernal while it was being done; one bulldozer sank into the mud and had to be pulled free by another. But by midsummer the new grass was sprouting, the encircling flagstones were in place, the blue plastic tinted the water a heavenly blue, and it had to be admitted that the Turners had scored again. They were always a little in advance of their friends. He was a tall, hairy-backed man with long arms, and a nose flattened by football, and a sullen look of too much blood; she was a fine-boned blonde with dry blue eyes and lips usually held parted and crinkled as if about to ask a worrisome, or whimsical, question. They never seemed happier, nor their marriage healthier, than those two summers. They grew brown and supple and smooth with swimming. Brad would begin his day with a swim, before dressing to catch the train, and Linda would hold court all day amid crowds of wet matrons and children, and Brad would return from work to find a poolside cocktail party in progress, and the couple would end their day at eleven, when their friends had finally left, by swimming nude, before bed. What ecstasy! In darkness the water felt mild as milk and buoyant as helium, and the swimmers became giants, gliding from side to side in a single languorous stroke.

In May of the third summer, the pool was filled as usual, and the usual after-school gangs of mothers and children gathered, but Linda, unlike her, stayed indoors. She could be heard within the house, moving from room to room, but she no longer emerged, as in other years, with a cheerful tray of ice and a brace of bottles, and Triscuits and lemonade for the children. Their friends felt less comfortable about appearing, towels in hand, at the Turners' on weekends. Though Linda had lost some weight and looked elegant, and Brad was cumbersomely jovial, they gave off the faint, sleepless, awkward-making aroma of a couple in trouble. Then, the day after school was out, Linda fled with the children to her parents in Ohio. Brad stayed nights in the city, and the pool was deserted. Though the pump that ran the water through the filter continued to mutter in the lilacs, the cerulean pool grew cloudy. The bodies of dead horseflies and wasps dotted the still surface. A speckled plastic ball drifted into a corner beside the diving board and stayed there. The grass between the flagstones grew lank. On the glass-topped poolside table, a spray can of Off! had lost its pressure and a gin-and-tonic glass held a sere mint leaf. The pool looked desolate and haunted, like a stagnant jungle spring; it looked poisonous and ashamed. The postman, stuffing overdue notices and unanswered solicitations into the mailbox, averted his eyes from the side yard politely.

Some June weekends, Brad sneaked out from the city. Families driving to church glimpsed him dolefully sprinkling chemical substances into the pool. He looked pale and thin. He instructed Roscoe Chace, his neighbor on the left, how to switch on the pump and change the filter, and how much chlorine and Algitrol should be added weekly. He explained he would not be able to make it out every weekend—as if the distance that for years he had travelled twice each day, gliding in and out of New York, had become an impossibly steep climb back into the past. Linda, he confided vaguely, had left her parents in Akron and was visiting her sister in Minneapolis. As the shock of the Turners' joint disappearance wore off, their pool seemed less haunted and forbidding. The Murtaugh children—the Murtaughs, a rowdy, numerous family, were the Turners' right-hand neighbors—began to use it, without supervision. So Linda's old friends, with their children, began to show up, "to keep the Murtaughs from drowning each other." For, if anything were to happen to a Murtaugh, the poor Turners (the adjective had become automatic) would be sued for everything, right when they could least afford it. It became, then, a kind of duty, a test of loyalty, to use the pool.

July was the hottest in twenty-seven years. People brought their own lawn furniture over in station wagons and set it up. Teen-age offspring and Swiss *au-pair* girls were established as lifeguards. A nylon rope with flotation corks, meant to divide the wading end from the diving end of the pool, was found coiled in the garage and reinstalled. Agnes Kleefield contributed an old refrigerator, which was plugged into an outlet beside the garage door and used to store ice, quinine water, and soft drinks. An honor-system shoebox containing change appeared upon it; a little lost-and-found—an array of forgotten sunglasses, flippers, towels, lotions, paperbacks, shirts, even underwear—materialized on the Turners' side steps. When people, that July, said, "Meet you at the pool," they did not mean the public pool past the shopping center, or the country-club pool near the first tee. They meant the Turners'. Restrictions on admission were difficult to enforce tactfully. A visiting Methodist bishop, two Taiwanese economists, an entire girls' softball team from Darien, an eminent Canadian poet, the archery champion of Hartford, the six members of a black rock group called The Good Intentions, an ex-mistress of Aly Khan, the lavender-haired mother-in-law of a Nixon adviser not quite of Cabinet rank, an infant of six weeks, a man who was killed the next day on the Merritt Parkway, a Filipino who could stay on the pool bottom for eighty seconds, two Texans who kept cigars in their mouths and hats on their heads, three telephone lineman, four expatriate Czechs, a student Maoist from Wesleyan, and the postman all swam, as guests, in the Turners' pool, though not all at once. After the daytime crowd ebbed, and the shoebox was put back in the refrigerator, and the last *au-pair* girl took the last goosefleshed, wrinkled child shivering home to supper, there was a tide of evening activity, trysts (Mrs. Kleefield and the Nicholson boy, most notoriously) and what some called, overdramatically, orgies. True, late splashes and excited guffaws did often keep Mrs. Chace awake, and the Murtaugh children spent hours at their attic window with binoculars. And there was the evidence of the lost underwear.

One Saturday early in August, the morning arrivals found an unknown car with New York plates parked in the driveway. But cars of all sorts were so common—the parking tangle frequently extended into the road—that nothing much was thought of it, even when someone noticed that the bedroom windows upstairs were open. And nothing came of it, except that around suppertime, in the lull before the evening crowd began to arrive in force, Brad and an unknown woman, of the same physical type as Linda but brunette, swiftly exited from the kitchen door, got into her car, and drove back to New York. The few lingering baby-sitters and beaux thus unwittingly glimpsed the root of the divorce. The two lovers had been trapped inside the house all day; Brad was fearful of the legal consequences of their being seen by anyone who might write and tell Linda. The settlement was at a ticklish stage; nothing less than terror of Linda's lawyers would have led Brad to suppress his indignation at seeing, from behind the window screen, his private pool turned public carnival. For long thereafter, though in the end he did not marry the woman, he remembered that day when they lived together like fugitives in a cave, feeding on love and ice water, tiptoeing barefoot to the depleted cupboards, which they, arriving late last night, had hoped to stock in the morning, not foreseeing the onslaught of interlopers that would pin them in. Her hair, he remembered, had tickled his shoulders as she crouched behind him at the window, and through the angry pounding of his own blood he had felt her slim body breathless with the attempt not to giggle.

August drew in, with cloudy days. Children grew bored with swimming. Roscoe Chace went on vacation to Italy; the pump broke down, and no one repaired it. Dead dragonflies accumulated on the surface of the pool. Small deluded toads hopped in and swam around and around hopelessly. Linda at last returned. From Minneapolis she had gone on to Idaho for six weeks, to be divorced. She and the children had tan faces from riding and hiking; her lips looked drier and more quizzical than ever, still seeking to frame that troubling question. She stood at the window, in the house that already seemed to lack its furniture, at the same side window where the lovers had crouched, and gazed at the deserted pool. The grass around it was green from splashing, save where a long-lying towel had smothered a rectangle and left it brown. Aluminum furniture she didn't recognize lay strewn and broken. She counted a dozen bottles beneath the glass-topped table. The nylon divider had parted, and its two halves floated independently. The blue plastic beneath the colorless water tried to make a cheerful, otherworldly statement, but Linda saw that the pool in truth had no bottom, it held bottomless loss, it was one huge blue tear. Thank God no one had drowned in it. Except her. She saw that she could never live here again. In

September the place was sold, to a family with toddling infants, who for safety's sake have not only drained the pool but sealed it over with iron pipes and a heavy mesh, and put warning signs around, as around a chained dog.

THE LESSON *by* JAMES PURDY

"Among those who know his work, the opinion is violent and various," Edward Albee wrote about JAMES PURDY (b. 1923) in 1966. Thirty years later, the enigmatic Brooklynite's body of more than forty published works remains uniquely unconventional and unsettling. Set in a private club, "The Lesson" pits a stubborn swim instructor against an equally obstinate heiress.

"THIS IS NOT LADY'S DAY AT THE POOL," Mr. Diehl said. "I can't admit her."

"But she pleaded so."

Mr. Diehl was about to give his lesson to a young man and wanted no women in the pool. He knew that if a woman entered the pool during the lesson she would distract the young man, who was already nervous about learning to swim. The young man was quite upset already, as he was going to have to go to a country house where there was lots of swimming and boating, and if he didn't know how, his hosts would be very put out with him. They might never invite him again. At any rate that was his story, and besides, he was the commander's son.

"But my grandmother always wants as many people to come into the pool as possible," the girl said. Her grandmother owned the pool.

"I have worked for your grandmother for a long time," Mr. Diehl, the swimming instructor said, "and I'm sure that she would not want a woman in the pool at this hour who does not belong to the club and so far as I know doesn't even know how to swim."

"Well, I asked her that," the girl said.

"And what did she say?" the swimming instructor wanted to know.

"She said she could swim."

"Just the same she can wait until the lesson is over. It takes only half an hour."

"I told her that, but she wanted to go in the pool right away. She has gone downstairs to change."

"For Christ's sake," Mr. Diehl said.

His pupil, the commander's son, was already splashing around in the shallow water, waiting for the lesson.

"Go and tell her in a half hour."

The girl looked as though she was not going to tell the woman.

"If your grandmother were here she would back me up on this," Mr. Diehl said.

"But she's not here and my instructions were to do as best I thought."

"As best you thought," Mr. Diehl considered this, looking at the girl. She was sixteen, but he knew she had a slow mind and he wondered what had ever made Mrs. Schuck leave the pool in the hands of such an immature person.

"Look," Mr. Diehl said. "Just go and tell the woman

that I can't have her in the pool while I am giving this special lesson."

"Well, I can't forbid her the pool very well, now, can I. If she wants to come in! This club isn't that exclusive and she knows one of the members."

"I don't care if she knows the man who invented swimming, she can't come in. Is that clear?"

"Mr. Diehl, you forget that I am the granddaughter of the owner of the pool."

"I am responsible for what goes on in the water, am I not?"

"Yes, I'll go along with you there."

"All right then," Mr. Diehl said, as though having made his point. "Go tell her I can't have her in the water until after the lesson. Can't you do that?"

"No," the girl said. "I can't tell that to a perfectly good customer."

"You have this pool mixed up with a public dance hall or something. This is not exactly a money-making organization, as your grandmother must have told you. It is a club. Not open to everybody. And this unknown woman should not have been allowed in here anyhow. Not at all."

"I know better," the girl said. "Many nice people come here just for an occasional swim."

"Not unless they are known," Mr. Diehl said.

"But she knows a member," the girl pointed out.

"Who is the member?" Mr. Diehl wanted to know.

"Oh, I can't remember," the girl told him.

"But I know every member by name," Mr. Diehl was insistent. "I've been swimming instructor here now for nine years."

"I know, I know," the girl said. "But this woman has every right to come in here."

"She's not coming in the water."

"Well, I don't know what to tell her. She's already putting on her suit."

"Then she can take it right off again," Mr. Diehl said.

"But not here, though," the girl tried to joke. Mr. Diehl did not laugh.

"What I'm trying to get you to see, Polly," Mr. Diehl said, and it was the first time he had ever called her by name, "is that this is a pretty high-class place. Do you know by chance who that boy is who is waiting for the lesson."

Mr. Diehl waited for the girl to answer.

"I don't know who he is," she replied.

"That is Commander Jackson's son."

"And he doesn't know how to swim?"

"What has that got to do with it?" the swimming instructor said.

"Well, I'm surprised is all."

"Look, time is slipping away. I don't want to have any more argument with you, Polly. But I'm sure your grandmother would back me up on this all the way if she were here. Is there any way we can reach her by telephone?"

"I have no idea where she went."

"Well, this strange woman cannot come into the pool now."

"I am not going down to the locker room and tell her to put her clothes back on, so there," Polly said.

She was very angry, but she had also gotten a little scared.

"Then I'm going to have to tell your grandmother how nasty you've been."

"How nasty *I've* been?"

Mr. Diehl went up to the girl and put his hands on her shoulder as he often did to his students. "Look here now," he said. He did not realize how he was affecting the girl and how the water fell from him on her blouse. She looked at his biceps as they moved almost over her mouth and the way his chest rose and fell. She had always lowered her eyes when she met him in the hall, avoiding the sight of his wet, dripping quality, the many keys held in his hand, his whistle for the days when they practiced champion swimming. He had seemed to her like something that should always remain splashing about and breathing heavily in water.

"Polly, will you please cooperate with me," Mr. Diehl said.

"I don't think I can," she said.

He put down his arms in a gesture of despair. "Will you please, please just this once go down to the ladies' dressing room and tell that woman that you've made a mistake and that she can't come into the pool just now?"

Polly looked out now into the water where the commander's son was floating around by holding on to a rubber tire.

"I just can't tell her," Polly said, turning red.

"You can't tell her," Mr. Diehl observed. Then: "Look,

do you know who the commander is?"

"Well, doesn't everybody?" Polly answered.

"Do you know or don't you?" Mr. Diehl wanted to know. Some more water fell from him as he gesticulated, wetting her blouse and her arms a little, and she was sure that water continued to fall from him no matter how long he had been out of the pool. She could hear him breathing and she could not help noticing his chest rise and fall as though he were doing a special swimming feat just for her in this room.

"Polly!" he said.

"I can't! I can't!" she cried.

He could see now that there was something else here, perhaps fear of something, he could not tell, he did not want to know.

"You're not going to run into any difficulty in just telling her, are you, that you didn't know the rules and that she will have to wait until the lesson is over."

"I can't and I won't," Polly said, and she refused to look at him.

The commander's son was watching them from the middle of the shallow part of the pool, but he did not act as though he was impatient for the lesson to begin, and Polly remembered what a severe instructor Mr. Diehl was said to be. Sometimes while she had sat outside in the reception room she had heard Mr. Diehl shout all the way from the pool.

"Look, do we have to go all over this again?" Mr. Diehl said. "You know the commander."

"I know the commander, of course," she said.

"Do you know he is the most influential member of the club here?"

Polly did not say anything.

"He built this pool, Polly. Not your grandmother. Did you know that?"

She felt that she might weep now, so she did not say anything.

"Are you hearing me?" Mr. Diehl wanted to know.

"*Hearing* you!" she cried, distracted.

"All right now," he said, and he put his hand on her again and she thought some more drops of water fell from him.

"I can't see how anybody would know," she said. "How would the commander know if a young woman went into his pool. And what would his son out there care."

"His son doesn't like people in the pool when he is taking a lesson," Mr. Diehl explained. "He wants it strictly private, and the commander wants it that way too."

"And the commander pays you to want it that way also."

"Polly, I'm trying to be patient."

"I'm not going to tell her she can't come in," Polly said.

She stood nearer now to the edge of the pool away from his moving arms and chest and the dripping water that she felt still came off them.

"Step away from the edge, please, Polly," he said, and he took hold of her arm drawing her firmly over to him, in his old manner with special pupils when he was about to impart to them some special secret of swimming.

"Don't always touch me," she said, but so faintly that it was hardly a reproach.

"Polly, listen to me," Mr. Diehl was saying to her. "I've known you since you were a little girl. Right?"

"Known me?" Polly said, and she felt the words only come vaguely toward her now.

"Been a friend of your family, haven't I, for a good long time. Your grandmother knew me when I was only a boy. She paid for some of my tuition in college."

"College," Polly nodded to the last word she had heard, so that he would think she was listening.

"You'll feel all right about this, Polly, and you will, I know, help me now that I've explained it to you."

"No, I can't," she said, awake again.

"You can't what?" Mr. Diehl said.

"I can't is all," she said but she spoke, as she herself recognized, like a girl talking in her sleep.

The hothouse heat of the swimming pool and the close presence of Mr. Diehl, a man she had always instinctively avoided, had made her forget in a sense why they were standing here before the water. Somewhere in a dressing room, she remembered, there was a woman who in a little while was going to do something wrong that would displease Mr. Diehl, and suddenly she felt glad this was so.

"Mr. Diehl, I am going," she said, but she made no motion to leave, and he knew from her words that she was not going. They were going on talking, he knew. It was like his students, some of them said they could never be champions, but they always were. He made them so. Some of the timid ones said they could never swim, the water was terror to them, but they always did swim. Mr. Diehl had never known failure with anything. He never said this but he showed it.

"Now you listen to me," Mr. Diehl said. "All you have to do is go and tell her. She can sit outside with you and watch television."

"The set isn't working," Polly said, and she walked over close to the edge of the pool.

"Please come over here now," Mr. Diehl said, and he took hold of her and brought her over to where he had been standing. "Polly, I would never have believed this of you."

"Believed what?" she said, and her mind could not remember now again why exactly they were together here. She kept looking around as though perhaps she had duties she had forgotten somewhere. Then as she felt more and more unlike herself, she put her hand on Mr. Diehl's arm.

"Believed," he was saying, and she saw his white teeth near her as though the explanation of everything were in the teeth themselves—"believed you would act so incorrigible. So bad, Polly. Yes, that's the word. Bad."

"Incorrigible," she repeated, and she wondered what exactly that had always meant. It was a word that had passed before her eyes a few times but nobody had ever pronounced it to her.

"I would never want your grandmother to even know we

have had to have this long argument. I will never tell her."

"I will never tell her," Polly said, expressionless, drowsily echoing his words.

"Thank you, Polly, and of course I didn't mean to tell you you didn't have to. But listen to me."

She put her hand now very heavily on his arm and leaned there.

"Are you all right, Polly," he said, and she realized suddenly that it was the first time he had ever really been aware of her being anything at all, and now when it was too late, when she felt too bad to even tell him, he had begun to grow aware.

"Polly," he said.

"Yes, Mr. Diehl," she answered and suddenly he looked down at her hand on his arm, it was pressing there, and he had become, of course, conscious of it.

He did not know what to do, she realized, and ill as she felt, the pleasure of having made him uncomfortable soothed her. She knew she was going to be very ill, but she had had at least, then, this triumph, the champion was also uncomfortable.

"You'll go and tell her then," Mr. Diehl said, but she knew now that he was not thinking about the woman anymore. The woman, the lesson, the pool had all lost their meaning and importance now.

"Polly," he said.

"I will tell her," she managed to say, still holding him tight.

"Polly, what is it?" he exclaimed.

He took her arm off him roughly, and his eyes moved about the room as though he were looking for somebody to help. His eyes fell cursorily upon the commander's son, and then back to her, but it was already too late, she had begun to topple toward him, her hands closed over his arms, and her head went pushing into his chest, rushing him with a strength he had seldom felt before.

When they fell into the water it was very difficult for him to get hold of her at all. She had swallowed so much water, and she had struck at him so hard, and had said words all the time nobody could have understood or believed but him. It was her speaking and struggling, as he said later, which had caused her to swallow so much water.

He had had to give her partial artificial respiration, a thing he had not done really in all his life, although he had taken all the courses in it as befitted a champion swimmer.

"Get out of the pool for God's sake and call somebody," Mr. Diehl yelled to the commander's son, and the boy left off hanging to the rubber tire, and slowly began to climb out of the shallow water.

"Get some speed on there, for Christ's sake," he said.

"Yes, sir," the commander's son replied.

"I can't be responsible for this whole goddam thing," he shouted after the retreating boy.

"Now see here, Polly, for Christ's sake," Mr. Diehl began looking down at her.

She opened her eyes and looked at him.

"You certainly pulled one over me!" he cried looking at her, rage and fear on his mouth.

She lay there watching his chest move, feeling the drops of water falling over her from his body, and smelling behind the strong chemical odor of the pool the strong smell that must be Mr. Diehl himself, the champion.

"I'll go tell her now," Polly said.

Mr. Diehl stared at her.

"She must never come here at all," Polly said. "I think I see that now."

Mr. Diehl stretched out his hand to her to lift her up.

"Go away, please," she said. "Don't lean over me, please, and let the water fall from you on me. Please, please go back into the pool. I don't want you close now. Go back into the pool."

THE SWIMMER *by* JOHN CHEEVER

JOHN CHEEVER's (1912–1982) "The Swimmer" was written in 1964, after John F. Kennedy's assassination shook the American psyche. In it, a man decides to find his way home by swimming from pool to pool, but the journey takes him further than he could have imagined. Originally published in The New Yorker *and later included in the bestselling book* The Stories of John Cheever, *this tour de force was made into a movie in 1968 starring Burt Lancaster.*

IT WAS ONE OF THOSE MIDSUMMER SUNDAYS when everyone sits around saying, "I *drank* too much last night." You might have heard it whispered by the parishioners leaving church, heard it from the lips of the priest himself, struggling with his cassock in the *vestiarium*, heard it from the golf links and the tennis courts, heard it from the wildlife preserve where the leader of the Audubon group was suffering from a terrible hangover. "I *drank* too much," said Donald Westerhazy. "We all *drank* too much," said Lucinda Merrill. "It must have been the wine," said Helen Westerhazy. "I *drank* too much of that claret."

This was at the edge of the Westerhazys' pool. The pool, fed by an artesian well with a high iron content, was a pale shade of green. It was a fine day. In the west there was a massive stand of cumulus cloud so like a city seen from a distance—from the bow of an approaching ship—that it might have had a name. Lisbon.

Hackensack. The sun was hot. Neddy Merrill sat by the green water, one hand in it, one around a glass of gin. He was a slender man—he seemed to have the especial slenderness of youth—and while he was far from young he had slid down his banister that morning and given the bronze backside of Aphrodite on the hall table a smack, as he jogged toward the smell of coffee in his dining room. He might have been compared to a summer's day, particularly the last hours of one, and while he lacked a tennis racket or a sail bag the impression was definitely one of youth, sport, and clement weather. He had been swimming and now he was breathing deeply, stertorously as if he could gulp into his lungs the components of that moment, the heat of the sun, the intenseness of his pleasure. It all seemed to flow into his chest. His own house stood in Bullet Park, eight miles to the south, where his four beautiful daughters would have had their lunch and might be playing tennis. Then it occurred to him that by taking a dogleg to the southwest he could reach his home by water.

His life was not confining and the delight he took in this observation could not be explained by its suggestion of escape. He seemed to see, with a cartographer's eye, that string of swimming pools, that quasi-subterranean stream that curved across the county. He had made a discovery, a contribution to modern geography; he would name the stream Lucinda after his wife. He was not a practical joker nor was he a fool but he was determinedly original and had a vague and modest idea of himself as a legendary figure. The day was beautiful and it seemed to him that a long swim might enlarge and celebrate its beauty.

He took off a sweater that was hung over his shoulders and dove in. He had an inexplicable contempt for men who did not hurl themselves into pools. He swam a choppy crawl, breathing either with every stroke or every fourth stroke and counting somewhere well in the back of his mind the one-two one-two of a flutter kick. It was not a serviceable stroke for long distances but the domestication of swimming had saddled the sport with some customs and in his part of the world a crawl was customary. To be embraced and sustained by the light green water was less a pleasure, it seemed, than the resumption of a natural condition, and he would have liked to swim without trunks, but this was not possible considering his project. He hoisted himself up on the far curb—he never used the ladder—and started across the lawn. When Lucinda asked where he was going he said he was going to swim home.

The only maps and charts he had to go by were remembered or imaginary but these were clear enough. First there were the Grahams, the Hammers, the Lears, the Howlands, and the Crosscups. He would cross Ditmar Street to the Bunkers and come, after a short portage, to the Levys, the Welchers, and the public pool in Lancaster. Then there were the Hallorans, the Sachses, the Biswangers, Shirley Adams, the Gilmartins, and the Clydes. The day was lovely, and that he lived in a world so generously supplied with water seemed like a clemency, a beneficence. His heart was high and he ran across the grass. Making his way home by an uncommon route gave him the feeling that he was a pilgrim, an explorer, a man with a destiny, and he knew that he would find friends all along the way; friends would line the banks of the Lucinda River.

He went through a hedge that separated the Westerhazys' land from the Grahams', walked under some flowering apple trees, passed the shed that housed their pump and filter, and came out at the

Grahams' pool. "Why, Neddy," Mrs. Graham said, "what a marvelous surprise. I've been trying to get you on the phone all morning. Here, let me get you a drink." He saw then, like any explorer, that the hospitable customs and traditions of the natives would have to be handled with diplomacy if he was ever going to reach his destination. He did not want to mystify or seem rude to the Grahams nor did he have the time to linger there. He swam the length of their pool and joined them in the sun and was rescued, a few minutes later, by the arrival of two carloads of friends from Connecticut. During the uproarious reunions he was able to slip away. He went down by the front of the Grahams' house, stepped over a thorny hedge, and crossed a vacant lot to the Hammers'. Mrs. Hammer, looking up from her roses, saw him swim by although she wasn't quite sure who it was. The Lears heard him splashing past the open windows of their living room. The Howlands and the Crosscups were away. After leaving the Howlands' he crossed Ditmar Street and started for the Bunkers', where he could hear, even at that distance, the noise of a party.

The water refracted the sound of voices and laughter and seemed to suspend it in midair. The Bunkers' pool was on a rise and he climbed some stairs to a terrace where twenty-five or thirty men and women were drinking. The only person in the water was Rusty Towers, who floated there on a rubber raft. Oh, how bonny and lush were the banks of the Lucinda River! Prosperous men and women gathered by the sapphire-colored waters while caterer's men in white coats passed them cold gin. Overhead a red de Haviland trainer was circling around and around and around in the sky with something like the glee of a child in a swing. Ned felt a passing affection for the scene, a tenderness for the gathering, as if it was something he might touch. In the distance he heard thunder. As soon as Enid Bunker saw him she began to scream: "Oh, look who's here! What a marvelous surprise! When Lucinda said that you couldn't come I thought I'd die." She made her way to him through the crowd, and when they had finished kissing she led him to the bar, a progress that was slowed by the fact that he stopped to kiss eight or ten other women and shake the hands of as many men. A smiling bartender he had seen at a hundred parties gave him a gin and tonic and he stood by the bar for a moment, anxious not to get stuck in any conversation that would delay his voyage. When he seemed to be surrounded he dove in and swam close to the side to avoid colliding with Rusty's raft. At the far end of the pool he bypassed the Tomlinsons with a broad smile and jogged up the garden path. The gravel cut his feet but this was the only unpleasantness. The party was confined to the pool, and as he went toward the house he heard the brilliant, watery sound of voices fade, heard the noise of a radio from the Bunkers' kitchen, where someone was listening to a ball game. Sunday afternoon. He made his way through the parked cars and down the grassy border of their driveway to Alewives Lane. He did not want to be seen on the road in his bathing trunks but there was no traffic and he made the short distance to the Levys' driveway, marked with a PRIVATE PROPERTY sign and a green tube for *The New York Times*. All the doors and windows of the big house were open but there were no signs of life; not even a dog barked. He went around the side of the house to the pool and saw that the Levys had only recently left. Glasses and bottles and dishes of nuts were on a table at the deep end, where there was a bathhouse or gazebo, hung

Japanese lanterns. After swimming the pool he got himself a glass and poured a drink. It was his fourth or fifth drink and he had swum nearly half the length of the Lucinda River. He felt tired, clean, and pleased at that moment to be alone; pleased with everything.

It would storm. The stand of cumulus cloud—that city—had risen and darkened, and while he sat there he heard the percussiveness of thunder again. The de Haviland trainer was still circling overhead and it seemed to Ned that he could almost hear the pilot laugh with pleasure in the afternoon; but when there was another peal of thunder he took off for home. A train whistle blew and he wondered what time it had gotten to be. Four? Five? He thought of the provincial station at that hour, where a waiter, his tuxedo concealed by a raincoat, a dwarf with some flowers wrapped in newspaper, and a woman who had been crying would be waiting for the local. It was suddenly growing dark; it was that moment when the pin-headed birds seem to organize their song into some acute and knowledgeable recognition of the storm's approach. Then there was a fine noise of rushing water from the crown of an oak at his back, as if a spigot there had been turned. Then the noise of fountains came from the crowns of all the tall trees. Why did he love storms, what was the meaning of his excitement when the door sprang open and the rain wind fled rudely up the stairs, why had the simple task of shutting the windows of an old house seemed fitting and urgent, why did the first watery notes of a storm wind have for him the unmistakable sound of good news, cheer, glad tidings? Then there was an explosion, a smell of cordite, and rain lashed the Japanese lanterns that Mrs. Levy had bought in Kyoto the year before last, or was it the year before that?

He stayed in the Levys' gazebo until the storm had passed. The rain had cooled the air and he shivered. The force of the wind had stripped a maple of its red and yellow leaves and scattered them over the grass and the water. Since it was midsummer the tree must be blighted, and yet he felt a peculiar sadness at this sign of autumn. He braced his shoulders, emptied his glass, and started for the Welchers' pool. This meant crossing the Lindleys' riding ring and he was surprised to find it overgrown with grass and all the jumps dismantled. He wondered if the Lindleys had sold their horses or gone away for the summer and put them out to board. He seemed to remember having heard something about the Lindleys and their horses but the memory was unclear. On he went, barefoot through the wet grass, to the Welchers', where he found their pool was dry.

This breach in his chain of water disappointed him absurdly, and he felt like some explorer who seeks a torrential headwater and finds a dead stream. He was disappointed and mystified. It was common enough to go away for the summer but no one ever drained his pool. The Welchers had definitely gone away. The pool furniture was folded, stacked, and covered with a tarpaulin. The bathhouse was locked. All the windows of the house were shut, and when he went around to the driveway in front he saw a FOR SALE sign nailed to a tree. When had he last heard from the Welchers—when, that is, had he and Lucinda last regretted an invitation to dine with them? It seemed only a week or so ago. Was his memory failing or had he so disciplined it in the repression of unpleasant facts that he had damaged his sense of the truth? Then in the distance he heard the sound of a tennis game. This cheered him, cleared away all his apprehensions and let him regard the overcast sky and the cold air with indifference. This was the day that Neddy Merrill swam across the county. That was the day! He started off then for his most difficult portage.

Had you gone for a Sunday afternoon ride that day you might have seen him, close to naked, standing on the shoulders of Route 424, waiting for a chance to cross. You might have wondered if he was the victim of foul play, had his car broken down, or was he merely a fool. Standing barefoot in the deposits of the highway—beer cans, rags, and blowout patches—exposed to all kinds of ridicule, he seemed pitiful. He had known when he started that this was a part of his journey—it had been on his maps—but confronted with the lines of traffic, worming through the summery light, he found himself unprepared. He was laughed at, jeered at, a beer can was thrown at him, and he had no dignity or humor to bring to the situation. He could have gone back, back to the Westerhazys', where Lucinda would still be sitting in the sun. He had signed nothing, vowed nothing, pledged nothing, not even to himself. Why, believing as he did, that all human obduracy was susceptible to common sense, was he unable to turn back? Why was he determined to complete his journey even if it meant putting his life in danger? At what point had this prank, this joke, this piece of horseplay become serious? He could not go back, he could not even recall with any clearness the green water at the Westerhazys', the sense of inhaling the day's components, the friendly and relaxed voices saying that they had *drunk* too much. In the space of an hour, more or less, he had covered a distance that made his return impossible.

An old man, tooling down the highway at fifteen miles an hour, let him get to the middle of the road, where there was a grass divider. Here he was exposed to the ridicule of the northbound traffic, but after ten or fifteen minutes he was able to cross. From here he had only a short walk to the Recreation Center at the edge of the village of Lancaster, where there were some handball courts and a public pool.

The effect of the water on voices, the illusion of brilliance and suspense, was the same here as it had been at the Bunkers' but the sounds here were louder, harsher, and more shrill, and as soon as he entered the crowded enclosure he was confronted with regimentation. "ALL SWIMMERS MUST TAKE A SHOWER BEFORE USING THE POOL. ALL SWIMMERS MUST USE THE FOOTBATH. ALL SWIMMERS MUST WEAR THEIR IDENTIFICATION DISKS." He took a shower, washed his feet in a cloudy and bitter solution, and made his way to the edge of the water. It stank of chlorine and looked to him like a sink. A pair of lifeguards in a pair of towers blew police whistles at what seemed to be regular intervals and abused the swimmers through a public address system. Neddy remembered the sapphire water at the Bunkers' with longing and thought that he might contaminate himself—damage his own prosperousness and charm—by swimming in this murk, but he reminded himself that he was an explorer, a pilgrim, and that this was merely a stagnant bend in the Lucinda River. He dove, scowling with distaste, into the chlorine and had to swim with his head above water to avoid collisions, but even so he was bumped into, splashed, and jostled. When he got to the shallow end both lifeguards were shouting at him: "Hey, you, you without the identification disk, get outa the water." He did, but they had no way of pursuing him and he went through the reek of suntan oil and chlorine out through the hurricane fence and passed the handball courts. By crossing the road he entered the wooded part of the Halloran estate. The woods were not cleared and the footing was treacherous and difficult until he reached the lawn and the clipped beech hedge that encircled their pool.

The Hallorans were friends, an elderly couple of enormous wealth who seemed to bask in the suspicion that they might be Communists. They were zealous reformers but they were not Communists, and yet when they were accused, as they sometimes were, of subversion, it seemed to gratify and excite them. Their beech hedge was yellow and he guessed this had been blighted like the Levys' maple. He called hullo, hullo, to warn the Hallorans of his approach, to palliate his invasion of their privacy. The Hallorans, for reasons that had never been explained to him, did not wear bathing suits. No explanations were in order, really. Their nakedness was a detail in their uncompromising zeal for reform and he stepped politely out of his trunks before he went through the opening in the hedge.

Mrs. Halloran, a stout woman with white hair and a serene face, was reading the *Times*. Mr. Halloran was taking beech leaves out of the water with a scoop. They seemed not surprised or displeased to see him. Their pool was perhaps the oldest in the country, a fieldstone rectangle, fed by a brook. It had no filter or pump and its waters were the opaque gold of the stream.

"I'm swimming across the county," Ned said.

"Why, I didn't know one could," exclaimed Mrs. Halloran.

"Well, I've made it from the Westerhazys'," Ned said. "That must be about four miles."

He left his trunks at the deep end, walked to the shallow end, and swam this stretch. As he was pulling himself out of the water he heard Mrs. Halloran say, "We've been *terribly* sorry to hear about all your misfortunes, Neddy."

"My misfortunes?" Ned asked. "I don't know what you mean."

"Why, we heard that you'd sold the house and that your poor children..."

"I don't recall having sold the house," Ned said, "and the girls are at home."

"Yes," Mrs. Halloran sighed. "Yes..." Her voice filled the air with an unseasonable melancholy and Ned spoke briskly. "Thank you for the swim."

"Well, have a nice trip," said Mrs. Halloran.

Beyond the hedge he pulled on his trunks and fastened them. They were loose and he wondered if, during the space of an afternoon, he could have lost some weight. He was cold and he was tired and the naked Hallorans and their dark water had depressed him. The swim was too much for his strength but how could he have guessed this, sliding down the banister that morning and sitting in the Westerhazys' sun? His arms were lame. His legs felt rubbery and ached at the joints. The worst of it was the cold in his bones and the feeling that he might never be warm again. Leaves were falling down around him and he smelled wood smoke on the wind. Who would be burning wood at this time of year?

He needed a drink. Whiskey would warm him, pick him up, carry him through the last of his journey, refresh his feeling that it was original and valorous to swim across the county. Channel swimmers took brandy. He needed a stimulant. He crossed the lawn in front of the Hallorans' house and went down a little path to where they had built a house for their only daughter, Helen, and her husband, Eric Sachs. The Sachses' pool was small and he found Helen and her husband there.

"Oh, *Neddy,*" Helen said. "Did you lunch at Mother's?"

"Not *really,*" Ned said. "I *did* stop to see your parents." This seemed to be explanation enough. "I'm terribly sorry to break in on you like this but I've taken a chill and I wonder if you'd give me a drink."

"Why, I'd *love* to," Helen said, "but there hasn't been anything in this house to drink since Eric's operation. That was three years ago."

Was he losing his memory, had his gift for concealing painful facts let him forget that he had sold his house, that his children were in trouble, and that his friend had been ill?

His eyes slipped from Eric's face to his abdomen, where he saw three pale, sutured scars, two of them at least a foot long. Gone was his navel, and what, Neddy thought, would the roving hand, bed-checking one's gifts at 3 A.M., make of a belly with no navel, no link to birth, this breach in the succession?

"I'm sure you can get a drink at the Biswangers'," Helen said. "They're having an enormous do. You can hear it from here. Listen!"

She raised her head and from across the road, the lawns, the gardens, the woods, the fields, he heard again the brilliant noise of voices over water. "Well, I'll get wet," he said, still feeling that he had no freedom of choice about his means of travel. He dove into the Sachses' cold water and, gasping, close to drowning, made his way from one end of the pool to the other. "Lucinda and I want *terribly* to see you," he said over his shoulder, his face set toward the Biswangers'. "We're sorry it's been so long and we'll call you *very* soon."

He crossed some fields to the Biswangers' and the sounds of revelry there. They would be honored to give him a drink, they would be happy to give him a drink. The Biswangers invited him and Lucinda for dinner four times a year, six weeks in advance. They were always rebuffed and yet they continued to send out their invitations, unwilling to comprehend the rigid and undemocratic realities of their society. They were the sort of people who discussed the price of things at cocktails, exchanged market tips during dinner, and after dinner told dirty stories to mixed company. They did not belong to Neddy's set—they were not even on Lucinda's Christmas-card list. He went toward their pool with feelings of indifference, charity, and some unease, since it seemed to be getting dark and these were the longest days of the year. The party when he joined it was noisy and large. Grace Biswanger was the kind of hostess who asked the optometrist, the veterinarian, the real-estate dealer, and the dentist. No one was swimming and the twilight, reflected on the water of the pool, had a wintry gleam. There was a bar and he started for this. When Grace Biswanger saw him she came toward him, not affectionately as he had every right to expect, but bellicosely.

"Why, this party has everything," she said loudly, "including a gate crasher."

She could not deal him a social blow—there was no question about this and he did not flinch. "As a gate crasher," he asked politely, "do I rate a drink?"

"Suit yourself," she said. "You don't seem to pay much attention to invitations."

She turned her back on him and joined some guests, and he went to the bar and ordered a whiskey. The bartender served him but he served him rudely. His was a world in which the caterers' men kept the social score, and to be rebuffed by a part-time barkeep meant that he had suffered some loss of social esteem. Or perhaps the man was new and uninformed. Then he heard Grace at his back say: "They went for broke overnight—nothing but income—and he showed up drunk one Sunday and asked us to loan him five thousand dollars..." She was always talking about money. It was worse than eating your peas off a knife. He dove into the pool, swam its length and went away.

The next pool on his list, the last but two, belonged to his old mistress, Shirley Adams. If he had suffered any injuries at the Biswangers' they would be cured here. Love—sexual roughhouse in fact—was the supreme elixir, the pain killer, the brightly colored pill that would put the spring back into his step, the joy of life in his heart. They had had an affair last week, last month, last year. He couldn't remember. It was he who had broken it off, his was the upper hand, and he stepped through the gate of the wall that surrounded her pool with nothing so considered as self-confidence. It seemed in a way to be his pool, as the lover, particularly the illicit lover, enjoys the possessions of his mistress with an authority unknown to holy matrimony. She was there, her hair the color of brass, but her figure, at the edge of the lighted, cerulean water, excited in him no profound memories. It had been, he thought, a lighthearted affair, although she had wept when he broke it off. She seemed confused to see him and he wondered if she was still wounded. Would she, God forbid, weep again?

"What do you want?" she asked.

"I'm swimming across the county."

"Good Christ. Will you ever grow up?

"What's the matter?"

"If you've come here for money," she said, "I won't give you another cent."

"You could give me a drink."

"I could but I won't. I'm not alone."

"Well, I'm on my way."

He dove in and swam the pool, but when he tried to haul himself up onto the curb he found that the strength in his arms and shoulders had gone, and he paddled to the ladder and climbed out. Looking over his shoulder he saw, in the lighted bathhouse, a young man. Going out onto the dark lawn he smelled chrysanthemums or marigolds—some stubborn autumnal fragance—on the night air, strong as gas. Looking overhead he saw that the stars had come out, but why should he seem to see Andromeda, Cepheus, and Cassiopeia? What had become of the constellations of midsummer? He began to cry.

It was probably the first time in his adult life that he had ever cried, certainly the first time in his life that he had ever felt so miserable, cold, tired, and bewildered. He could not understand the rudeness of the caterers' barkeep or the rudeness of a mistress who had come to him on her knees and showered his trousers with tears. He had swum too long, he had been immersed too long, and his nose and his throat were sore from the water. What he needed then was a drink, some company, and some clean, dry clothes, and while he could have cut directly across the road to his home he went on to the Gilmartins' pool. Here, for the first time in his life, he did not dive but went down the steps into the icy water and swam a hobbled sidestroke that he might have learned as a youth. He staggered with fatigue on his way to the Clydes' and paddled the length of their pool, stopping again and again with his hand on the curb to rest. He climbed up the ladder and wondered if he had the strength to get home. He had done what he wanted, he had swum the county, but he was so stupefied with exhaustion that his triumph seemed vague. Stooped, holding on to the gateposts for support, he turned up the driveway of his own house.

The place was dark. Was it so late that they had all gone to bed? Had Lucinda stayed at the Westerhazys' for supper? Had the girls joined her there or gone someplace else? Hadn't they agreed, as they usually did on Sunday, to regret all their invitations and stay at home? He tried the garage doors to see what cars were in but the doors were locked and rust came off the handles onto his hands. Going toward the house, he saw that the force of the thunderstorm had knocked one of the rain gutters loose. It hung down over the front door like an umbrella rib, but it could be fixed in the morning. The house was locked, and he thought that the stupid cook or the stupid maid must have locked the place up until he remembered that it had been sometime since they had employed a maid or a cook. He shouted, pounded on the door, tried to force it with his shoulder, and then, looking in at the windows, saw that the place was empty.

THE ISABEL FISH *by* JULIE ORRINGER

"The Isabel Fish" first appeared in The Yale Review *and shows how a teenage girl struggles to learn scuba and make peace with her grief-stricken brother after an accidental drowning. Quietly confident and hauntingly compassionate, this story shows why JULIE ORRINGER (b. 1973) has been called a major new talent.*

I am the canker of my brother Sage's life. He has told me so in no uncertain terms. Tonight as we eat hamburgers in the car on the way to our first scuba class, he can't stop talking about the horrible fates that might befall me underwater. This, even though he knows how scared I am after what happened last November.

"You could blow out your eardrums," he says. "Or your lungs might implode from the pressure."

"Shut up, Sage," I say.

"Did you know that one in twelve scuba divers gets attacked by sharks?"

"Not in a pool," I say.

Sage is sixteen, plays drums, smokes unfiltered cigarettes, and drives his beat-up black Pinto to school every morning, with me practically hanging onto the rear bumper because I'm slow getting ready. I know he sees me as a problem, a younger and more stupid version of himself, and a girl, not popular, sort of plain, with my hair pulled back in a knot most days and a walk some people make fun of. He used to be cruel to me in the normal sibling sense, but now it's worse. He is far from forgetting Isabel, and who can blame him? She'd been his girlfriend for six months before the accident, and it's only been four months since. Four months is a short time in the grand scheme of things, shorter than it's taken Sage's shaved hair to grow long again, shorter than it's taken me to grow twenty-six fighting fish from eggs for my science experiment, "The Relationship Between Aggression and Hypertension in *B. Splendens*." I got the eggs one month before the accident. When I showed them to Isabel, red and clumped together in a small tank, she laughed and said she could hardly believe that bunch of caviar would become real animals. Well, guess what? They are now.

Every day I feed them and give them liquid vitamins and alter their blood pressure with drugs, and still get my homework done and make it to school just as if I were fully recovered. Which I'm not, in many ways. My parents are aware of this. As a kind of remedy, they came up with the idea of a spring-break trip to St. Maarten in the Dutch Virgin Islands. We're not a family that tends to take spring-break trips. We've never taken one, in fact. So when my father rose from his chair at the dinner table and asked Sage and me what we thought about going to St. Maarten, I took it to mean we'd reached a state of emergency.

They've been talking about the problem between Sage and me for months, our psychologist mom trying to give us counseling, our dentist dad distracting us with jokes. Now scuba lessons, in preparation for the trip. What our parents don't understand is that their son has become cruel and unusual, and he shows no sign of changing.

We stop at a red light and Sage eats a handful of fries all at once. I stare out the window. Beneath the streetlights, snowflakes swarm like moths. It's hard to remember a time when it wasn't winter. Sage crumples the greasy bag in his lap and tosses it into the back seat.

"Anyone could fuck with your tank underwater," he says. "One turn of a knob. That's all it would take."

I lower my sandwich from the eating position. The feeling I remember is being in Isabel's car with the water coming in, filling my mouth with its cold fishy taste, and me groping in the dark for my seat belt, my lungs already hot and tight, and Isabel in the seat beside me bleeding into the darkness. Sage must know what I'm thinking about, but he won't look at me or say anything more. He revs the motor hard, three times, and then the light turns green and we're off.

At the YMCA I follow Sage into the lobby, where the chlorine smell of the pool stops me cold. Sage doesn't notice. He doesn't even look back. He just disappears down the hall toward the men's locker room, leaving me standing there alone. I look at the trophies in a glass display case, silver swimmers and wrestlers and softball players, all frozen mid-sport. The lobby is full of kids and old people milling around and getting snacks from the machines. I sit down on a bench and think about my tropicals, my pet fish, the ones I don't do experiments on. It calms me to imagine them swimming in their pH-balanced environments, the clown loaches loaching around near the bottom of the freshwater tank, the pearl gouramis flirting in a stand of bamboo plant. I have a marine tank too, with three yellow tangs and two fireworks anemones and a dusky angelfish. Tonight, for the first time, I'll begin to know what my fish have known all their lives: how to breathe underwater.

When I get calm enough I go to the women's locker room and find an empty locker. All around me, teenagers are tying back their hair and putting their naked bodies into tank suits. Someone in the next row of lockers says she heard we're not actually scuba-ing today, just learning about the equipment and doing some laps with fins to get used to the feeling. That makes me feel a little better. When I go to St. Maarten I will have my own fins, according to my father; we have already looked at examples in the window of Arbor Valley Sea and Ski, and I have admired a translucent blue pair with a matching mask. They seem like they'd be almost invisible underwater.

Looking at those fins made it easy to imagine swimming, but now that I'm here at the Y it seems crazy. Sure, in St. Maarten there are a lot of fish you can see living their lives around coral reefs if you happen to know how to scuba. That kind of thing is attractive to an ichthyophile like me. But I am also a person who almost drowned. When my dad told us about St. Maarten, with its great diving, I wanted to ask if he and my mother were crazy. Did they think I would voluntarily walk into the ocean and let it close over my head? Before I could respond, my mother said she'd found us a scuba certification class at the Y. She and my father gave Sage and me these hopeful, anxious looks. I was speechless for a moment, and then I blurted, "Scuba?"

"We think it'll be good for you," my mother said. "We think it'll help you form positive associations with water."

"You don't have to dive at all, of course," my father said. "But we hope you'll consider it."

After all their planning, how could I say no thanks? Even Sage, who for months had hated everything, seemed interested in the trip. The next day he called the Y and signed us up for scuba lessons, and the rest of the week he walked around with a strange half-smile on his face. Now I think he was already coming up with mean things to say to me, things that would make me feel as scared as I do now.

As I get into my tank suit I cannot help noticing the mistakes of my body. The magazine look nowadays is breasts but no hips; I am the opposite. Thin, still, but with hipbones like cup handles. My chest is too flat, my legs too skinny, and there is a scar running the length of my left thigh. Under the water, car metal sliced me in a neat line. I didn't even feel it. Only at the edge of the pond afterward did I look down and see the blood. One doctor sewed it badly in the emergency room, and another had to take the stitches out the next day and do it again. Meanwhile I was in a kind of trance, not wanting to believe what my parents had told me about Isabel. Now the scar is thin and white, like a dress seam. I turn my leg back and forth, looking. A dark-haired girl in a red suit notices, then glances away.

"It's okay," I say. "It's just a scar. You can look if you want to."

She bends down and looks, and when she meets my eyes again she seems unimpressed. "I also have a scar," she says. She pulls her hair up to show me a jagged pink keloid at the back of her neck. It looks as if someone tried to cut her head off and failed.

"Wow," I say.

The girl looks about my age, but she speaks like the Romanian women who work at the bakery near our house. "My sister threw a broken glass," she says. "She was little, six years old."

"Ouch," I say. "Are you in the scuba class?"

"Yes," she says. "You?"

"Me and my brother."

I see her giving me a side-eye look, and it occurs to me that she might recognize my picture from the news or newspapers. Then I realize this is an extremely egotistical thought, given how many unfortunate things there are on the news and in newspapers over four months. She locks her locker and throws her towel over her shoulder, then adjusts the strap of her goggles. I realize there are probably only ten or fifteen minutes between me and the experience of getting underwater again. For a moment I wish my mother or father were here. Then I remember I am fourteen and lucky to be alive.

"Ready?" the girl says. And I am, I think.

But nothing has prepared me for the experience of actually seeing the pool. It seems to go on forever, lanes and lanes of water strung with red-and-white dividers. Lines of black tile stretch along the bottom, all the way to the diving part of the deep end, where the water darkens to a holy blue. Sage is nowhere to be seen. I sit down on a bench and put my head between my knees to feel better. All around, the echoes of voices bounce off the water and the high ceiling. I'm hoping Sage will come out and just sit near me, and not say anything about messing with my tank, but when I look up again I see him talking to some guys at the other end of the bleachers, as far away from me as possible.

The instructor is a college student, a girl with blond hair and muscular thighs. She wears two tank suits like they do on swim teams. My brother is obviously looking at her breasts, which surprises me because of how much I know he still misses Isabel. But I suppose certain things do not go on hold. As we learn the names of different parts of the gear, we are required to take notes in the small notebooks we bought for the class. The girl in the red suit sits beside me writing very neatly in her notebook. She writes *buoyancy control device*, *pressure gauge*, *primary regulator*, *mouthpiece*, with small pictures next to each word. I try to make mine as neat as hers. We learn what seems to be a basic fact but one I never knew, that scuba stands for Self-Contained Underwater Breathing Apparatus. Over on his end of the bleachers, Sage is writing fast and using a lot of pages. Later he won't be able to read what he wrote and will come crawling to me for help. In my notes I write *Too bad your handwriting sucks so much, Sage!* but then I cross it out, thinking of how Isabel saved all of Sage's notes to her, those scrawls on torn notebook paper that they found in a Japanese box under her bed.

When we have gone through the basic principles of the equipment, the instructor invites us down to select a pair of flippers. At first it looks like there won't be enough to go around. I wait until everyone has a pair, then take my own, realizing nothing will save me now from going in the water. The girl in the red suit clomps around with her toes turned out. "Like a duck," she says, and smiles at me.

We learn that the fins are supposed to fit snugly but without smashing our toes. Everyone puts them on and sits at the side of the pool to get the feel of them in the water. The instructor tells us we'll have fifteen minutes of laps and then a water polo game to increase our agility. It sounds like fun, and it should be fun, but I look at my feet waving in the water and wonder if I'm going to brick. It's one of the main reasons I didn't want to take the class, the possibility of me freaking out and Sage having to take me home while everyone else learns deep dives and repressurization. Sage probably expects me to freak out too. I watch him moving his feet back and forth in the water with great concentration. Just to spite him I decide I will not brick. Cognitive therapy, like what my mother had me do to get comfortable in the bath again: I will not drown here with all these people watching, and me a good swimmer, and with fins on my feet. At least today there will be no tank for Sage to fuck with underwater. The girl in the red suit grins at me as we splash our feet in the pool. If I brick, I tell myself, this nice Romanian kid will think I'm an idiot.

We all line up to swim laps, starting at the deep end of the pool. Why we have to start at the deep end is quickly explained:

We're practicing our roll entry, where we have to crouch down with our backs facing the water, the way you go backward off the boat with all your gear on. If the water were too shallow, people might clonk their heads. Once you fall in you're supposed to orient yourself and swim down to the shallow end of the pool, kicking in the fast smooth way you do when you're wearing fins, and then get out and wait by the starting blocks.

This would be a good time to have a brother who cared if you were feeling shitty about getting into the water, but Sage is not that kind of brother. He won't stand anywhere near me. I go to the back of my group, hoping to have more time to get calm, and I think about my sea anemones because they are the calmest of the fish, though technically they are not fish at all but flowerlike polyps of the order Actiniaria. My two anemones, a purple and a pink *Pachycerianthus mana*, are similar in size but have different personalities. The pink is shy and smart and retracts its tentacles fast when something brushes by, but the purple is slower and perhaps less smart, though when it waves its arms it looks more graceful. Thinking of them makes me forget that I am about to fall backward into a pool, gallons and gallons of water, with at least thirty people watching, including my brother and the girl in that red suit, who has already done her roll entry and is now whip-kicking toward the lighter blue of the shallow end. Sage shoots me a look that says *You'd better not fuck up.* Then it's his group's turn to fall in, and he crouches at the edge and goes backward at the count of three. It's true that I could learn something from his confidence, if only he weren't always using it to smash me down.

Finally it's my turn. The instructor gives me a smile and pats my shoulder. I stand at the edge of the pool and pretend there is no water behind me at all, but instead my bed with the quilt I wrap myself in when I get depressed, and there will be no moment when the water covers me, and I will not remember the plunge in the car as we hit the surface and started going down. The instructor begins the countdown. I bend my knees. The flippers on my feet are cold and awkward. Somewhere at the other end of the pool, my brother is watching.

"Go!" cries the instructor, and I push off the edge. There is a whirling moment as the high-up natatorium ceiling flies by, and then I plunge backward into the cold shock of water and sink almost immediately. My arms and legs go numb with panic, and my mouth fills with the bleach taste of pool water. It feels like I'm going down to that place where I was before, the cold dark pond on that November night, and if I go down farther still I will reach Isabel, her hair floating mermaidlike around her. Up above there is a commotion of water, and the echo of shouting, and then the shadow of someone following me down.

In the car on the way home, Sage says nothing. He might as well be made of igneous rock. I keep thinking of the way the red-suit girl looked, scared and sorry for me, when they heaved me up onto the deck of the pool. Through the rest of the class, as everyone finished the laps and played water polo, I was in the locker room getting dry and dressed and then waiting on a wooden bench. All I could think about was how mad Sage would be on our way home. Once again I'd given him evidence of what a non-hero I am. Both of us can plainly see how I might have failed at a crucial moment, missed my chance to pull Isabel out of the car. The thing the police told him, the thing the autopsy confirmed, was that she was already unconscious and wedged into the crushed driver's side, the steering wheel pinning her ribs. It might have been possible for me to pull her out, but if I'd tried I might have drowned too. And she might not have survived anyway. Everyone says I did the right thing by swimming up and climbing out to run for help. Still I know Sage blames me, and in my heart I agree.

At home Sage goes upstairs and closes the door of his room, leaving me in the hallway to explain everything to my dad with his anxious smile, and our mother in her nightgown and socks. After I tell them, we sit down together on the couch. They wedge me in between them the way they used to when I was little. My dad puts an arm around my shoulder. My mother looks miserable, as if she's done this to me herself.

"You swam, though," my father says. "Didn't you?"

"I fell in the water and sank."

"That's a start," he says.

My mother gives him a stern look. We all know that falling in the water and sinking is hardly an accomplishment, and my mother's not the kind of person who pretends something is what it's not.

"I don't think scuba's for me," I say. "Maybe someday, but not now."

"But think about the fish you'll get to see in St. Maarten if you do finish the class," my father says. "Otherwise it'll just be me and Sage diving, while you and your mom play tennis."

"Don't push her, Robert," my mother says. "She knows what she can do."

"I'm not. I'm just stating the facts."

"Anyway," says my mother, "what's so bad about tennis?"

"Nothing," my father says. "But it doesn't have quite the appeal, for some people, of seeing a coral reef with triggerfish and orange spiny tangs and things of that nature."

"It's up to you, Maddy," my mother says. "We're not going to make you dive if you don't want to."

I tell them I'll think about it, and that seems to satisfy them. We get up and they hug me goodnight. Then my mother goes up to check on Sage, who is undoubtedly sitting in his room thinking about Isabel, and my father kisses me on the top of my head and goes into his study.

When I climb the stairs, I see a line of light at the bottom of my brother's door. From inside I can hear the rise and fall of his voice and my mother's. I stand still outside the door, listening. "It's not my responsibility," I hear my brother say, and my mother says something too quiet for me to make out. Very faintly, from the crack at the bottom of the door, come the fumes of cigarette smoke. I imagine them both in there smoking, my mom trying to blow it out the window so as not to smoke up the carpets and furniture, Sage not caring. I'm not much of a smoker. Once or twice I had puffs of Isabel's cigarettes in the garage during band-practice afternoons, but it was never as great as she made it look. Sometimes my mom would come out and smoke a thin cigarette of her own, sitting there on the car bumper and telling us about high school and old boyfriends, stories that tended to embarrass me. But Isabel laughed like my mom was another high school girl, and my mom, who always secretly seemed to distrust Sage's girlfriends, liked Isabel in return.

Finally I hear Sage tell my mom he's going to bed, and I skeet off down the hall before I am discovered. In my bedroom the fish are awake, making their rounds. The pink anemone is shut tight, and the purple one waves smoothly. The loaches are mouthing algae from the side of the freshwater tank. Beside them, my science-experiment fish seem to be sleeping in their plastic containers. Even when they're still I could watch them all night—the red-purple of their bodies, the tiny flick of their gills. The control-group fish look particularly tired, their fins not even finning. Perhaps their natural aggressions have exhausted them. I've tried to learn everything they can teach me about the chemistry of anger, what makes it ebb and flow, how it can be controlled. Twice a day I give them their special food and make behavioral observations and take their blood pressure. It's easier than you might think to take the blood pressure of a fish. Hewlett-Packard makes a sensor that can feel the force and rate of their pulse through the water. My father likes to ask me where's the little cuff, where's the little stethoscope. He thinks it's a big joke that some fighting fish seem to die of heart attacks from so much aggression, but it's no joke if you're a fighting fish.

To be professional I tried not to name my science experiment fish, but then I realized the coincidence of there being twenty-six of them, one for each letter of the alphabet, and now they all have names. Amy, Ben, Carl, Dan, and so forth. I won't, of course, use any of their names in my report; they all have scientific tags like "Control 17." The Isabel fish is in the experimental group, fed a calming drug a couple times a day. She has a blue mark at the center of her dorsal fin, a distinction I happen to know is very rare in members of her sex and species. The Sage fish is a control, reddish-brown in color, mean and small with high blood pressure. At times, when I have been particularly mad at my brother, I've been tempted to give the Sage fish little zaps with an electrode. As a scientist, though, I have refrained.

I roll up my sleeve, put an arm down in the marine tank, and tear off a leaf from one of the underwater plants. After rinsing it in a stream of distilled water, I use it to stroke the backs of the experimental fish. No one pets fish, I know, but these fish seem to enjoy it. It calms *me*, anyhow. I pity these fish, them not knowing what's going on and being in isolation except during the aggression trials. As I stroke them I think about the girl in the red bathing suit, the look she gave me as I lay coughing on the pool deck, and then later, in the locker room, how she said in her Romanian accent that she hoped I was *ollright*. That is the normal way of things, trying to make a person feel less bad about a stupid thing they've done, as opposed to Sage's way, which is to make you feel worse.

He wasn't always that way, particularly when Isabel was around. One time the two of them caught me singing "Louie Louie" in the garage when I thought I was alone. Isabel laughed, but not in a mean way. She had her electric bass there in the garage beside Sage's drum kit, and she picked it up and asked what other songs I knew and did I want to sing while she played. She was like that, taking something I considered embarrassing and trying to make it into something cool. She said I had a retro voice like girl bands in the sixties, and she convinced Sage to play drums while she and I belted out a couple of verses of "Respect." We sounded good. Even Sage said so. Nowadays he would sooner spit in my face than let me sing with him. I keep telling myself he cannot be angry at me forever, though maybe I am wrong.

The next morning at the breakfast table, Sage does not appear. My father, eating oatmeal with honey, tells me Sage has one of his headaches and that I'll have to catch the bus to school. Sage gets random migraines that lay him out flat for days.

As I eat my Cheerios I feel bad for my brother, even though he's been mean to me for months. Being sick is something he and I have tended to do together. Last spring, when neither of us could imagine anything like the accident ever happening in our lives, we both came down with mononucleosis. We spent a week at home by ourselves, ordering videos our parents would never have let us watch and shooting Chloraseptic into each other's throats. Years before that, we had the chicken pox together. Sage made an oxygen chamber for us out of blankets and couch cushions and told me I was not allowed to leave. We stayed in there for hours, watching cartoons and sweating through our fevers, while our mother brought us soup and juice and Children's Tylenol. This was in our house in Baltimore, with one very small room for both of us. We slept in bunk beds and played with the same toys and even wore some of the same clothes.

When I finish breakfast my father asks me to take Sage some Imitrex and a glass of water. I go up to his room but he's in the bathroom, so I leave the pills and water on his desk. As I'm leaving I see Isabel's bass lying beside the bed. Her parents let Sage keep it after she died, which makes me think they must have known how much she loved him. I pick it up and touch the smooth neck and the polished black body. The name ISABEL is painted on the bass in silver paint, my brother's work, the letters long and crooked and childlike. I pull the strap over my head, feeling the weight of the bass in my shoulders. Then the bathroom door opens. Sage comes out in just pajama pants, his hair wild. When he sees me with the bass he crosses the room in three swift steps, grabs the bass by the neck, and jerks the strap from around my shoulders.

"Don't *ever* come in here," he says, his ribs pumping, his eyes glassed with hate and headache. "Get out, or I'll fucking kill you."

I go to the door. "There's some medicine on the desk."

He gives me a shove toward the hall. When he slams the door behind me, the whole wall shakes.

I go to my bathroom, close the door, and sit down on the edge of the bathtub. Though I don't have time to cry, I cry anyway. My father says goodbye to me through the bathroom door, and I say goodbye back, trying to make my voice sound normal. To my surprise, he buys it. I wait until I hear the garage door go down, and then I wash my face, say goodbye to the fish, and get my books and lunch money. I am late again. I have to run through the snow to catch the bus, and along the way my shoe comes off and I take one cold wet step. Everyone finds this hilarious, even the bus driver.

School offers me no comfort today. In History we watch a movie about the Civil War, with cheerful fife music and reenactments of people being shot to pieces. During Biology there's a fire drill. We all stand outside shivering for half an hour. In Math I find out that the two sisters I usually eat lunch with, Salma and Meena Padmanabhan, are out of school for a Hindu holiday. So at lunchtime I go down to the loading dock near Auto Shop to smoke a crushed cigarette stolen from Sage's pack. It's bent at the end and smells like raisins. I try to light it with someone's thrown-away Bic, but the lighter won't stay lit and the cigarette's too wet and stale to do anything. I sit down on a milk crate and watch the wind blow dead leaves and bits of hard dirty snow.

This afternoon there are only two other kids out smoking: Mike Milldow, a tall stringy kid in a plaid flannel shirt, and Althea London, a girl with chopped black hair and a purple eyebrow ring. Althea, a senior, used to be friends with Isabel. She's talking to Mike about some band called Manila, which she likes and he hates. "They're even worse than Hangtooth," Mike says, and Althea says, "Hangtooth rocks." She blows smoke and flicks ashes in my direction, her eyes narrow and green and ringed with black makeup.

I know she's thinking about Isabel when she looks at me,

maybe wishing it had been me who died instead. Althea was one of the last people to see Isabel alive. She'd been with us earlier that night, when we sneaked into the backyard of a new house and used the hot tub. It was Ty Thibodeaux's idea, a friend of my brother's. Ty worked weekends as a hot tub installer and knew where all the tubs were, the places where people were building houses on the north side of town. Sometimes he got the tubs hooked up weeks before the owners moved in.

I would never have gone along if I hadn't been standing around in the garage with Sage and Isabel and Althea London when Ty drove up in his old Buick. He and a couple of other guys came into the garage to fool around with Sage's equipment and smoke cigarettes. There was talk about going to check out a new hot tub. Everyone was excited except me. I'd been having a great time there in the garage, and now everyone was going to leave. I turned to go inside, and that was when Isabel said, "Hey, Maddy, you can come if you want."

"No she can't," Sage said, looking up from his drums.

"Sure she can," Isabel said.

"Yeah, why not?" said Althea London, who had no reason to hate me then.

"She's just a kid," Sage said. "She can't."

"Go get your jacket, Maddy," Isabel said, and that seemed to settle it. If Sage had been driving he probably would have fought harder, but this was before the black Pinto. So I ran inside to get a suit and towel, and then we were off, me and Sage and Isabel and Althea London, all piled in Isabel's Toyota, Isabel singing along with the radio. I felt lucky and cool and older, and a little nervous. I wished Sage would stop sulking and act like it was okay for me to be there. He sat in the passenger seat with his feet up on the dashboard, scowling.

"Sit normal," Isabel said, but he refused.

We followed Ty past broken-down farms and wooded hills and a water tower lit up yellow, all the way to the new developments, where half-built houses stood on bare dirt lots. Out on one of the cul-de-sacs there was an almost-finished house, a blue two-story with white shutters and a three-car garage. They hadn't put down sod in the yard or finished pouring the concrete of the walkway, and one wall of the garage still had to have its siding put on. But around back, in the middle of a redwood deck, was a brand-new eight-person Jacuzzi. Ty unclipped the cover and hit a switch on a control panel, and the tub lit up and starting bubbling. Everyone cheered. We were out in the middle of nowhere, with no one around to hear us.

I unrolled my bathing suit from the towel and looked for a place to change, but suddenly all around me people were taking their clothes off—shirts, pants, underwear, everything. I couldn't keep myself from staring at Sage as he pulled off his shirt and jeans. I hadn't seen him naked since we were kids, and suddenly there was the dark hair between his legs, and his pale penis. Isabel was naked too, her arms crossed over her chest. She looked nervous at first, but then she opened her arms and let the wind hit her and she laughed and shivered, her hair all loose and messed up, her skin going pink. She was so beautiful that for a minute I forgot to be freaked out by what was happening. I started taking off my clothes like everyone else, feeling the wind hit my skin. Then I saw Sage looking at me, waiting for me to take my shirt off, his mouth curling as if he were getting ready to say something mean. So I went down some stairs to the side of the deck and put my suit on. It was freezing down there, in no clothes, with nothing but hard ground beneath my feet.

As much as I wanted to go up and get in the hot tub, it seemed better to wait until everyone else was already in, their parts mostly submerged. I climbed a couple of stairs and watched them. Ty was in the tub, laughing and splashing Althea London, who had one nipple pierced. Isabel got in next to Ty, and Sage next to her. Someone passed beers around. I was seeing the secret world of cool older people, the world Sage slipped off into every weekend while I stayed at home with my fish or made cookies with the sisters Padmanabhan. I took a breath and looked up at the stars. It was November. Orion was bending his bow in the sky above us.

"Hey, Maddy," Isabel called from the hot tub. "Where are you?"

I climbed the stairs and headed for the Jacuzzi as if this were the kind of thing I did all the time. Isabel moved over to make space for me, and I got in. Our thighs pressed together under the water, her skin slick-smooth. The water steamed and rolled and burbled around us. Ty Thibodeaux handed me a beer, and I sank down in the water up to my neck and drank. The beer was bitter and bready and cold. I thought maybe I could develop a taste for it if I tried.

There was some talk about people at school, kids I'd seen but never spoken to. Someone had gotten a tattoo gun from his cousin in New York; someone else had thrown up in Calculus class from eating pot brownies. I laughed along with everyone, as if the people they were talking about were friends of mine. After a while, when I was feeling braver, I told a story of my own: Last week a wiener dog had run into our gym class and peed on a rack of basketballs before anyone could stop him.

"I heard about that," Isabel said. "I heard Miss Cortland freaked."

"She completely freaked!" I said. Ty laughed and handed me another beer.

Then, as if he couldn't stand that people were talking to me and acting like I belonged there, Sage had to start telling the story about my fifth birthday, the pool story. I tried to make him stop, but he wouldn't. "She was drinking Sprite all morning," he said. "Gallons of it. We only got to drink soda on our birthdays, because of our dad saying it would rot our teeth." People were listening, lowering their beers and leaning forward so they could hear him over the bubbles. "We were on the pool deck," he went on, "and she's dancing around like she has to pee, and our mom's like, 'Maddy, do you have to go wee-wee?' "

"Shut up, Sage," I said.

"No," Sage said. "I'm just getting to the good part." He winked at Ty Thibodeaux across the rolling water. "So I look in the pool five minutes later and there's Maddy with this peaceful expression on her face. Our mom saw it too. She got everyone out of the pool in like five seconds flat. She made them go in and have cake. Everyone was like, 'Why can't we swim anymore?' Meanwhile Maddy tried to act like she hadn't done it. She still won't admit it, will you, Maddy?" He poked me in the shoulder.

"So what?" Isabel said. "Little kids pee in the pool all the time."

"I called her the Mad Pisser that whole summer," Sage said.

"That story's a lie," I said, though probably everyone knew it wasn't.

"You'd better not have too much to drink," he said, grabbing my beer away and taking a sip. "The Mad Pisser might ride again."

He wouldn't let it rest. He kept poking me in the shoulder and saying, "Think you can hold it?" with me staring into the water and wishing he'd stop, until Isabel climbed out of the tub and stood there shivering in a towel, looking out at the empty backyard. When she started putting on her clothes Sage tried to stop her, but she pulled away and zipped her sweatshirt up.

"Why do you have to be such an asshole?" she said.

"It was funny," Sage said, and looked at Ty. "Wasn't it funny?"

"I don't know, man," Ty said, as if he didn't want to take sides.

"It wasn't funny," Isabel said, pulling her jeans on.

Sage turned away and kicked a beer bottle off the deck, and I wondered whether we'd all just go home now. Part of me hoped we would. Then the next minute floodlights were flashing and a shrill alarm was screaming. The house security system had gone off. We hadn't even known there was one. Althea London had triggered it when she tried to climb in through a window to use the bathroom.

Suddenly everyone was screaming and running around, elbowing one another as we tried to get our jeans and shoes and coats on. I was so scared I couldn't even manage to put on my pants, and Isabel had to grab my hand and run us to the front of the house where her car was parked. We got in and she started the motor.

"What about Sage?" I said. In my side mirror I could see him coming around the side of the house, his shirt bunched against his crotch.

"He can find another ride," Isabel said. Then she hit the gas, and we were off.

We tore out of the cul-de-sac at what must have been sixty miles an hour, windows down, Sonic Youth blaring from the tape player. "Woo-hoo!" Isabel screamed. Her hands were shaking as she held the steering wheel, and I couldn't tell if it was because she was cold or because she was excited. I'd never seen anyone drive so fast. The night was cold and clear, the sky shot with stars, the bare trees whipping by. The vinyl car seat was like ice against my legs, and my teeth were clacking so hard I could feel it in the top of my skull. Isabel was singing along with the tape as we roared over those roads. Every now and then she'd look at me and grin.

"We can drive all the way to Chicago," she said. "I feel like driving."

I imagined the two of us walking down Michigan Avenue, parents three hundred miles away, hot dogs in our hands. "We'd be in such deep shit," I said, and laughed.

"No, we wouldn't," she said. "I have an aunt there. She's cool. We could stay with her tonight and come back tomorrow."

"Chicago," I said. "That's crazy, Isabel."

"Let's do it," she said. "Let's go right now."

We turned in at Gettyswood Townhomes, a shortcut to US 23, and all at once I knew she was serious. I felt lightheaded and frightened and almost in love with her. Together we would zip out along the open highway. We wouldn't even call our parents until we got there, and God only knew what they would say. Sage would be so jealous he would spontaneously combust. Isabel laid on the gas, and as we came around the curve near the pond I felt the jolt of the curb and a sudden hollow rush in my chest and we were airborne.

The car hit the pond nose-first. The windshield crunched and everything was dark and water poured in through the open windows, so cold it erased every part of me it touched, and suddenly it was in my mouth with its pond-scum taste and I couldn't breathe. I hardly knew what was happening. In the darkness I felt for Isabel, straining against my seat belt, and my hands brushed something warm and soft, but I couldn't make my fingers hold on to anything. My lungs began to burn. I shrugged out of the seat belt and felt for the edge of the open window, pushing through, trying to kick up to where the moon wavered like a reflection of itself. I struggled through what seemed like thick black honey, broke the surface, breathed, swam to the edge, and crawled out onto the frozen bank. Kneeling on the wet grass I coughed out water, waiting to see Isabel come up. I screamed to her. The trees beside the pond clicked in the wind. On my left leg a widening cut ran black and hot with blood. I got up onto the numb blocks of my feet and ran toward the townhouses, toward a phone, shouting for help.

Now, four months later, Althea London sits on the edge of the loading dock, shooting me mean glances, blowing cigarette smoke at me like she's trying to make me cough. I'd like to remind her that she was the genius who tripped the alarm. She has no idea what it was like between Isabel and me in the car, or what happened down under the water.

I crush the wet cigarette with the toe of my shoe and jump off the edge of the loading dock, six feet down, to land hard on hands and knees on the pavement, and then I am limping toward home.

Crime and punishment. That is the pattern between my brother Sage and me. A quiet private criminal justice system is what we've created, with Sage as judge, jury, jailer, and executioner. Our system has no checks and balances, and it allows multiple punishments for the same crime. If, in a real court, I'd been proven guilty of killing Isabel, I would have gotten my punishment and been left to live with it. In the world of Sage and me, however, I must pay and pay—even though Sage is guilty in some ways himself.

God only knows how he killed them, whether he fed them poison or put ice cubes in their water or something even worse, but when I got home from school I find eleven of my fighting fish dead, the Sage fish and the Isabel fish among them. They float on top of the water in their plastic containers, still and cold. My fish, the animals I raised from eggs. Their fins are limp, their mouths open, their little round eyes looking at nothing. Five experimental-group fish and six control-group ones. If he were smart he would have killed all the experimental ones, making me think I was somehow at fault. But I know whose stupid fault this is, from beginning to end.

Though I know it won't help, I throw the dead fish into

the aggression-trial tank and administer a few electric shocks. Nothing. It's just as well. If they did wake up, they'd attack each other to death in three seconds flat. I scoop them out, put them all in an empty yogurt container, and snap the lid on. They weigh almost nothing. I take them to bed with me and wrap myself in the quilt. And though I don't want to let myself cry, I do, because they're dead beyond the reach of hope or science, and Sage is the one who did it, and no matter what I do to get back at him—burn his room, trash his car—he'll just find a way to get me back worse.

That night, after a quiet dinner at which Sage does not appear and at which I pretend to my parents that nothing is wrong, I take the yogurt container and walk the mile to the pond, which isn't even a real natural pond but an ornamental small lake near the east entrance of Gettyswood. I crouch in the grass near a fake dock and unwrap the fish and throw them into the water, one by one. It doesn't take me long to realize how ridiculous I must look, hurling tiny fish into a pond. They float on top, dark shapes against the moonlit surface, and I know they will probably be eaten by birds or by other fish.

It's the first time I've been to the pond since the accident. Things look almost the same as they did that night, the trees without leaves, the grass patchy and frozen. In the weeds beside me I find a piece of thick glass, blue at the edge, and I can't help wondering if it belonged to the Toyota windshield. Though I know the car was dragged out months ago, I imagine it there beneath the surface of the water, Isabel still trapped inside. It's impossible to believe how gone she is, how untouchable. She's the only one who doesn't have to know what it's like here on Earth without her.

The next day I'm waiting for my dad to take me to school, thinking maybe I'll tell him about the fish, but at the last moment Sage comes down with his car keys in hand. He looks exhausted after his long headache.

"I'll drive," he says, his voice scratchy and low.

"You sure?" our dad says.

Sage nods. I kiss our dad goodbye and follow Sage to the car. All the way to school he seems to be getting ready to say something to me. He keeps giving me a squinty look, as if he's trying to figure out what I'm feeling, but I'm not about to let him know. I keep my face still as stone, just as he did when we were driving home from scuba class. School is not far from our house. We get there before he manages to talk.

"See you at three?" he says as we climb out.

"Whatever," I say.

I wait for him to say something else, to confess or apologize, but he just turns and lopes across the parking lot.

When we get home from school I find a blue plastic bag on my bed. I open it to find the swim fins and mask I'd admired at Arbor Valley Spa and Ski. There's no note, but at the bottom of the bag I find a credit card receipt with my mother's signature. The fins look even better in person than they did in the store window, the translucent blue plastic shot through with green swirls, the glass of the mask almost iridescent. I kick off my shoes and pull the fins on. They fit.

I am so happy, clomping around the room in my new SeaQuest Thrusters, that it's a fresh shock to pass by my experimental fish and see the empty containers among them. I take off the fins and mask and put them back in the bag. I pull the experimental notebook from my backpack. I have not recorded blood pressure data in two days, and it almost seems not worth continuing the experiment. Out of habit, though, I feed the fish their flakes and vitamins and take their blood pressures with the HP device. Everyone's blood pressure is slightly high today. It makes me wonder if they can sense that something went wrong, that they themselves have only narrowly escaped disaster. As I sit down on the bed to record my results, there is a soft knock at the door. "Come in," I say, hoping it will be Sage. Instead it is my mother.

"You look nice today," I say, and she does, in black pants and a gray sweater and scarf. Her cheek feels cold when she kisses me, as if she has just come in from outside.

"How are they?" she says, looking into the plastic fish containers. Because she was the one who drove me to Detroit to buy the eggs, and helped me set up the experiment with its control and experimental groups, she knows something's wrong when she sees the empty containers. She gives me a puzzled look.

"Some of the research subjects died," I say.

"Why?" she says. "What happened?"

"I don't know." I could tell her it was Sage's doing, but I don't. What happened is between him and me.

She has me walk her through the water temperatures and chemistry, the blood-pressure sensing mechanisms, the fish's diet. Of course she can find nothing that would have caused the random deaths. She stands there looking into the containers as if an answer might emerge from the water. If it occurs to her that Sage might have killed the fish, she doesn't say so.

"I'm sorry, Maddy," she says finally. "You took such good care of them."

I don't respond, because I know I will cry if I try to speak.

"Maybe they got some kind of virus," she says. "That can happen. You just have to carry on with the experiment. Note the deaths in your log and move on."

"I'll try," I tell her.

"You know," she says, fingering the edge of one of the containers, "I had lunch with your father today. Afterward he cleaned my teeth and bleached them." She smiles, and her teeth are as white as sleet.

"Nice," I say.

"We wondered if you were going to go to class again tonight."

"I wasn't planning to. But those are excellent fins." I take them out of the bag again and put them on, flopping around the room to demonstrate. Then I put on the mask. "How do I look?" I ask her.

She takes me by the shoulders, turning me back and forth. Despite the dead fish, despite my failure in the swimming pool, despite everything that has happened in the past four months, she looks almost proud of me. "*Très* Jacques Cousteau," she says. "*Très magnifique.*"

On the way to scuba that night I watch Sage as he drives and eats, the grease shining on his fingers. He steers with one hand and grabs chicken nuggets with the other. If he had another hand, he would be using it to smoke. He seems to want to keep his mouth full so he doesn't have to talk to me. I don't eat anything. Usually he'd finish my nuggets and fries too, but tonight he leaves my food alone.

We pull into the parking lot and find our space, and then we get out so Sage can have a cigarette. It is cold and windy March, still frozen, without a hint of spring. Sage has a hard time getting the lighter to stay lit, but finally his cigarette catches. He takes a drag and then extends the pack toward me.

"Yeah, right," I say.

He blows out a plume of smoke, throwing his head back to get his hair out of his eyes—a gesture Isabel once told me she loved, but which to me seems like the kind of thing people do when they're trying to look cooler than they really are. "I know you steal them sometimes," he says.

I take the pack from him and swizzle the cigarettes around inside. Their smell reminds me of the lunch I spent out on the loading dock. I tell him I'll pass.

As Sage smokes he shoots quick glances at my fins, trying to look at them without being obvious. I lean against the car and slap them against my leg. Finally he says, "How come I didn't get any fins?"

"I don't know," I say. "Maybe because you're such a dickhead."

He takes the pack of cigarettes from me and stuffs it into his pocket.

"You can't just not mention the fish, Sage." I look him hard in the eye. "You can't pretend nothing happened."

He leans against the car and crosses his arms. Very quietly he says, "I'll get you some replacement fish."

"Do you know how ridiculous that is? I raised those fish from eggs, just for the experiment. Under controlled conditions. It took months!"

"Okay, okay."

My throat goes tight. I sling my towel over my shoulder and begin to walk toward the door of the Y. Already I can hear the sound of little kids inside, playing as they wait to be picked up. Sage comes up behind me and grabs my wrist, but I whick it away.

"Maddy," he says, and I turn to look at him. He's so cold I can see him shivering. Behind him the Y glows with yellow light, its entryway toothed with icicles. "I wouldn't have to get you fish for your experiment," he says. "I could get you some pet fish."

"Just forget it, Sage."

"Listen to me," he says. "I'm an asshole. I admit it."

"You didn't use to be," I say. "Not such a major asshole, anyway."

Cars sweep by, honking for the kids waiting inside. When the door of the Y opens, the sound of the kids' voices grows sharper. Somewhere farther inside is the pool with its tiled depths.

"You make me wish I died instead of her," I say.

He stands there staring at me as if I've hit him. A fine dry snow has begun to fall, speckling his jacket with flakes. He drops his cigarette and grinds it into the asphalt with his heel. "I followed you the other night," he says. "When you went to the pond."

"You followed me?"

"You went sneaking out of the house. I didn't know what you were going to do."

I hate the thought of him watching as I threw my fish into that pond. It seemed a stupid enough thing to do when I thought I was unobserved. "Don't follow me around, Sage," I say. "If I want you to go somewhere with me, I'll ask you."

"No, you won't," he says. "Why would you?" He takes out another cigarette, then puts it back in the pack. Finally he speaks again, so quiet I have to lean close to hear him. "I can't believe I turned out to be such a shitty person," he says. "I wasn't even nice to her."

"What are you talking about?"

"I was a terrible boyfriend. I got mad at her for no reason during band practice. I didn't listen to her enough. I forgot her birthday. I made fun of her car."

"You weren't a terrible boyfriend," I say. "Isabel loved you."

"How do you know?"

"I just do," I say. "I could see it."

Just then the girl from last week walks by, swinging a gym bag over her shoulder. She lifts a hand and waves as if she's never seen me coughing out water on the side of the pool. I wave back.

"We're going to be late," Sage says.

I follow him into the Y, and we split off toward our separate locker rooms.

Among the rows of yellow lockers I unpack my suit and towel, my new mask. As I change clothes, the girl in red comes over and picks up my swim fins.

"SeaQuests," she says in her Romanian accent. "Very professional."

"My mom got them for me."

"They match you," she says, holding them up against my bathing suit.

"You can try them later if you want," I say, and she looks pleased.

When I see the pool again, the place where I went down last time, nausea slams me. I try to take some slow breaths. Out on the bleachers some kids are talking about different kinds of equipment, single tanks versus double, but Sage is sitting off to one side, scratching his ankle. The blond swim-team-looking instructor whose name I have forgotten is hauling complete scuba sets and wetsuits out of a storeroom. No one's bothering to help her. The red-suit girl and I go down there and start hauling out tanks, and by the time we're finished my nausea has gone away.

"All right," the instructor says, dusting off her hands. "Who wants to dive?'

People yell and clap. Even Sage looks interested.

She says we're going to do a five-minute ten-foot dive, and tells everyone to get into wetsuits. The suits are the one-piece back-zip kind; the Romanian girl and I zip each other in. The instructor gives us each a weight belt and a scuba set and shows us how to fasten the tanks to the buoyancy control device. We learn how to attach the regulator to the tank, how to turn on the air, and how to test the regulator by pushing the purge button. We learn that we're supposed to use the hang-ten sign to say *cool* to each other, because the thumbs-up sign means to go to the surface. We lift the gear onto each other's backs and secure all the buckles. Then we stagger toward the deep end and take practice breaths just standing on the side of the pool. The air from the tank is metallic and very dry. The last thing we do before going in is to put on fins and masks. My new flippers look sleek and aqua blue against the white tiles of the floor.

Finally it is time again for all of us to get into the water. Sage moves close to me as we line up to splash in, him shivering, me trying not to look over the edge into the mouth of the water.

"Quit thinking about last time," he says. "It's going to be different."

"We'll see," I say.

"Practice measuring your breaths, like she told us."

I practice measuring my breaths, and it calms me a little. We watch our classmates line up and fall backward into the pool. I see them down there beneath the surface, not coming up for a breath, and all of a sudden a great excitement fills me. Although I know it is stupid, I feel as if we're going to find ourselves in the ocean when we splash down, surrounded by coral reefs and fish, seeing things we'd never even imagined. When I crouch for my roll entry, Sage crouches beside me. Together we fall back and splash down. At first I forget to breathe. We're underwater, after all. But when my lungs start getting tight I suck in a breath. The air is cold and surprising in my lungs, and suddenly I'm scuba diving, shooting out bubbles of used breath into the pool, and Sage is finning beside me.

When I think of Isabel this time it's not as a mermaid but as the living girlfriend of my brother, wearing blue jeans, playing bass in the garage, telling me to try singing. She would have liked to see us diving, Sage and me, going down into the richest blue of the bottom. We tread water, watching each other through our masks. I cannot see his eyes through the glass, but I can see, reflected small and blue, a girl wearing swim fins and a metal tank, self-contained and breathing underwater.

272 **MELCHER MEDIA** wishes to thank David E. Brown, Hilary Laffer, Lauren Nathan, Clive Piercy, Lia Ronnen, Shoshana Thaler, Anna Wahrman, Betty Wong, Megan Worman, and Liz Zang.